MW01231976

Order your autogra~~phed copy~~ ~~...~~
30% discount at <u>www.jihadwrites.com</u> And family, please
post a review on <u>www.amazon.com</u> and e-mail Jihad at
<u>jihadwrites@bellsouth.net</u>

AUTOGRAPH PAGE

To be used exclusively to recognize that special King or
Queen for their support.

This is a work of fiction. Any references or similarities to actual events, locales, real people, living or dead are intended to give the novel a sense of reality. Any similarity in other names, characters, places and incidents is entirely coincidental.

Envisions Publishing, LLC
P.O. Box 83008
Conyers, GA 30013

DARK HORSE ASSASSIN: RISE OF THE MESSIAH: copyright © 2014 Jihad

ISBN: 978-0-9706102-9-4

First Printing October 2014
Printed in the United States of America

10 9 8 7 6 5 4 3 21

Submit Wholesale Orders to: Envisions Publishing, LLC Envisions2007@gmail.com P.O. Box 83008
Attn: Shipping Department, Conyers, GA. 30013

DARK HORSE ASSASSIN: *Rise of the MESSIAH*
Is dedicated to my uncle **REVEREND JAMES C. BOYCE** who's walk inspired me far more than any words spoken from a pulpit. Uncle Jake you said that everyone has two dates and a slash. The date we came into the world and the day we left this world. These dates are reference points. Most important is the slash. It represents what we have contributed to mankind. Well, Uncle Jake I apologize for having to abbreviate your slash, there is just not enough paper in production that can make your slash big enough to reflect the impact that you had on so many.

THE FACE OF A MAN

JANUARY 21, 1946 – NOVEMBER 20, 2013

Uncle Jake I hope this book makes you proud and is worthy of your name being in it. I will never forget you, but then again, no one that has ever spent five minutes with you will.

More important I will carry on your work to uplift and as you were I am and as you did I will do. I saw you Unc. I saw the God in you. As you breathed the spirit of brotherly love into me I will continue breathing it onto and into others through my words and my actions. IF THE WORD MANHOOD HAD A FACE, I HAVE NO DOUBT THAT IT WOULD BE YOURS UNC.

Envisions
PUBLISHING COMPANY

APPRECIATION PAGE

First and foremost I wanna thank the Creator, without your inspiration and your spirit to guide my mind, my action, and my fingers this work would still be a culmination of thoughts and beliefs

KING Uncle Jake this is for you, for without you being who you were I wouldn't be who I am. You got me to see through your actions. QUEEN Dr. Georgene Bess Montgomery if it weren't for you injecting African centered spirituality in our class readings I would have never challenged your teaching, and yes tis is one of the times I am so happy that I was wrong, without you I wouldn't have told the truth in this book. King Rev. Dr. Mukungu Akinyele, the most valuable lesson you taught me was in South Africa, it was the lesson of controlling my anger that helped me write this book. My friend and mentor KING dr. Akinyele Umoja, your book "WE WILL SHOOT BACK" and the ancestors you revealed to me helped tell our story, Thank you. QUEEN Rev. Dr. Shirlene Holmes, thank you for inspiring me with your words and your wisdom, your walk inspired me to give First Afrikan Church a chance. KING Rev. Dr. Michael Omawale Lomax your absolutely amazing African Centered spiritual teaching seriously helped inspire this book. Without your presence in my life there is no way I would have done the research, communed with the right ancestors to produce the reality that is typed on these pages. My man, the baddessssstttttttt, realessttttttt, 'Keep it 100' bout it – bout it pastor I have ever heard, Reverend Daniel 'DK' Kelly you are my hero… If any do not know this man, you need to come to Lithonia Georgia to meet and hear him at First Afrikan Church, he is the UNDISPUTED TRUTH. So much of this book has come form the messages I heard on Sunday Mornings between January 2014 and June 2014. Mom, you have always supported me in my writing and of course I wanna thank you. Andre Frazier, my brother, I said my last book was going to be my last, but it was the first book you ever read and your questions and your understanding of what I wrote made me throw the notion to STOP writing out of the window, thank you. I WANNA GIVE A SPECIAL THANKS TO FIRST AFRIKAN CHURCH AND ALL THE KINGS AND QUEENS THAT HAVE SHOWN ME AND EVERY ONE ELSE THAT WALKS THROUGH ITS DOORS UNCONDITIONAL LOVE. You truly embody the mission we all recite every Sunday. For more info on this spiritual experience go to firstafrikanchurch.org.

Of course I will never leave out my fans and the Captives held in America's prisons – men and women who are the sole reason that I am able to write. If half as many people in the freeworld supported my stories – our stories I truly believe that we would be so much closer to FREEDOM. I need you fam. Keep on doing what you do buying, reading, and becoming the Kings and Queens that I know we are.

I need help fam. I CAN NOT CONTINUE TO WRITE WITHOUT YOU SPREADING THE WORD. YOU READ ME, YOU FEEL ME, PLEASE BUY DARK HORSE ASSASSIN OR WORLD WAR GANGSTER FOR A FRIEND AND GET THEM TO SEE WHAT YOU DO.

SUPERFANS

Queen Ann Joiner of Norfolk thank you. Queen Kariymah of Philly thank you. Queen Tazzy Fletcher thank you. Queen Iliene Butler, New York thank you. Queen Martha and the queens of IPS transportation Indianapolis, Thank you.

And again I want to give a very special thanks to the Kings and Queens living behind America's prison walls. I personally read all of your letters. And I may not respond to all letters, but just know that I read every one of them.

THEY SAY BLACK MEN DON'T READ. FOR ALL THE KINGS ON THE INSIDE AND OUTSIDE KEEP PROVING THAT MYTH WRONG.

By supporting my books, you help our young brothers and sisters realize the kings and queens that they are.

And I'd like to give a very special thanks to President Barack Obama. If a man with the name of Barack Hussein Obama can get past the hate so can a man with the name Jihad Shaheed Uhuru. Please don't judge me by what you think my name means, judge me by my actions and by my character.

Please log onto www.jihadwrites.com to find more about Jihad or to purchase any of his books 30% less than the store price, and if you purchase 3 books anytime on www.jihadwrites.com you get the 4th book absolutely FREE. Please tell others what you think by posting a review on www.amazon.com. Log on to www.jihadwrites.com to sign Jihad's guestbook.

Also by Jihad/J.S. Free

Friction Fiction
STREET LIFE
BABYGIRL
RHYTHM & BLUES (PREACHERMAN BLUES PREQUAL)
MVP: **M**urder **V**engeance **P**ower
PREACHERMAN BLUES
WILD CHERRY (BOOK 2 IN PREACHERMAN BLUES SERIES)
PREACHERMAN BLUES II
MVP RELOADED
WORLD WAR GANGSTER
DARK HORSE ASSASSIN: *Rise of the MESSIAH*

Self Help
THE MESSAGE: 16 Life lessons for the Hip Hop Generation

Anthologies
GIGOLOS GET LONELY TOO
THE SOUL OF A MAN

Please pick up any of Jihad's books at a 30% discount at **jihadwrites.com** and if you buy 3 books you get any one of your choice FREE only at **jihadwrites.com**. and books ordered from **jihadwrites.com** will be shipped FREE. You can also order at Amazon.com or get Jihad's books at your local bookstore. All of Jihads books are available on kindle and nook.

And I looked, and behold a pale horse: and his name that sat on him was Death, and Hell followed with him. And power was given unto them over the fourth part of the earth, to kill with sword, and with hunger, and with death, and with the beasts of the earth.

Revelations: 6:8

DARK HORSE ASSASSIN:
Rise of the Messiah

Jihad S. Uhuru

THE BEGINNING OF THE END

April 3, 2002
Langley, Virginia

Arguably, the three most powerful men in the world were sitting at the Trilateral Commission roundtable a hundred feet below the historic Waldorf Astoria hotel in Manhattan.

If the dictionary were to describe what an average middle-aged, white male banker looked like, Bernard Schwartz's picture would have saved Mr. Webster from wasting words to capture the definition. Bernie, as he was called, was definitely not what Hollywood would deem your leading man type. Standing flatfooted at five-seven, with a vampire complexion, he was one hundred sixty pounds and that's with two wet bricks in each pocket. Bernie was far from being a physically imposing figure. But what his physical attributes lacked, his mental prowess more than made up for. Akin to beautiful people sleeping their way to the top, Bernie used his analytical prowess and sociopathic cunning to rise to his now Wizard of Oz-like status as Chairman of the Federal Reserve Bank.

Bernie was a planner; everything in his life, his successes, his failures, all had been planned down to the minutest detail. That's why it was odd to see him seemingly lost in thought as he stared straight ahead at the gray concrete underground walls while the head of the CIA, known as the National Director of Intelligence argued his case.

"XR13 has had five assignments since nine eleven. Five. All executed flawlessly. Eight kills. In those months he has not done anything to suggest that he has ulterior motives," Gerald Bush, the director of the CIA explained from his chair.

General Maurice Lesure's quick temper would have derailed his NSA appointment six months ago if he hadn't had a garbage dump full of dirt on one too many movers and shakers in government. The physical opposite of Bernie, the NSA chief was a former standout college hoops star. At six-five, he had the height but his width and muscular disposition made him the prototype professional NFL lineman. To this very day, Lesure still held the record for heaviest starting basketball player in Rutgers' history. Thirty-five years after leading Rutgers to its first NCAA championship, Lesure's three hundred pound Iron Man physique had jellied into three hundred sixty pounds of Michelin Man fat. Like his weight redistribution, his hair had done the same. As time went by, his hair slowly started to relocate from the top of his head to his ears, back and nose. Although his hair and weight had made a transition, his penetrating blue eyes and the force of his baritone voice still had the power to make the strongest man quiver.

"Are you frigging kidding me?" General Lesure hammered his melon-sized fist on the walnut oak roundtable before extending an arm toward the CIA director. "All you need is a friggin' mini skirt, a halter, and some frigging Pom-Poms. For Christ's sake, Gerald, we found a thumb drive in his mother's home on September second, nine days before we took out the towers. A thumb drive that had an unauthorized conversation with you and him on it."

Gerald leaned forward, clasped his hands in front of him and stared into the riveting blue eyes of the NSA chief. The staredown lasted fifteen seconds before the director spoke in a calm tone. "Your feeble attempt to belittle and emasculate me, your loud accusatory tone, the tintinnabulation of your fist banging on the table, nor does your unwanted presence intimidate me in the least, so I would suggest that if you really must open your mouth and regurgitate the pre-school thoughts that are swirling around in that liver spotted bald head of yours, the least you can do is exercise some modicum of respect when speaking in my presence. I respect your opinion Maurice and your passion for what and how you believe," he pointed a finger in the air, "but, remember, at the end of the day," he pointed the finger at himself, "you answer to me."

The general bounced out of his seat. "Who in Sam hell…"

Chairman Schwartz retrieved his titanium briefcase from the floor beside him before standing up and slamming it onto the dark wood conference table. "Gentlemen." His neutral position shifted to the NSA chief. "Sit down, Maurice." Once the general was seated, Bernie sat down and turned his attention to the director. "Give us the facts, Gerald."

"The facts are this… I personally ordered the investigation into XR13, not because I suspected him of foul play. I ordered investigations into any and everyone that was involved with our plans to take out the towers and the pentagon. It was an added security measure. Do I know why XR13 had a recording of he and I innocently speaking about nothing on a thumb drive, no, but what I do know is that if XR13 knew that we tortured and killed his mother he would come for us by any means necessary. Do I think he suspects us? Yes, I do, but he will not act out of suspicion. Do I think his mother was innocent? Yes I do, but in war there are always innocent casualties, and although we are not at war, we would potentially be in a civil war if America knew what we did on nine-eleven.

"We even put his mother through some of the most painful torture techniques… that is, until her heart gave out. Her torture was a waste of the government's time and resources. She didn't give us anything because she didn't know nothing." The director turned to the NSA chief, "And before you ask, we did not interrogate XR13 because he would only tell us what he wanted us to know. No amount of torture or sodium pentothal would loosen his tongue."

"And how do you know this?" Bernie asked.

"Because I trained him."

"In the end, Frankenstein turned on his creator," the head of national security said.

"First, General Lesure, Frankenstein is a fictitious figment of its creators' imagination, Treble XR13 Frazier is a living, breathing problem."

"Bottom line, Gerald," The bookish-looking chairman of the Federal Reserve interjected, "What would be the potential fallout if XR13 were to go rogue?"

Gerald took a deep breath and exhaled. "As you know XR13 has been with us since '68. He was one of the recruits after we eliminated the agents that were involved with taking out King. We recruited XR13 right out of the military. Navy Seal. For the last thirty-four years, he's been the number one sharpshooter in the world, and one of only a handful of people that can build a nuclear bomb. In the over thirty years he's been with us, he's taken down 413 targets."

The head of National Security rose from his seat. "Gerald, stop pussyfooting around the real issue. Bernie asked you what the bottom line was."

"If you would sit down and let me finish, Maurice."

The grossly overweight middle-aged NSA chief pointed a finger at the gray haired, Mitt Romney look alike. "You are finished, Gerald. You're the one who cultivated the relationship between the Bin Laden's, the Saudi government and XR13. I voted against the terror campaign. I warned you."

"I'm what? You warned me? General Maurice Jefferson Lesure, I am your superior, what you just said is insubordination."

"I don't work for you." The NSA chief's face twisted into a mask reminiscent of someone swallowing spoiled milk. "I just answer to you. Like yourself, the department of defense pays my salary. You don't have the authority to remove me."

Gerald nodded. You're right. I don't, but I can make your job pure hell. Now if we wanna start pointing fingers," the director pointed, "you wrote the AFOC bill. The American Foreign Oil Campaign is your baby Maurice."

"I never agreed to take out the twin towers or the pentagon."

"You didn't have to. The dollar was and still is on the verge of collapsing. We have nothing to secure the national debt and we have nothing to back the American currency that's in circulation. If China calls in our debt America is screwed. We had no choice."

The NSA chief exploded. "There's always a choice. At the end of the day, XR13 was your man. You don't even know how much or what he has recorded over the years."

Bernie stood up. "The only way to contain this is to eliminate XR13, his family and every agent he's worked with over the last five years, which is about the time we began planning nine-eleven. Unfortunately, time is of the essence and we don't have time to interrogate his family, just the agents he's worked with.

"I agree, but before we go after his family or the agents we have to take out XR13 first," the CIA director said.

"I detect a little trepidation in your voice, Gerald," the General said. "Scared that the big bad Black 007 is going to come for you?"

"No, I'm scared that he's coming for you, Maurice. You see when he comes for me, I'm sending him to your doorstep. I'm sure he'd enjoy inserting his big black manhood into Jessica and Janine. I wouldn't be concerned about Julie, if she's too ugly for the dog to play with, then I'm sure she's too ugly and let me add, too fat, for XR13's taste."

"My wife and girls…" The chief pointed a finger at the director. "As God is my witness, Gerald, one day I am going to – "

"Sit down and shut up Maurice so we can get this over with," the chairman said. "Gerald, please continue."

"Thank you Bernie." The director nodded. "XR13 knows that we know that he knows something."

"Friggin' idiot," the General mumbled.

Bernie made a stopping gesture with his left arm while shuffling some papers in front of him. "Gentlemen, placing blame gets us nowhere." He looked down at a paper in front of him. "XR13 has a ten-year-old son, Zion Uhuru Jones by off-and-on girlfriend, Malia Jones. Eliminate her and the boy. That will draw him out."

"He'll know we did it. Do we really want to risk XR13 going to the press?"

"With what?" Bernie asked. "Is he in possession of some damning evidence? Is there something you haven't told us, Gerald?"

"Of course there isn't. But, we don't know what hard copy Intel he has in his possession. He did have a level four security clearance."

"Level four?" Bernie sounded surprised. "No agent should ever have a level four security clearance," Bernie said. "Oh well," he shrugged his shoulders, "too late to cry over spilled milk, now. We just have to clean this mess up and fast." The chairman turned to the director. "Get to the family, we get to him."

"Bernie," Gerald explained, "XR13 is by far the best counterintelligence specialist we have ever trained. If we get close to his son, he'll know and he will be ready."

"We are talking about one man, Gerald. I don't care how good and well-trained he is, we are the American friggin' government. Our resources are unlimited." The general gave the CIA director a stern look. "So, do you know where the woman and the boy are or not?"

Gerald nodded, "I do."

In a calm quiet tone, the chairman said, "Gerald, make sure this woman and the boy don't see another sunrise. I don't care how you do it, but do it today. And by the end of the week, I want XR13 and everyone associated with him dead or we will begin to question your loyalty."

"You can't threaten me. I'm the director of the CIA," Gerald burst out.

"I know who you are, where you live, what church you attend and what school your children go to. I even know where your mistress gets her nails done every Tuesday. You are right, I can't threaten you. I'm just the chairman of the Federal Reserve Bank." Bernie took off his glasses and leaned forward. His voice dropped to a decibel above a whisper. "But, let me tell you what I can do, Gerald. I can use the resources of the American government to do to you what needs to be done to protect this nation. And if this means arranging for you to fall on the pointy end of a bullet headfirst and replacing you with someone competent enough to do as I ask, then I will not hesitate to act in whatever way I deem is in the interest of America.

"And the recordings?" the general asked.

"Find them, Maurice, and any other evidence implicating the American government in any wrongdoing. I don't have to tell you what will happen if XR13 has physical evidence of the government's involvement with nine eleven.

Chapter 1

April 3, 2002
Same day: Atlanta, Georgia

Like an Italian sports car, the black limo zipped in and out of Atlanta early afternoon traffic. No matter how tense the situation, Treble "XR13" Frazier was trained to stay calm. He learned long ago that panicking in any situation did not produce any quicker results. As a matter of fact, it often hindered progress. That's why America's most skilled CIA specialist filed his nails while silently singing the Earth, Wind and Fire classic, "Reasons."

Treble dropped the nail file before checking his Movado. 2:23pm. His flight departed at 3:15pm. He would have to do a Flash Gordon if he was going to make the flight. He reached down to his left and pulled his briefcase onto his lap. There he opened and removed two metal rods with four half dollar sized wheels attached. A few minutes later, the Middle Eastern limo driver slammed on brakes in front of Delta's South Terminal.

Treble reached inside his powder blue double-breasted tailored suit jacket and pulled out a money clip full of endless hundred dollar bills. "Shokran Akhee." Treble thanked the driver in his native Arabic language while peeling a hundred-dollar bill from his platinum money clip.

"Afwan Akhee," the driver replied.

Gate agents, passengers, shuttle bus drivers, taxi drivers, everyone outside of the Atlanta airport's South terminal was focused on the long and slender elegantly dressed black man rolling to the airport's sliding doors on what appeared to be supercharged motorized roller blades.

Treble Frazier could easily pass for an Olympic athlete. Built like a professional sprinter, Treble was in better shape than most professional athletes half his age. He had never eaten processed foods, pork, or red meat. For forty-five of his fifty-five years, he'd exercised his body and mind for hours daily.

The main difference in his training and the training regimen for professional athletes was the motivation. Although athletes are highly motivated to train for their sport, people like Treble are motivated in ways that athletes would never be. Athletes often regroup and train harder when they lose to the competition. The loser in Treble's profession didn't live to train another day. There can be no stronger motivation than competing for your own mortality. While racing toward his gate, Treble pulled out the cell phone he'd not long ago purchased and dialed the number of the man's home he just left, Reverend Dr. John Boyce.

"Hello?"

"Rev?"

"Finished installing the infra red barrier around my estate already, Treble?"

"No, I have to get home. I have a situation."

"Okay, give me a minute, I'm walking out of the convention hall now so I can hear you. London is so beautiful this time of year," Dr. Boyce said. "Okay I'm outside."

Treble began, "Seven months ago, right before nine-eleven, they searched Malia's, Hattie Mae's, and my apartment in DC, Frisco, and Chicago. Hattie Mae went missing around this time."

"And why are you just now telling me this?"

"You didn't need to know until now."

"You didn't think that your mother being abducted elicited a phone call?"

"I never said she was abducted."

"If you can't find your mother, then she's been abducted. Can you feel her energy, Treble?"

"No." Treble shook his head.

"She's gone?" Dr. Boyce's statement came out as a question.

"Yes. She is." Treble's tone became melancholy. "That's why I didn't call. Before I knew she was missing, I felt her life-force leave my body. There was nothing you or any of the others could have done. By acting against my bosses, I'd only alert them that I knew that they were the enemy."

"You sure it was the Agency?"

"If it wasn't them, it was another faction. At the end of the day, they must all be destroyed."

"Hattie Mae was a phenomenal woman," the reverend said. "I am so sorry, Treble."

"I am, too."

"Any Intel to corroborate your theory?" the reverend asked.

"While reviewing and analyzing footage from the hidden surveillance cameras at the apartment in Indianapolis, I saw Hattie Mae going through my pants pockets before preparing my clothes to go to the cleaners. She found a thumb drive. It must have been defective because I deleted its contents, but for some reason the deletion didn't fully take."

"So, Hattie Mae accessed the content?"

Treble nodded. "On one of my laptops."

"Okay, let me get this straight, almost seven months ago, less than two weeks before the towers went down, your mother found and accessed a thumb drive on one of your laptop computers in the high rise apartment downtown on Meridian. The contents on this thumb drive were partially deleted."

"That's right," Treble said.

"And how soon did Hattie Mae come up missing after she accessed the content?"

"Within two hours."

"And how can you be so sure of the timeline that she went missing?"

"I had and still have surveillance on my handler."

"You what?" Dr. Boyce exploded. "You have surveillance on the director of the CIA?"

"Yes, and others," Treble said. "As soon as Hattie Mae accessed the drive, I knew. Unfortunately, I had to act as if I didn't, so I wouldn't arouse suspicion."

"So, you have surveillance showing that Hattie Mae was picked up?"

"No, she was not on my property, or at her house. They probably grabbed her out in the open," Treble said.

"What exactly was on the jump drive?"

"Originally, it was a conversation between Director Bush and I. I was being given an assignment to take out Jihad Umoja, the famous author/activist. The CIA felt that due to Mr. Umoja's popularity and because of the too-close-to-home content in his books that he would give the government problems after we orchestrated the national *Muslim Smear, Fear Campaign.* The only thing that was left on the thumb drive was the director thanking me for my service."

"No! If you are correct, then they tortured your mother for information. God rest her soul. Hattie Mae didn't deserve that."

"I know, Rev." Treble nodded. "I know. Since her disappearance, I stepped up my surveillance efforts on some and pulled back on others. I'm calling you now because all hell is going to break loose shortly. Less than an hour ago, I received Intel that the agency is going after Malia and Zion. I'm headed back to Indianapolis now. Rev, if anything happens to me, I need you – "

"First, nothing's going to happen that you don't want to happen and second you don't have to ask me to do what I was born to do. You know I will raise him in the light."

"Two thousand years," Treble said. "We've been preparing, praying, and training for this. Unfortunately, I may not live to see the outcome, but you must make sure Zion finishes what we started."

"Treble, before you were a twinkle in your daddy's eye, your destiny had been mapped out, you just didn't know what your role was until recently."

"Yeah, you thought I was the Messiah. You and Baba even convinced me that I was the Dark Horse Assassin. All those years living under the palace, training my body and mind to defeat the Pale Horse and its rider."

"We never lied to you, Treble. We deceived you, for your own good, but we never lied. We always knew who you were." The Reverend paused to allow his words to seek in. He continued. "Zion is an extension of you, son. He is not just your sun, but he is everyone's sun, just like he was when he was born in Bethlehem two thousand years ago. Zion's success depends on you setting the stage like John the Baptist did. You had to go through the burning sands, just like Zion will have to. Whether it be in body or spirit, you have to help prepare him, you have to protect him by any and all means. The Pale Horse rider is only getting stronger."

"Old friend, do not worry. I will do my part as I have always done."

"You and Zion are the last descendants of Shango. Shango's soul and his blood runs through both of you, but it is Zion who was born to be the Dark Horse Assassin," Dr. Boyce said. "Treble, remember back in '65 after Malcolm was assassinated, we vowed to make his dream a reality? Now that day is coming close."

"Yes, it is. It will be a long, arduous process but tearing down the white patriarchal racist system and rebuilding it into a truly democratic American system of government will be well worth the blood that we've spilled and the blood that we have yet to spill."

"All rows for flight 724 to Indianapolis are boarding now," the pleasant voice sounded over the airports intercom.

"Rev…"

"I heard… You be safe and don't worry about my end. The church is ready. If you need anything…"

"I know. And Rev?"

"Yes."

"I love you."

"I love you, too Treble. Now get home to your woman and son."

"Shit!"

Treble disconnected and looked at his watch. 3:00. Zion got out of school at 3:05. Malia would be home waiting. He pressed one on his speed dial.

"Boarding pass?" an airport attendant asked as he made his way up to the gate.

His undivided attention was on the ringing cell phone he had to his ear.

"Sir, I need your boarding pass," she requested again.

"Uno memento," he said while holding up a finger. He reached inside his Hugo Boss suit jacket pocket and felt his other cell phone along with his boarding pass. That's when he remembered that his ten-year-old wouldn't answer a number that wasn't programmed into his phone. He replaced the untraceable throwaway minute phone with his personal cell.

"Thank you and have a nice flight Mr. Rodriguez," the attendant said using the name that was on Treble's passport and boarding pass. Being light skinned with wavy straight long black hair, Treble could pass for a multitude of different ethnic groups.

Treble was taking a huge risk pulling out his regular cell phone and putting the battery back in it. The CIA could easily track him, but he had no alternative. Zion would not answer a call from an unknown number.

While walking down the corridor to the plane, Treble called his son.

Chapter 2

April 3, 2002
Same day: **Indianapolis, Indiana**

Donnie Emerson was a polar bear, big, fat, hairy, and dumber than a doughnut. Typical elementary school bully on the fast track to a career of crime, incarceration, and death, not particularly in that order. Zion didn't know his true age, but what he did know was that the fat, stringy-brown-haired, zit faced kid was older than any kid in school and that it had taken him two years to go from the fifth grade to the sixth and now he was serving his second term as a sixth grader.

It was Friday. The Indianapolis Spring sun felt like summer. Zion's jacket was in his backpack with his books. Before Zion got onto the school bus, he heard Donnie's loud, obnoxious voice. While Zion made his way toward the back of the bus, he glimpsed Donnie leaning over his seat about to flick a kid on the ear. Zion took his seat and thought that he had nothing against white people, but Donnie was just plain mean. Zion hated mean, and would have done something about his bullying back in September when he started riding the school bus, but his dad had told him to exercise patience and to not bother anyone unless they bothered him repeatedly. And Zion had never disobeyed his dad or his mom.

Zion was three when he began studying eastern forms of self-defense. And he could think of several ways to inflict bodily harm on Donnie. Zion didn't want to hurt Donnie or anyone else but he didn't want Donnie or anyone else bullying others.

Donnie was always starting trouble, especially on the school bus. He'd never bothered Zion, probably because Zion stayed to himself and didn't socialize much with kids at school. At lunch and at recess Zion was always off somewhere to himself, his face usually engrossed between the pages of some book. Most kids thought he was weird. While most ten-year-old boys played video games, watched cartoons, and did what most ten year olds did, Zion's first love was reading. He often spent hours reading everything from the Bible and Holy Quran to a Walter Dean Myers novel. While reading was his first love, target shooting and running were at the top of the list as well. Writing was a close third.

Zion was sitting in his seat writing in his notebook while he thought of the competition tomorrow. He was the youngest and only kid from the Midwest to reach the finals. He didn't expect to place first in the five-mile obstacle course, but he did expect to win the self-defense and the shooting competition. His smile broadened at the thought of all the happy faces and full stomachs he would be responsible for after he won the competition. He wished he could feed all the homeless people in the world, but five thousand dollars would only pay for so much barbequed chicken and fried fish.

Donnie reached over his seat and grabbed the notebook.

"Tomorrow is the big day. The biggest," Donnie read out loud from Zion's notebook. "I can't wait to see all the happy faces after I use the prize money to throw a barbeque for Atlanta's homeless."

Zion remained seated. In a cool measured but stern tone, he said, "Donnie give me my notebook."

Donnie continued in a singsong girly tone. "I would be the youngest by five years to ever win the hunting skills challenge."

"Now, that everyone knows that you can read, I'll ask you one more time. Please give me my notebook back?"

"What you gon' do if I don't, punk?" Donnie spat. "Go on, tell Mr. Sams and make him pull the bus over. Show everyone how much of a little snitch you are. Don't make me no never mind, punk. I'm gon' tear a mudhole in your behind if you tell or not."

Zion was more relieved than angry – relieved that Donnie was writing checks with his mouth that his behind couldn't cash – relieved that he could smash the big-mouthed bully without disobeying his father.

Zion shook his head. "I'm not going to tell."

Donnie slipped into the bench seat next to Zion. "Then, who's gon' make me give this," Donnie held the notebook in the air, "back?"

Zion hit him with a chopping blow to the neck. Donnie dropped the notebook and fell out of the seat hyperventilating while trying to catch his breath.

"Mr. Sams," Zion shouted while bending over Donnie who was on his knees trying to breath. Before the bus driver could make it to the back, Zion whispered in his ear, "Now show everyone how big of a snitch you are."

*****

Ten minutes later, Mr. Sams restored the bus to some semblance of order. Donnie remained seated next to Zion.

He pinched Donnie's arm.

"Ow," the fat kid squealed before turning to Zion.

"Nobody saw what I did to you, and we can keep it that way, do you understand?"

Donnie nodded his head up and down at the much smaller Zion.

Donnie was in a trance-like state as he stared into Zion's eyes. "From this point forward you will use your size to protect and defend others from harm. You will be a gladiator for good. You are a son of God and you will walk in His light. You will stop hating yourself. You will love yourself unconditionally and you will love others more. This love will inspire and motivate you to train your body and your mind to benefit and uplift others."

Donnie's lip quivering nods were Zion's indication that his words were having no effect on the bully. He decided to get off the bus a couple stops early, before Donnie's lip quivering turned into crying and crying turned into finger pointing.

He reached into an outside flap of his red backpack. He pulled out his cell phone. Seventeen missed calls. All of them from his dad. His first instinct was to panic. Instead, he took a few deep breaths and closed his eyes. He could feel his dad's energy. He could hear Treble's bumpety-bump heartbeat. He searched the clouds inside his mind for his mother. He couldn't feel her. This wasn't unusual. His dad and he were connected in a way that he didn't understand. He and his mom were close but he could rarely feel her energy and he only felt her heartbeat when she was close by. But still, something wasn't right. He could feel it.

He pressed redial. His dad's phone went straight to voicemail. He dialed his mom. No answer. He couldn't quite see the house from where he stood, so he decided to take the back way through the alley. As he got closer, the something-wasn't-right-feeling got stronger with each step. The hairs on his arms began to rise.

Mom was home waiting on me so why didn't she pick up and more importantly, why had dad called me seventeen times? And why was his phone going straight to voicemail? Dad always says that if something doesn't seem right, then it usually wasn't.

Zion always took his dad's words to heart and this wasn't an exception. He decided to cut through Dr. Bess's yard next door. He disappeared behind the five-foot azaleas that surrounded the five-acre estate. As he got closer to his own home, the something-wasn't-right-feeling manifested as a pale-like darkness, sort of like a cloud but pale and transparent. This darkness was rising from the ground and began slowly swallowing up the house, the ground and everything in its path. Zion's concern for his mother overruled the fear that kept telling him to run as fast and as far away from the house as humanly possible.

Instead of running away, Zion inched closer. He relied on the skills his dad had taught him – the skills to move without being seen. His dad had taught him how to use the surrounding environment for cover. He'd gotten so good that he could get within a few feet of a deer without it noticing.

The pale darkness had moved toward him as he moved toward it. He moved with as much stealth as he could muster, but the pounding of his heart reverberated in his ears. A few more steps and he would be totally immersed inside the pale darkness. Fear twisted inside his stomach, but he stepped forward anyway. There was no way he was going to leave his mom in the darkness.

Thoughts about his father swirled in his head while he hid and watched.

His dad wasn't aware but Zion knew… well, sort of… He knew his dad wasn't an international business consultant for the government. When his dad would come home from work after days, weeks, sometimes months, he often carried the same scent that the darkness carried. Although he didn't know what his dad actually did for a living, he knew that it had something to do with guns.

Dad always had some super cool guns and was an even better shot than Zion was. But Zion was a better spy, though. Like now. He sat behind Dr. Bess's azaleas, while looking at his house less than ten yards away. The TV in the sitting room wasn't on. If it was, he would've been able to see the glare and his mother watching "Guiding Light."

He picked up the phone to dial his dad again. Voicemail. He watched. He prayed. He meditated.

As the day grew old and the sun's light and warmth diminished, so did his hopes. He looked at his watch. It was 6:30. A couple more hours and it will be completely dark, he thought. He could go to ground then. He shook his head. No. Going to ground meant he had to get to the basement. While he was trying to figure out his next move, his phone vibrated in his hand.

"Dad?"

"You all right, sun?"

"Yes. You know that pale white cloud I told you – "

"Sun, don't say any more. I need you to listen closely."

Zion nodded as if his dad could see him.

Treble began to sing. "After the morning after…. After the night before… when all the fun is over..." He paused. "Remember where I taught you that song?"

Zion nodded. "Yes. Frankie Beverly and – "

"Can you get to that location?"

"I think… Yes. I can get there."

"Hurry, and move like you're invisible – the way I taught you."

"But, what about – "

Treble didn't give his son time to complete his thought. "I love you, sun." The phone disconnected.

Treble passed on his love for 60', 70's, and 80's R&B music to his son. Zion thought about the private concerts he and his dad would give for the birds, the trees and any and everything that was in listening distance when they jogged together.

Day had turned into evening and soon, evening would turn into night. The crickets were getting warmed up while Zion was setting his phone to navigation mode. He typed in `Wes Montgomery Park, Indianapolis, In.`

It was near the bleachers by the dilapidated park's basketball court that Treble had taught Zion the lyrics to "The Morning After" by Frankie Beverly and Maze.

Four-point-two miles.

Music was sort of like Zion and Treble's personal Morse code. After re-lacing up his Nike's, he took a deep breath before looking north, south, east, and finally west before taking off. Like the biblical Lott, Zion didn't look back, at least not until he'd put at least two blocks between him and the house.

That's when a massive explosion made the ground under him tremble so hard that he stumbled into someone's overflowing trashcan. He turned to the light he saw out the corner of his eye.

"Moooommmmmmm!" he shouted while reaching his arms out toward the flames. "Nooooo!!!!!!" he screamed, while banging his fists on the gray concrete alley floor. The raging flames that burned in the distance robbed the night of its darkness, making it easy for Zion to see that it was his house that was on fire. A huge cloud of gray smoke billowing toward the heavens and beginning to spread its arms made him cough. His mother was gone. He was sure of it.

Most ten-year-olds would've completely lost it, but Zion was far from being like most ten-year-olds. In his reality, death did not exist. At the end of existing in the physical form, he was taught that the life source transitioned into another dimension of reality.

Knowing that his mother had transitioned and that there was nothing he could do for her, Zion got to his feet and turned back toward his destination and ran as if his life depended on it. As far as he knew, it did.

His lungs were on fire. His legs felt like jelly. He was on automatic pilot. Dogs barked as he ran through alleys and back yards. Grundy's Funeral Home came into view as he ran.

He bent over in the shadows of the rear entrance of the funeral home to catch his breath. Moments later, he looked up. Across the street, he could see lights on in the Elbert Lee Frazier Sr. Rec center next to Wes Montgomery Park. He checked his phone. No missed calls or texts. He looked left and then right. Traffic was sparse. His biggest test would be crossing over Northwestern Avenue's four-lane highway-like street. The park was right on the other side. He looked both ways and when he saw an opening, he took off running. Every muscle in his body cried out for relief.

He could smell weed as he crossed the street. A minute later, he saw some older kids kicking it on some swings while puffing on some Loud. (Kids called this type of weed Loud because of the extra strong, pungent odor).

So busy looking at the older kids getting high, he ran smack dab into an older man dressed in black leather.

While bending down to help Zion to his feet, the man extended a hand.

Before the man made another move, Zion elbowed him in the nose.

"Bismillah," the reddish brown black man spoke in Arabic after grabbing his nose and falling back down.

Zion sprang to his feet and jumped in the air and delivered a spinning roundhouse kick to the man's temple, knocking him out.

Without hesitation, he went through the man's pockets. No wallet or ID. Just two cell phones. Zion picked up the first one. It was a minute phone with only one number programmed into it – a number with a 404 area code. Oddly, no name was assigned to the programmed number.

He checked the other phone. It was loaded with contacts. He didn't recognize any of the names so he began reading the stranger's latest text messages. He stopped at the third text.

NOW... AFTER THE MORNING AFTER.... AFTER THE NIGHT BEFORE... WHEN ALL THE FUN IS OVER...

"Oh, nooo. I just knocked out one of Dad's people. Shoot!" Zion bent down and slapped the man a couple times, attempting to stir him awake.

"Yo, shorty, what's crackin'?" One of the boys that was puffing on weed by the swings asked as he and another boy walked up.

"Set that shit out, shorty," the boy wearing the white kufi said, pitching a hunting knife from one hand to the other. "If we gotta run after you, we gon' carve you up like a Thanksgiving turkey."

Zion rose from the ground beside the old man he'd just incapacitated. "Man, I don't know what y'all talking about. I think this old head needs help."

"Shorty, we don't care nothin' about pops, all we care about is them ends." The kufi-wearing leader said as he waved the hunting knife at Zion and the older man that was regaining consciousness.

"Young man," the man that Zion had incapacitated moments ago was slowly rising to his feet. "Are you Muslim?"

"No question," the boy wearing the white kufi said with pride.

"I'm Imam Abdullah Hakim Fast."

The boy pointed. "Oh shit... You are Imam Fast." The boy stared on as if he was in a daze.

"Miss us with that shit, ole man," the other boy said. "Don't nobody care if you Christ himself. All we care about is what you got in - "

The boy wearing the Islamic headdress slapped his buddy upside the head. "Have some respect fool, that's Dr. Fast."

"Who?" the boy said, rubbing the back of his head.

"Dr. Hakim Fast. The most thorough Muslim scholar and Imam on the planet."

The other boy puffed up. "Nigga, I'm here to get paid, not preached to." The man-child that stepped up had the build of an NFL linebacker and the face of an angry boy.

The Muslim cleric extended his arms. "Son, you don't wanna do - "

The kid swung. The middle-aged half Native American, half African, Muslim leader ducked under the boy's swing and came up with an uppercut, cracking the rushing boy in the jaw. The boy was out cold before he hit the ground.

The boy wearing the kufi said, "May Allah have mercy on him and me. Allah hu Akbr," the boy shouted before turning and running off into the darkness.

Dr. Fast turned to Zion. "Your dad sent me."

"I know. I'm sorry for - "

Dr. Fast said, "We have to go now."

Zion ran after the Imam. Moments later, they were behind the Elbert Lee Frazier rec center standing next to a mean looking triple black Suzuki Hyabusa in the parking lot. Zion had a million questions, but he knew they had to wait until they were safe. The Muslim pastor took a black helmet off the bike's mirror.

"Put this on, sun."

Zion did as he was told. He quickly mounted the dark horse. Once the mechanical beast roared to life, the two sped off into the night. Zion held on for dear life as the wind cut through his brown leather jacket. His teeth chattered as he tried to hold it together. He had no idea how long they'd been riding when they finally pulled onto a dark and deserted gravel street, past a gated field of junked cars. Two big black Rottweilers ran beside the fence as they pulled up to a huge rusted metal gate. Two signs quickly caught Zion's attention. The smaller black and red sign read: DOGS ON DUTY. The huge black and white sign read: HAND OF GOD RECYCLING AND USED AUTO PARTS.

The gated fence electronically began to open. Zion's eyes searched the night. He could feel the dogs near, but there was no sign of them as they drove through the gate. Zion held his legs up as high as he could as the mechanical black horse's wheels kicked up gravel while slow rolling through the automotive graveyard. They rode up to a large garage. Dr. Fast reached inside his black leather biker's jacket and pulled out a small remote. After pressing one of two buttons, two large gray metal doors opened sideways to reveal a lot of motors and car parts, and a plain looking white Ford Taurus station wagon.

They were dismounting when Imam Fast said, "Sun, I know you are confused and have a lot of questions, but right now is not the time." He took off his helmet, revealing short reddish brown hair that matched the mustache and beard he wore. "You just have to trust us."

"Who's us?" Zion asked while giving the helmet back.

"We are the Council of Clerics, but right now I am a counsel of one for the moment."

None of this made sense.

"You're wearing a look of disbelief on your face, sun. Let me alleviate your worries." Dr. Fast began snapping his fingers and tapping his feet on the garage's concrete surface. "Wake up everybody... No more sleeping in bed... No more backward thinking.... Time for thinking ahead..."

Zion tried his best not to laugh.

"Oh, you don't like my singing?"

"I've heard dogs howl better." He laughed. By the time Zion was five, Treble had drilled into his son's head that anyone who came up to him and sang the first bar of the old school Harold Melvin and the Bluenotes song was someone to be trusted and followed.

He pointed to the station wagon. "Sun, there are Turkey sandwiches, chips, and a cooler of Gatorade in the back." Then, Dr. Fast pointed to a door in the garage. "I need you to go use the restroom. We have a very long ride. I will explain everything once we are out of Indiana, but you mustn't rise from under the blankets in back." He reached out. "Here, give me your hand, I'll guide you to the restroom."

"I'm good. I can see just fine."

Chapter 3

April 2, 2002
REWIND TO YESTERDAY: **Columbia Maryland**

He flushed the toilet and walked over to the bathroom sink. He really wanted to shower, but time was of the essence. He was still trying to gather himself. Too much alcohol and way too much of her, he thought while staring at the stranger that stared back in the Double Tree Hotel bathroom mirror.

His throwback fifties always-perfect-in-place, James Dean hairstyle was anything but. Agent FX02 was too hungover to be horrified at the Marilyn Manson identical spiked hair twin that stared back at him in the mirror. It had taken eight shots of Absolute and three Apple Martini's to get his latest chocolate conquest up to his suite. By then he was too drunk to perform. All he wanted to do was lie down, but the dainty, baby faced, Victoria Secret's model turned into a sex-crazed wild woman. Agent FX02 was as fit as a professional boxer, but in his inebriated condition, he was no match for the vixen that awaited on the other side of the suite's bathroom door.

Ronald "FX02" Reagan turned his attention to the jiggling bathroom doorknob.

"Come on, Bob, a few more minutes," the vixen pleaded from behind the bathroom door.

"I told you, I have to go home to my wife," he lied.

"I'm not stupid, Bob. That was a man's voice on the phone earlier."

"My wife," he repeated. "Me and Bob have been together for five years."

"Bob, you know what? You are full of it. I can't believe that you think I am stupid enough to believe that you are in a relationship with another man named Bob."

"I'm not. . . I. . . "

"Save it. It's shit like this that made me step outside of my race in the first place, but you know what, Bob or whoever you really are, it doesn't make any difference if I date a brotha or an other, all men are the same."

Agent FX02 had a preference for dark meat although he hated Black men. Jungle savages, not much better than primitive beasts, he'd once said. That's why he was overly excited about the opportunity to black bag the CIA's version of Jason Bourne.

As he was getting dressed, he heard scurrying from behind the bathroom door. If he wasn't in such a rush, he would have found the situation he was in hilarious.

He shook his head while thinking. *I've taken down twenty-seven targets in the last eighteen months and that's not counting the civilians that I had to kill in order to get to the intended target, and now I'm hiding from a dog dumb, twenty-year-old black whore.*

"Lose my number, asshole. And before I leave, I just wanna let you know that you've proven the myth true. Black men are way bigger than white men."

The front door made a clicking sound as it closed.

Five minutes later, the front door to the suite made another clicking sound as the CIA assassin made a hasty exit.

While parked in the Double Tree Hotel's parking lot at a quarter 'til three in the morning, Reagan downloaded and read the file that Director Bush had sent to his PDA.

"Indianapolis, Indiana," he said aloud. He had a twelve to eighteen hour window to travel six-hundred thirty nine miles, enter the exclusive half-million dollar plus Indianapolis Golden Hill estate home community, plant just enough C4 to take out the house and everyone in it, and then sit and wait until the target arrives. When agent XR13 arrived FX02 would have a direct shot from the upstairs bedroom of the empty house across the street to the right of the Jones home, just in case he didn't walk into the house.

After studying the blueprints to the seventy-year-old five-thousand plus square foot home, FX02 used his agency PDA to order the C4, wire, exploding caps, an integrated cell phone, a .50 caliber NTW-20 rifle with a infra red Bushnell scope, two fold-up tripods, and a hundred rounds of ammo. There was no reply, which was standard. The supplies, along with a clipboard, a tool belt, and a service uniform would be inside the Indianapolis Gas and Light van the CIA would provide once the private jet landed at the Eagle Park airstrip in the Indianapolis suburb of Speedway.

*****

Seven hours later, FX02 pulled into the open gates and around the horseshoe shaped driveway. He got out of the van and looked up at the clouds.

"I guess if I believed in You, then I would ask that You not let it rain before I finished what I came to do." The agent shrugged. "But since I don't, I'll just let the fate of my actions order my way."

He checked his watch after walking to the front door. Five after ten, his Patek Phillipe read. The high-tech, military-designed watch also read radiation levels, as well as a host of other things that would determine if there were any immediate lethal threats such as land mines or other booby traps that are active in the watch wearers immediate vicinity. After determining no imminent threat, he rang the doorbell.

"Yes? Can I help you?" A female voice with a strong Hispanic accent came over the intercom.

"My name is Nathan Beckford." He loved using his hero's identity, especially when his target or targets were Black. No one he'd killed ever questioned his name. None of his previous black targets ever knew that Nathan Beckford was the man that started the Ku Klux Klan. "There's a gas leak in the area, I need to get inside to check your levels."

"The meter's on the side of the house," she replied.

"Yes ma'am, I am aware of that, but I have to check the level inside of the house to see if there's any danger."

He could see through the thick stained glass front door window. The front room looked like a mini-museum. African-looking artifacts, masks, and pictures were all over the walls and the sparse but tasteful eclectic furniture.

"Invite him in, Cara," the agent heard another woman say.

A minute later, the clicking sound of locks and bolts turning made agent FX02 smile.

A portly young Hispanic woman held out her hand. "I need to see another form of ID."

One punch to the neck crushed her Adam's apple.

She reached for her throat and silently gagged as FX02 lightly pushed her aside, closed the door and headed in the direction of the live body that his watch's heat source detected.

Malia Jones was in the kitchen stirring cake batter. Agent FX02 walked in the kitchen.

Malia looked up.

"Hello," the CIA assassin said before raising his gun. "Goodbye," he said before shooting her in the face.

She was dead before she hit the ground. FX02 had to hurry before the bowl of batter fell to the hardwood kitchen floor.

He put it back on the table, removed a black glove and dipped a finger in the bowl and placed it in his mouth. "Not bad. Not bad at all."

An hour later, the house was wired and ready. He thought it best to wait inside for the kid to come home from school, but the agency didn't know where XR13 was. And he'd received direct orders to wait and watch from the foreclosed home across the street. From there the director had said, he'd be able to see the boy getting off the school bus in front of the subdivision. This would give him enough time to get back over to the house and grab the boy for bait, just in case XR13 didn't show or somehow got away.

Getting into the foreclosed house across the street undetected proved to be much more difficult than getting into the Jones's home. Designer burglar bars were on the first floor windows and doors on all fours sides of the two-story brick Tudor style home. After driving the van into the alley he carried surveillance equipment, gun, and a rope and anchor into the back yard and placed the equipment inside the poolhouse a few feet from the main back doors. Director Bush had called the agent's cell phone three times in the last ten minutes. He couldn't scale the wall and get in the house and set the surveillance equipment up fast enough.

*****

McLean, Virginia

The director's home office looked like a library at a hunting lodge. The heavily wooded log cabin office boasted a wall full of books – all hard cover and many first editions. An impressive glass cabinet full of hunting rifles dating back to the sixteenth century took up another wall, while a moose, bear and a cougar's head were mounted on the same wall where three 42-inch computer monitors hung. After yesterday's tense meeting at headquarters, the director decided to work from home, where he could drink his brandy while keeping abreast of FX02's progress. The situation was tense. XR13 had been his recruit, his real life 007. Over XR13's thirty-year plus unheralded career, Gerald had been his only handler. Only a handful of people knew the true identity of XR13.

No one outside of restricted circles in the spy community would ever believe that the world's most dangerous killer was an African-American. But just like all good things, everything comes to an end. It didn't matter that nothing damaging was recovered from the thumb drive, what mattered was that XR13 had recorded an unauthorized interaction, which was a level four security breach.

Gerald's peers had done exactly what he would have in a similar situation – pass the death sentence on XR13. Because Gerald had been remiss in his own security measures in allowing himself to be compromised on the recording, he, too, was well aware that his own mortality hung in the balance if he didn't quickly contain the situation.

On one monitor staring back at him was the agent assigned to snatch the boy if he didn't go straight home and on the other two monitors, Gerald could see the bright green manicured lawn and the long cobblestone driveway that led to the Jones's restored two-story 1930's four sided cobblestone home.

"Any word on the boy?" the director asked, while intently monitoring all three screens.

"Still, no sign," FX02 said while watching the house across the street through a high-powered two-way camera scope. "The heat sensors I planted around the perimeter haven't registered any human movement."

The director's voice was laced with concern. "It's getting dark. The kid should have been home by – "

41

"Sir, do you still have a visual?"

"Yes, yes, zoom in closer," the director ordered as he stared at the Black Lincoln that just pulled in front of the Jones's.

"It's him," FX02 said.

Treble was getting out the back of a Black Lincoln.

"What do I do?"

"Take the shot," the director said.

"The shot? I don't even have my rifle set up. You never told – "

"Shit." The director cursed. "I'm sending in a team."

"Sir?"

"In the meantime, if he leaves that house," the director began before a thought crossed his mind. "Shit, he won't leave out the front once he discovers the boy's mother."

"Sir?"

"Shit! Why didn't I have someone covering the rear? Shit. Shit. Shit."

Louder, FX02 said, "Sir?"

"What?" the director finally acknowledged his field agent.

"I planted enough C-4 on both floors to level the house."

"I didn't authorize . . . Why? Never mind. Good Job," the director congratulated. "Do you have remote access?"

"Yes, sir. Cell phone digital code frequency." FX02 spoke with an air of pride in his voice.

"By now he's discovered the body," the director commented. "Do it. Do it now!"

Two seconds after being given the order, a massive explosion rocked the forty estate homes in the upper crust neighborhood. Several homes were damaged, including the home that Agent FX02 was set up in.

"FX02, are you there? FX02?"

Ronald 'FX02' Reagan was disoriented as he slowly rose to his feet. Despite the ringing in his ears, he still could hear his boss's voice. Pitch black a minute ago, now the upstairs bedroom where FX02 was perched was lit up like the noon sun.

"FX02, come in," the director said. "I've lost visual. FX02, come in."

Glass and sheetrock were moving around the battered and bleeding agent. The ringing in his head was almost unbearable. He closed his eyes and slowly crawled over to where he thought he heard the director's voice.

The rising smoke made the agent cough, which caused excruciating pain in his abdominal area.

"FX02, please respond. I've lost visual."

The agent assassin noticed the blood on his hands as he picked up the high-powered camera scope. He slowly inserted the four-way scope's earpiece back into his ear, allowing the director to regain his multidirectional visual.

"FX02," the director said. "You have several shards of glass protruding from your mid-section."

The agent looked down. His Indianapolis Gas & Light uniform was soaked with blood. He noticed several large shards of glass lodged in his stomach and chest area. "I need an extraction, sir."

"I know, but first look out the window. Tell me what you see."

The agent slowly did as he was told. "Too much smoke and debris." He fought back the desire to cough.

"The house. What about the house?" the director asked.

"Gone, that one and the two houses on either side."

"Shit. Shit. Shit. You killed civilians," the director said.

"I don't understand. I planted just enough C4 to bring down that house."

"You made a mistake in your calculations."

"No disrespect, sir, but I do not make mistakes. I know how much C4 I planted." He doubled over and coughed. "How long before the extraction team? I'm bleeding pretty bad."

"The press and the locals will be swarming the area any minute. It will be impossible for us to get a team to you as long as the locals are on the scene."

"What are you saying?"

"You served your country well, son. Your wife and children will be well taken care of."

"Wife and children? I'm twenty-five. My wife is the agency and I have no children. Sir, I will die if no one comes soon."

"I suggest you take the cyanide capsule," the director said. "At least you won't suffer."

Chapter 4

April 4, 2002
***PRESENT DAY*: Early Morning: Blountville, Tennessee**

An average looking middle-aged black man wearing a priest's collar opened the huge gray metal doors as the white station wagon approached the private airport hangar. Once the station wagon came to a complete stop inside, Dr. Fast jumped out. "George Rawlings." Dr. Fast embraced the catholic archbishop. "It's been too long."

They broke their embrace.

"Yes, it has been," the archbishop replied. The archbishop looked at the sleeping form in the rear of the station wagon. "So, that's him?"

Dr. Fast nodded.

"The Messiah has risen," the archbishop said.

"Not exactly. I drugged him because of the trauma of losing so much in such a short time," the Muslim cleric said.

"The child has been through a lot over the last few hours, but of course, God won't put a burden on him that he can not carry," the archbishop said.

Dr. Fast looked through the window at Zion's sleeping figure. "The world is truly on his shoulders." He turned to the Archbishop. "Give me a hand. Let's get him onto the plane."

The Cessna's twin jet engines roared to life, causing the Catholic Archbishop and the Islamic scholar to shout over the noise.

"Does Dr. Boyce know that you gave the boy something?" the Archbishop asked while helping Dr. Fast carry Zion onto the plane.

"Yes, he didn't seem too happy about it."

The archbishop smiled. "Don't pay any mind to John, he thinks all drugs are bad."

"They are," Dr. Fast said, "but, sometimes you have to take the bad and pray that good will come out of it. In any case, let's just get the boy to Dr. Boyce in London."

"London?" The Archbishop wore a confused look on his face. "Dr. Boyce lives in Atlanta."

"I know but he's in London addressing this year's World Archaeological Society conference."

"I'm baffled."

"Did you forget that Dr. Boyce is one of the leading archaeologists in the world today?"

"No, of course I didn't forget," the archbishop said. "I guess I just assumed that you were taking Zion to Atlanta or to Momma Orthine's in Spartanburg."

"You know what they say about those who assume?" Dr. Fast said. "Besides, Nigeria is a lot closer to London than it is to Atlanta or South Carolina."

Chapter 5

April 4, 2002
NEXT DAY: **Mid morning CIA Headquarters**

"We interrupt this program for this late breaking news report," the CNN anchor said. "We want to go straight to Andre' Lamont, reporting live from Golden Hill Estates in Indianapolis. Andre' what's going on?"

"As you can see, three houses have been completely leveled. The fire department spent nine hours fighting the raging fire that erupted after a loud explosion that could be heard and felt for miles around."

The anchor's voice interrupted. "Andre', do the authorities know how the fire started?"

"I've been told that the fire resulted from an explosion, inside one of the homes. We do know that there were nine casualties."

*****

The director sat in front of his computer screen on a teleconference call with the NSA chief and the Chairman of the

Federal Reserve. All three watched as the news reporter on the scene finished his story.

"Sir?" A female CIA analyst stepped into the director's office.

The director shook his head. "Not now."

"But, sir?"

The director turned his head. "Agent Reynolds, I said – "

"Sir, I really think you need to see this now."

The director turned back to the screen. "Excuse me, gentlemen."

The director rose from his seat and walked around his desk before escorting the analyst out of the office and into the hall.

"What do you have?"

She whispered, "FX02 wasn't in the house across the street."

"Okay, then where did you find him?"

She exhaled. "We didn't."

"That's odd. Hmm," the director pondered. "What about the blood? Where did the trail end?"

"Sir, there was no blood. Not even a trace sample."

Can't be. I saw the explosion. If somebody was working with XR13, I'm dead. "Thank you, agent Reynolds."

"I'll have the full report to you within the hour."

"That won't be necessary. This one stays off the books."

"You're Red Flagging it?" She was referring to the term used when all records of a CIA mission were destroyed and that mission was deemed to have never happened.

"No need. As far as we know, agent FX02 could be anywhere. There was never an assignment where FX02 would have needed an extraction, right, Agent Reynolds?"

"Right, sir."

"That will be all," the director said before the young analyst turned around.

"By the way, Reynolds?"

She turned. "Yes, sir."

Good agent. Hate to have to eliminate her. And I won't have to if she chooses Dubai, he thought. "Keep up the great work. And you should apply for the senior analyst position in Dubai. You'll have your own team, a five thousand dollar a month living stipend and your salary will be substantially higher than it is now."

"I still have two years before I'm eligible for senior analyst, sir."

"Agent Reynolds?"

"Sir?"

"I'm the director. I said apply." He turned and headed back to his office, before he shouted, "Apply this week, Reynolds."

Someone moved FX02. A professional. This had XR13's stamp all over it. But, he was dead. No way he could have survived. The chances of FX02 surviving were minimal at best. These and other thoughts swirled around in the director's head. Before he did anything he knew he had to answer the Why, then the Who, the Where would be easy when he answered the first two questions.

The director sat back in his seat and faced the monitor. "Sorry about that."

The director's eyes were on the screen but his mind was analyzing and reanalyzing the events that unfolded right after the explosion.

All that blood. How did they get the carpet and FX02's body out so fast without anyone noticing? Only a professional could have cleaned that area and made it look like it had not been cleaned. This has XR13's writing all over it, and Treble knows that I can't implicate him, because I was his handler. My career would be finished. I would be finished if XR13 somehow lived and had a hand in killing and or abducting agent FX02.

The NSA chief's voice snapped the director out of his thoughts. "Gerald, you look like you just caught your best friend plucking your wife."

"I'm fine, Maurice. If we could get on with the briefing, gentlemen," the director said.

"While you were off playing with your pretty little analyst, I received DNA confirmation," the NSA chief said. "The bodies found in the Jones' house were positively identified as Malia Jones and Treble Frazier's. Both were burned beyond recognition. The lab had to use bone marrow for the samples."

Director Bush breathed a heavy sigh of relief, but that relief only lasted seconds when the director realized that someone else had to know about the mission. Finding FX02 was now a top priority Red Flag mission.

"Don't relax just yet, Gerald," the chief said. "The boy is still missing."

"So what, he's ten."

"Isaiah 11:6," the General remarked. "And the wolf shall dwell with the lamb, and the
leopard shall lie down with them."

"So melodramatic, we are not living in biblical times, Maurice," the director admonished.

The chairman of the Federal Reserve interrupted. "That may be so, but we still don't know if XR13 had any recorded or documented evidence of the government's involvement with nine-eleven."

"Who cares? If XR13 is dead, he won't be able to corroborate the validity of any future evidence discovered," Director Bush said.

"If?" the NSA chief said. "You sound like you don't trust the labs findings, Gerald."

"No, I trust them. DNA doesn't lie," Director Bush said, not sure if he one hundred percent believed the words that had just come from his mouth.

"There is still the issue of the other seven bodies," the NSA chief said.

"What issue? They're casualties of war," the director said.

"First, there is no war, Gerald and second they are, were American citizens. One of the so called casualties was a judge," the General said.

"You're an asshole, Maurice."

"An asshole that doesn't make mistakes or leave behind loose ends."

"Gentlemen please," the chairman pleaded. "Gerald, find a scapegoat fast, we don't want the locals or the FBI to spend too much time on this. Someone needs to answer for the seven bodies. Innocence or guilt doesn't matter. What matters is getting an ironclad conviction."

"How do I – "

The chairman interrupted. "Do I really need to tell you, Gerald? I mean, if we can fool the world into believing that two passenger jetliners brought down two structurally sound skyscrapers by attacking them from the top, framing someone for this should be a walk in the park. Do you foresee a problem with putting this Golden Hill Estate incident to bed, Gerald?"

"No, sir. No problem at all."

"Just one more thing, Gerald."

"Yes?"

"Find the boy."

"And do what with him?" the director asked.

"Do you really need me to answer that?"

"He's just a child," the director said.

"The child of the most dangerous killer in the history of the agency."

Chapter 6

April 9, 2002
Four Days Later: **Ile, Ife Nigeria**

"Whew," Dr. Boyce said as he used a handkerchief to wipe the sweat pouring from his brow. "It's hotter than a whore house in hell on nickel night. How can you stand to be outside in this Nigerian heat, Baba?"

If man were created in the likeness of God, then Baba was created in the likeness of Marcus Garvey. Short, stout and dark, he even had a commanding presence reminiscent of Garvey. Even his mannerisms were Garveyesque, Dr. Boyce thought as the blazing African sun beamed down on his mentor's sweating baldhead. The two men were out back, walking through the palace's eight-foot high maze of a million flowers. The man that answered to many names such as your highness, Ooni, Oduduwa and Baba, was dressed like a rich medieval king's sorcerer instead of the Ooni of Ile-Ife, also known as the city were creation began.

Oba is the name for king in Yoruba culture, with the exception of the king of Ile-Ife, which is the Mecca, or the Bethlehem of the Yoruba people. The Ooni is the name for the king of the sacred and legendary city of Ile-Ife, located in Southwestern Nigeria.

Baba's hands were clasped behind his back, as he seemed to float on air as he led Reverend Boyce through the winding five-acre maze of flowers and greenery.

"My Brother," the middle-aged dark skinned man stopped, closed his eyes and extended his heavily jewel clad hands and arms to the heavens. "What you feel are sun bursts of energy." Baba's chest rose as he tried to take in all the air out of the sky. Exhaling, he said, "Doesn't the warmth just invigorate you?"

"Yeah, I'm invigorated to get in some air conditioning. This African heat makes me think that the good Lord is hosting the world's biggest barbeque." Reverend Boyce stopped and looked at his friend's dress. "Baba, you have to be slow roasting in all that royal regalia."

There was a slight vibration in the earth as Baba bellowed out a deep good-natured laugh. "I'm used to the royal garments and head dress. I've been wearing them long enough."

"Can we please go inside the palace before all that red," the Reverend pointed at the heavy robe Baba wore, "catches on fire? And will you please take off that beaded head dress so I can see your face when we speak?"

"You know I can't remove my crown."

"It's only the two of us out here, Baba."

"You only see two of us, but I assure you there are more. And you know if any of them look into my eyes they will burn to ashes."

"They might as well look into your eyes and get it over with instead of being slow roasted in this oven heat."

Baba placed a huge dark hand on Reverend Boyce's back. "Come, let's go inside. I feel Zion's energy stirring."

"He's awake?" Dr. Boyce asked as he followed the Nigerian king into the royal palace.

"Not yet."

This was his fourth time visiting the palace in the last half century. Each time, the face and body were different. The other Ooni's bodies had died, but the spirit and soul in all of the Ooni's were that of Baba Ududuwa.

*****

His first encounter with Baba was in '55, a few days after he'd spoken at the Bandung Conference in Indonesia. Dr. Boyce had flown straight from Indonesia to Nigeria on April 25, the day after the largest gathering of non-western world leaders was held. On the 26th Dr. Boyce was chest deep in sand and dirt. He had been on an archaeological dig two hundred miles northwest of the sacred city, Ile-Ife when he dug up a small hand-carved black jewelry box. He had tried to open it, but it had been locked, so he took it inside his tent and dug up enough dirt to bury it until he could get back to it later that evening.

By the time he'd dragged himself into the tent that evening, back in '55 all he had enough energy for was sleep. That night, the weirdest thing had happened. A god-like spirit had come to him in a dream. Normally, the reverend was a skeptic, but when he first met Baba Oduduwa in that dream forty-seven years ago, he had no doubt that the Ooni was who he proclaimed to be. To this very day, Dr. Boyce couldn't even begin to explain how he had been so sure that Baba had been sent by the Creator to prepare the twelve men that would serve as the "Council of Clerics" to help nurture and protect the Messiah until he acquired the 360 degrees of knowledge needed to defeat Evil.

The spirit had explained to the Reverend Dr. that it was a jewelry box that could only be opened by a direct descendant of the Yoruba goddess, Oba. Being that he was an archaeologist and a well-studied theologian, the Reverend Dr. was well versed in Vodun African centered spirituality. Dr. Boyce was one of a small handful of people living in the 50's that knew and had empirical evidence that Christianity was a derivative of Vodun spirituality.

At the time of his discovery, he was a twenty-eight-year-old African-American archaeologist working on his PhD in Christian theology. Thanks to Baba and the ancient texts he gave Dr. Boyce to study, he became the leading world scholar in Vodun, Islamic, and Christian spirituality. After several years of research, Dr. Boyce came to the conclusion that all three spiritual concepts were virtually the same, once you put them in their original context.

Each time Dr. Boyce had visited the Ooni over the years, it was a different face and body, but the sprit and voice were always the same.

*****

Baba and the Reverend Dr. were in the Ooni's library inside Baba's royal bedchambers. As if pressing in a code, Baba touched the number on the spine of six of the twenty-four volumes of the "Book of Knowledge" before the bookcase parted like the Red Sea. The two men stepped into the small elevator that the wall-to-wall bookcase opened up into. Dr. Boyce was wondering how far down they were going, and he was about to ask when the elevator slowed to a stop before the titanium doors opened.

"Amazing," Dr. Boyce said as he stepped out of the elevator and rubbed his hand across a gray rock wall. "Simply amazing." He rubbed his fingers together. "Gneisses, granite, and some other metavolcanic substance." Dr. Boyce continued studying the rock sediment on his hands. "No way to be sure without testing it, but I'm almost positive that this cave is Precambrian."

Baba stopped and turned to the Reverend Dr. "I don't know what that means?"

"It means that this cave is somewhere around two and a half to three and a half billion years old."

"Three-billion, six hundred thirty-seven million, four-hundred seventy-six thousand, eight hundred and nineteen years, but who's counting?" Baba said before he continued walking through the cave.

"That would mean – "

Baba finished the Reverend Dr.'s statement. "This cave was here before man."

Dr. Boyce stopped walking to marvel at the changing rock walls. "Amazing."

Baba smiled. "I assure you Reverend, they are real."

"When we brought Zion here four days ago," Dr. Boyce pointed at the three-story cave walls, "all of this was just rock."

"It still is." Baba looked over at the transparent enclosure that Zion was resting inside of before walking toward his unconscious guest. "He did this."

"How? Zion's been unconscious the whole time he's been here," Dr. Boyce said as he walked up next to Baba.

"Both men were looking into the glass-like chamber that held only a bed and Zion's ten- year-old unconscious form.

"Right here where we are standing is where creation began. Ile-Ife was the first city and once upon a time it was known as the city of Gods. Being that young Zion here is the last descendant of Shango, the god of fire, lightning and thunder, his subconscious mind has manifested enough energy to cause these walls to transform into the diamonds that you are looking at."

"The temperature would have had to be at least 2,200 degrees, probably a lot hotter for the rock to begin to change," Dr. Boyce said.

"Don't leave out the pressure," Baba said, "It would take at least 725,000 pounds per square inch after the rock is heated to 2,200 degrees."

"No man or animal can survive under those conditions, and this glass cage would have melted along with the bed," Dr. Boyce said.

"I agree. But as you know, Zion is so much more than man or animal." Changing the subject, Baba continued. "You know, before Shango's deification he was a warrior king, the third king of the Oyo Empire – a true unselfish servant of the people – one of the very few rulers to have never been corrupted by power. God, Allah or Oludamare as I like to refer to the Supreme Creator bestowed certain aspects of his supreme wisdom to some mortals. Shango was one such mortal. This supreme wisdom transformed mortal into a god – or for lack of a better word, an intermediary between man and Creator, sort of like Jesus, Moses, and Abraham. And remember my Christian friend; none of the four horsemen are mere mortals. And we know that Zion is destined to be the third horseman, the Dark Horse Assassin. And he has but one God-given mission."

Chapter 7

April 10, 2002
NEXT DAY: Ile-Ife, Nigeria

The Reverend and Baba stood on opposite sides of Zion's hospital bed in the glass-like enclosure.

Baba reached out and took Reverend Boyce's hand while both men held one of Zion's. Next, Baba closed his eyes and barely above a whisper he began, "I Baba Oduduwa, servant of the most high command you Zion Uhuru Jones, last descendant of Shango, god of fire, thunder, lightning, and the personification of strategy to open your eyes."

Dr. Boyce jumped at the sudden eruption of thunder that exploded. Streaks of zig zagging lightning lit up the underground darkness.

Then, silence.

Moments later, steam began to ooze from the rock floor and walls. Baba's face was calm. He seemed serene as he watched the metamorphosis around them. The glass-like structure protected them from the conditions outside of the bubble that they were in. The Reverend Dr.'s earlier amazement had turned to fear as he watched the floors and the walls heat up until they were a bright burnt orange.

The Reverend Dr. turned to Baba. "Make him stop before we start to cook."

"Don't be afraid, Reverend. This enclosure is resistant to weather or gravity. I designed it myself," Baba said as balls of fire jumped off the walls and flew across the cave like small meteors.

Reverend Boyce was too busy being terrified when Zion's eyes began to flutter.

The roof and the sides of the enclosure were suddenly assaulted by flaming hot falling rock, and soccer ball sized balls of fire. The concrete floor outside the bubble looked like orange taffy as it began to liquefy. The steam from the molten rock began to cloud the glass like structure. Visibility was almost zero.

As suddenly as the storm began, it stopped.

"Oduduwa," Zion said as he slightly turned his head to Baba.

Baba smiled.

Zion turned his head to the Reverend, who was now at Zion's side. "Uncle John."

Fifteen minutes later, the ground and walls had cooled enough for Baba and the reverend to roll Zion's bed into another cavern. This one was well lit, unlike the cavern they'd just left. The small cavern they were now in resembled a high tech clinic.

"Zion, I am going to remove the wrapping from your feet and legs first and then I will make my way up to your head," Baba explained.

"If you just changed his facial features, why the mummy wrap on his whole body?" the reverend asked.

"Purification. The linen strips are soaked in herbs that remove all impure substances on and inside the body. It also helps wounds heal miraculously fast without any scarification," Baba said as he removed the off white linen mummy wrapping.

"How does he know who we are?" Dr. Boyce asked.

"I can still hear you Uncle John," Zion said.

"Uhm. I apologize."

"No need. My dad told me who you were."

"Your dad… he's dead." the Reverend Dr. said.

"Transitioned," Zion said. "Dad, me, you, no one ever dies. We are all masses of energy. And Energy cannot be created or destroyed. It only transforms."

"So, you are in communication with your father?" the reverend asked.

"Dad speaks to me in my dreams. I have no control over how and when he comes."

"Actually, you do," Baba said.

"I do what?"

"You have the power to control these communications with your dad, and other spirits. You just don't know how."

"And this is what you are going to teach me?" Zion asked Baba.

"This and so much more."

Baba was unwrapping the linen from Zion's face.

Reverend Boyce's eyes got big as the wrapping was peeled away.

"What's wrong, Uncle John?"

"Nothing," he said in awe. "Nothing at all."

Baba put a hand mirror to Zion's face. "Sun, you are in danger and you will be in danger as long as you dwell the earth. The facial reconstruction provides you with anonymity for now."

"Anna who?"

"Anonymity. The enemy won't be able to recognize you, now that I have reconstructed your face," Baba said.

Zion looked at the foreign image that stared back at him in the mirror. He touched his nose and then his lips. "What about my name? Shouldn't we change it, too?"

Baba shook his head. "No. By the time the enemy does find you, it will be time for you to be found and your name will tell the world who you are."

Zion played with his new face while he listened to Baba.

"You'll get used to it," Baba said.

"It's cool." He opened his mouth as wide as he could then closed it. Zion repeated this several times. "My new face is really cool. I just hate that there are no scars."

"You want scar tissue on your face?" the Reverend Dr. asked.

"All great warriors have scars," Zion spoke in a knowing tone. "Scars mean you're battle tested."

"What makes you think that you are a battle tested warrior?"

"My Dad told me all about Shango, my great, great, great, times infinity grandpa. Dad said that Shango was one of the greatest warrior kings. He said he was a loved and popular ruler and warrior because of his meticulous strategizing, and fairness. Dad said that all the male descendants of Shango lived and fought so I could be here to complete the oracle. Only thing is Dad didn't tell me what the oracle was or how I was going to complete it."

"To complete the oracle you must defeat the author of confusion and division."

"Huh?"

"He's ten, Baba, you might wanna wait until he learns more African history."

"He may be ten, but he has the wisdom of a god," Baba said. "Besides, we only have seven years to teach him when it takes forty years to unlock all the mysteries of the human mind."

61

"Alexander was schooled for seven years in the sacred mystery schools in Ionia and he was able to conquer an empire that stretched from the Balkans to Pakistan," Dr. Boyce said.

Baba picked up where the Reverend Dr. left off. "Alexander the Great was also a paranoid schizophrenic who had many of his close friends executed because of his extreme paranoia. He died a very lonely man," Baba said. "Many thought that his paranoia came from his early exit from the mystery schools. And they were right. With only seven years in school, he didn't understand the information he had and that, Zion, drove him insane."

"So, does that mean that in seven years I'm going to go crazy?"

"I surely hope not," Dr. Boyce said. "With a destiny such as yours and a name like Zion Uhuru to wear as a badge, crazy won't be able to get into your head."

"Why was I named Zion?"

"Why not Zion?" Dr. Boyce replied. "It means promised land."

Baba intervened. "Which refers to the land of peace, and of course, you can't have peace without freedom, and that's what your last name means. Zion Uhuru. Peace and freedom. Man has been fighting for these two concepts since the Pale one manifested himself into a serpent and introduced mankind to sin and death.

Zion's eyes widened. "My mother... did the explosion...Is she...?"

Baba nodded. "I'm afraid so, but you already know this, sun."

"I... I didn't want to believe it."

"It's okay to show emotion, sun," Dr. Boyce said as he squeezed Zion's hand.

"I've been grieving in my sleep for however many days I've been sleep," Zion said. "Dad helped me to understand. Mom doesn't come to me in dreams like dad does. So, I miss

62

her way more, but dad tells me that mom is watching me and that her love is all around me and will never leave me."

"You've been through a lot for a ten-year-old," the Reverend Dr. said.

"That's what I told Dad. He said that I've gone through and will only go through forests and down roads that God has planned."

"Did Treble tell you the Creator's plan for you?" Baba asked.

"No. But he did tell me to trust you and Uncle John."

"Are you scared?" Baba asked.

"Of what?" Zion asked.

"Of today, tomorrow, your new life, anything, everything," Baba said.

"No."

"Good," Baba said. "Zion, three million one hundred and sixty thousand years ago, man was born of the Creator. He had only one date and that was a birth date. Death didn't exist until one of God's little gods, became jealous of Her. This jealously caused this god to try and thwart the Creator at every turn. So, Zion when God created this World, everything in it was in harmony. It was perfect; all of it was the Promised Land, and there was only peace until this jealous god came down to earth in physical form and introduced sin to this Promised Land world."

Zion turned to Dr. Boyce. "Uncle John, is a god the same thing as an angel?"

The reverend replied, "A god, little G, is a special angel – one that the Supreme Creator uses to help mankind understand the scope of the Creator's infinite wisdom and power."

"So, is that why in the Bible God says do not bring any god before me."

Dr. Boyce nodded. "I guess it is."

Zion turned his head back toward Baba. "I'm sorry, Baba. So, what happened after sin came to the world?"

"Well, when sin was introduced death followed as a result. And since that time, the Supreme Creator has sent Her spirit, which She made manifest in human form to teach the people of the World how to avoid being slaves to sin. Each time that messenger left, many of those people, particularly the well-to-do and ones that wielded earthly power over others reverted back to coveting objects that the author of Death put before them."

The reverend picked up without missing a beat. "And now, the most popular and powerful country in the world has morphed into a modern day Babylon," the reverend paused to let his words sink in. "Zion you are the last messenger of God. Christians refer to you as the Messiah; Muslims refer to you as the Mahdi. Revelations chapter six verse eight, 'and I looked, and behold a pale horse: and his name that sat on him was Death, and Hell followed with him. And power was given unto them over the fourth part of the earth, to kill with the sword, and with hunger, and with death, and with the beasts of the earth.'"

Baba added, "There was also another horse, a dark horse, it's rider a judge and an assassin."

"So, the pale horse rider is death, and I am the Dark Horse Assassin that has come to fight him?" Zion asked.

Baba shook his head. "No. You have been sent to defeat Death," Baba said, and you do know that when we refer to Death, we are talking about Evil. But, before I send you to the battlefield, I must devote the next seven years preparing you for war."

"Why seven years?"

"It was supposed to be forty," Baba said. "Your dad had just completed the fifth tier in his sixth tier priesthood education. He still had six years to go when doors in his conscious mind opened up and allowed him to briefly see through the Creator's eyes. He saw you, Zion. He saw you and your wife on dark horses."

"My wife?"

"Let me back up," Baba said. "Shango was more than a warrior king. He became a god, or one of the Creator's angels, whichever word you prefer. Oba was the first of Shango's three wives. She, too, was a fierce warrior. She even taught Shango knife fighting, but the strongest virtue Oba carried was her love for Shango. She loved him so much that she cut her own ear off and attempted to feed it to him in hopes of winning his love back, instead Shango was so angered that he banished her from the kingdom and she fell to earth.

"At the time, Shango didn't know that one of his other wives had tricked Oba into the self-mutilation. And since the banishment, Shango has never been the same. His strength decreased and he wasn't the supreme strategizer that he was when he was with Oba." Baba paused in hopes that he was not confusing Zion's young mind.

"Zion, you have to find the last descendant of Oba. Once you gain her unconditional love, then and only then will you have the strength and wisdom to defeat the Pale Horse rider."

"Okay, let me make sure I understand you correctly," Zion said. "I have to stay here, where ever here is, for seven years. In that time I have to acquire forty years of knowledge, then I have to find some girl that I have no idea what her name is and make her fall in love with me and then I have to go and save the world by killing Evil?"

Baba nodded. "Basically."

"Sounds like a low budget straight-to-DVD horror movie."

"What is a ten-year-old doing watching low budget horror movies?" the reverend Dr. asked.

"I don't watch them, Uncle John. I'm just saying…"

"What are you just saying?"

"I'm just saying that you two are putting a lot of pressure on a ten-year-old kid. Bay, Spielberg, and Cameron together couldn't sell this story line to Hollywood and you want me to do this in real life."

"Sounds about right," the reverend Dr. said. "How 'bout it, Baba?"

"Uhmm, more or less," Baba said. "As I help you expand your mind and body, you will grow more confident," Baba said. "The young lady, the last descendant of Oba, her whereabouts will not be as difficult to locate as you might think."

"Come with me, Zion, you, too, Reverend," Baba said as they walked back into the huge amphitheater-like hollow cave where Zion recovered over the past few days.

"Baba, when did my daddy know that I was the Dark Horseman?"

"Seven days ago?"

"The day before the explosion?" Zion said.

"Yes." The Reverend Dr. nodded. "I was in London at the time, but Treble was in Spartanburg with my sister. She initiated your father into the sacred Amun priesthood when it came to him in a vision. He said, we had been wrong, that you were the Messiah and he went on to explain to me what you needed to do in order to complete the oracle. Your dad was extremely disturbed. He was even more disturbed when I explained to him that we had always known who he was and who you are.

"The day of the explosion, Treble called from Atlanta. He said that he had to get to the airport, that you and your mother were in danger. That was the last time I spoke to him."

Zion looked at both men. "I think I might know the last descendant of Oba. I think she's a little girl around my age."

"What makes you think that?" Dr. Boyce asked.

"Well, every since I was a little kid, I've had these dreams."

"What dreams?" Baba asked.

"Well, when I was real little, a long time ago, she was real little, too. We played catch, pitching a soccer ball back and forth with our minds. The ball would stop right in front of our chests. Over time as I aged, she did, too. In one dream we were fishing, in another we were racing on our bicycles."

"How often do you have these dreams?" Baba asked.

Zion shrugged his shoulders. "I don't know. Maybe once, twice a year."

"When was the last time?" Baba asked.

"She and I were just about to get on the Mindbender at Six Flags before you woke me."

"Today?" the Reverend Dr. asked.

Zion nodded.

"What's her name? What does she look like? Where does she live?"

Chapter 8

April 10, 2002
SAME DAY: **Night: Lithonia, Georgia**

Pleasant Pointe apartments were anything but pleasant. Dekalb County should've fined the complex owners for misleading advertisement. The Rowdy Ridge apartment complex was a more fitting name for the low-budget housing complex in the Atlanta suburban area.

The big arrow, had just met up with the little arrow and they both were pointing due north on every accurate clock and watch in Atlanta. To a vampire, the night was young. On this Friday night the bloodsuckers were out in full swing. Pushers, prostitutes, tricks, and thieves waiting for an opportunity lingered in private and public areas in the one way in/one way out drug and crime infested community.

There wasn't even a full moon out and folks were acting more of a fool than usual. Used condoms, needles, broken glass, cigarette and cigar butts, and used diapers littered the complexes two playgrounds. There seemed to be more dope dealers than fiends hanging around the rear playground.

Millions changed hands weekly on the rimless half basketball court and over by the rusty swing set frame.

In middle class white suburbia, at midnight on Saturday night, most ten-year-olds were in bed, maybe even watching television or playing video games but here, they were running up to cars, exchanging nickel size ten foil packs filled with crack and powder cocaine for money.

"Yum-Yum!" Sunny shouted, catching the little boy's attention.

The boy turned his head to the two women.

"Get your narrow butt home, 'fore I knock you out."

Yum-Yum looked back at the three older boys that he ran dope for before turning back to Sunny. "What you need to do Ms. Brown is find you some business and leave mine alone 'fore you won't have no business at all."

Assata grabbed Sunny's arm. She knew her best friend too well.

"What did you just say? Did you just threaten me?" Sunny asked, stepping toward him.

The kid waved an arm as if shooing her away before turning around and heading back to the curb where the older boys were passing around a blunt.

"Oh shit," one of the older boys said.

When Yum-Yum turned around, Sunny was right there.

Pop! She slapped the little boy across the face.

"Bitch!" he shouted as he put a hand to his stinging jaw.

Sunny kicked off her heels and put the ten-year-old in a strangle hold, while using her other hand to take off his belt.

"Let me go. Stop! You ain't my momma!"

"Thank God for that," she said while removing his belt.

Whap!

"Owww!"

"Now, who you calling a bitch?"

Whap!

"Owwww!"

"Don't you ever talk back to grown folks, boy!" Sunny looked up at the three older boys. "Y'all oughta' be ashamed, using this baby to sell your dope."

The smallest of the three had his pants hanging below his knees, one foot on the ground the other on the building wall behind him. He turned his Miami Heat hat to the back. "Yo, sis, word up, on everything." He grabbed his crotch area. "You can get it. Straight up." He held a small bank roll out toward Sunny. "Just throw out a number, shawty."

Sunny ignored the dope boy for the moment. She pushed Yum-Yum away. "Now run home and tell your momma I beat your behind and tell her why I tore that tail up."

He turned and started walking.

She took off her shoe and threw it, intentionally missing the kid.

"I said run, boy," she shouted.

Yum-Yum took off down the street.

Next, Sunny turned and snatched the wad out of the dope boy's hand. "This will do."

The boy took his foot off the wall and used one hand to pull up his pants. "That's damn near a stack, sis." He reached an arm out toward her.

She put the money inside her bra and started unbuttoning her dress.

"Yo, whachu doin?" one of the other boys asked.

"I'm takin' off my clothes."

"Why?" the first boy asked.

"I'm 'bout to earn this money you just gave me. Now get naked, little man. We can do it right here." Sunny pointed to a small grassy area where a couple of fiends stood.

"Nah, sis, yo, I was just uh…"

"You was just talking out your ass and now shit coming out your mouth," she said as she began buttoning up her red form-fitting dress.

"Whateva, sis. But yo, you gon' have to come up off my cheddar," he said, holding out his hand.

The three didn't notice the shadow approaching from the left.

She pointed at her breasts. "You talkin' about this money I just earned?"

"Earned? If you don't unass my bankroll." He lunged forward as Sunny stepped back.

The boys froze at the sound of a bullet being chambered. Assata had her .380 inches from the lunging boy's forehead. "Now we can handle this one or two ways," Assata said. "I can make the world a better place and at the same time help bring your families together in one home or you can apologize to my girl."

After all three apologized, the little one asked, "What about my bankroll?"

Assata looked over at Sunny.

Sunny reached into her bra and pulled out the rubber-banded stack of cash, "You can get it, shorty," Sunny said.

"Yeah, little man, you can get it right now," Assata said as she grabbed at her crotch area.

"Pull it out, little man and you can get it all. I mean drop 'em down to your ankles, take off that big ass T-shirt. I wanna see what you workin' with. And if I think I can work with what you workin' with, than we can go back to my place and put in some work," Sunny said.

"Stop playin', sis. All that ain't even mine," the boy said.

"Do I look like you? I mean, really?" Sunny asked the boy.

"Nah," he said with a confused look on his face, "Why you ask that?"

"Cause you keep calling me sis, like we related, now drop 'em or we out."

The three boys just stood there doing nothing and saying nothing.

Sunny pulled out a twenty before she threw the wad at the boys. "Punk asses. You three best find you another corner, cause just like the eviction party me and my girl just left, you are evicted from this corner. Don't let me see you three here tomorrow night. Is that clear?"

"Yes ma'am," the three boys responded in unison.

Sunny held out the twenty she just removed. "Here, let me get a quarter of that mid. I don't want none of that loud, y'all smoking."

A few minutes later, the two best friends were sharing a joint on the back porch of Sunny's project apartment.

"Girl, you a plum fool. I can't believe you whipped that boy's behind in front of his friends."

"I don't know why you can't believe that. You know me. I can't stand no bad behind, disrespectful kids, I don't care whose they are. I might beat his little behind again next time he come over asking to play with Mira." She held her a hand up in front of Assata. "Little nappy head monster made me break one of my nails. I just had them done. Fifteen damn dollars down the drain."

"Girl, that fifteen dollars is nothing if one of those dope boys would have knocked your head into next week."

"Now you know," Sunny gave Assata a you-know-better-than-that look, "them boys may be dumb, but they not stupid," she said while puffing on the cannabis.

"I swear I thought the little Jermaine Dupree look-alike was about to pee his pants when I held Betsy to his forehead," Assata said.

"Let's just hope them boys are smart enough not to come back. I hate to have to spill blood on my own doorstep."

"It wouldn't be the first time," Sunny said.

"On another note, how many times is Butter gon' throw an eviction party, damn?" Assata asked.

Sunny held up three fingers. "This is the third one in three months and she still there."

"And we still go and pay our ten dollars each time, and we will be there next month when she does it again."

"And you know that's the truth," Sunny said while giving Assata a high-five before pulling five wallets out of Assata's purse and laying them out on the concrete in front of them. "Like taking money off the dead. Butter have it so dark in there, niggas be so close together tryin' to rub on somebody's ass, they don't even feel our hands in they pockets."

"I heard Butter made so much the first time that she caught up both months and paid all the late fees."

"Wouldn't have been difficult. Her rent ain't nothing but eighteen dollars. I don't even see how you can't come up with eighteen damn dollars every month," Sunny said. "She look all right. She still got her youth. She coulda' tricked off with one of these sorry ass dope boys to get that little money."

"Sunny," Assata said, "Butter ain't no ho."

"She needs to be whatever and do whoever if it means keeping a roof over her and them two little girls heads."

Assata made small clouds of smoke as she exhaled. "Heffa, every woman can't just spread her legs to get a bill paid."

"I don't see why not. Just cause you done been to church four Sundays in a row don't mean you earned a halo, ho. Remember Mr. Stokes," Sunny said.

"Girl, I was only fifteen. That don't count."

"Hell if it don't."

"I was gon' get held back. Ain't no way I was gon' repeat the tenth grade, and besides Mr. Stokes know he was full of fine."

"He was a married forty-year-old science teacher with kids older than we were."

Assata shrugged. "I was young and dumb, and besides it wasn't like I was no virgin."

"Stop making excuses, girl, just admit it," Sunny said. "You a ho."

"Hold on, if memory serves me correct," Assata crossed her arms and nodded her head, "Mr. Stokes had his way with you, too. So, what does that make you Ms. Lady?"

"First, Reginald didn't have his way with me."

"So, you on a first name basis with the father of his wife's children?" Assata said.

"Back then, I was," Sunny said. "After you told me how he made your river flow, naturally I had to see what all the flowing was about. And the difference between you and me is I got sixty dollars out of my test drive." Sunny pointed a finger in Assata's direction before continuing. "And that makes me a prostitute, not a ho."

"I know that sorry behind Raynelle didn't pay for nothing."

"Nothing but raping me," Sunny said.

Assata dropped the blunt on the concrete below. "Sunny, I'm sorry. I wasn't thinking."

Sunny put a hand on Assata's. "I'm used to it," Sunny said.

"Used to what."

Sunny smiled. "You not thinking."

"Seriously, Sunny, do you ever think about that night?"

"All the time."

"Mira is ten, so Raynelle has been in prison for a minute," Assata said. "Ever wonder if he's innocent?"

"Back then, I hadn't been with anyone else since Mr. Stokes. And I did him six months before Little Dave's going-to-jail party. Mira is proof that Raynelle raped me."

"You were drugged. You didn't remember what happened. All you know is that you woke up in a strange bed in a big ass mansion with your pants and panties at your ankles. I'm just sayin', you even said that the house was wall-to-wall bodies. What if someone else came into that bedroom, like Raynelle said?"

"Raynelle brought me to that party. If he didn't stick it in, he might as well have. I was fifteen at a kingpin's going-to-jail party. Raynelle was eighteen. He obviously left me alone."

"I know all that, but the man done did a dime and he still got eight cents left before he even comes up for parole and if he gets out then, he'll be branded as a sex offender for the rest of his life."

"Why are we even talking about this eleven years after the fact?"

"I don't know. Last Sunday, Dr. Lomax spoke about hate and forgiveness…"

"Damn, girl, you drinking the kool-aid for real. You know good and well that pastors ain't nothing but pulpit pimps."

"Not Dr. Lomax at First Afrikan. He puts the prosperity preaching pulpit pimps on blast. He even calls America what it really is, Amerikakaka," Assata said.

"You sound like all the rest of the deaf, dumb, and blind," Sunny remarked. "Besides Assata, ain't you the one that said, Black folks that go to church are modern day slaves because they still worshipping the same way the slave master made them, and they still praying to the slave master's God expecting to be saved?"

The patio door opened.

Her hazel brown zombie eyes stared right through Sunny. The sky blue gown she wore was the only thing that moved as the ten-year-old stood at the door. The little girl was a four foot six, coffee brown statue wearing an emotionless stare.

"Mira, what's wrong, baby?" Sunny asked.

"He's getting bigger," Mira said.

"Who's getting bigger, baby?"

"The boy."

"What boy?"

"My friend, the one I dream about."

Sunny held her arms out. "Come here, baby."

Mira took a couple timid steps forward.

Sunny got down on one knee and took her daughter in her arms.

Mira wrapped her arms around Sunny's neck.

Assata stood back admiring the scene unfolding between mother and daughter.

Sunny held Mira at arms length. "Baby, I told you that there is nothing wrong with dreaming. I don't know why you keep dreaming about this boy, but as long as the dreams are pleasant, there's no need for worry."

"But Momma, I think he's in trouble."

She put her daughter down and knelt down in front of her. "He's not real, Mira. How many times do I have to tell you that?"

"He is real, momma. He is."

"Did you just raise your voice at me, little girl?"

Mira shook her head.

"Answer me when I speak to you."

"No, ma'am."

"Go back to bed and I don't wanna hear another peep about that little boy in your dreams."

Mira stood in front of her mother, silently gritting her teeth.

"Do you hear me talking to you, little girl?"

"Yes, ma'am."

"You better act like it. Now you best take some of that huff out your voice and go on back to bed."

Mira turned and walked back in to the house.

"You make me sick," Mira mumbled while closing the patio door.

Sunny got up. "Let me get my belt."

Assata grabbed Sunny's arm. "Girl, don't let her get you all worked up, ruin a good night, with good company, good weed, and," she looked at the five wallets on the concrete, "those."

Sunny picked up one of the wallets after sitting back on the upside down paint bucket. "I love that little girl with everything I got, but I swear sometimes she makes me wanna reach out and smack her eyes in the back of her head. What's wrong with these disrespectful kids today?"

"They momma and daddy's are crazy and they bring babies in this world and they make them crazy, but Black folk just ignore crazy," Assata said.

"Whachu saying, Assata?"

"Don't get all defensive on me, girl. I'm just speakin' truth. 'Member Cornbread Gibson?"

"Man-man's brother," Sunny said. "Girl, how can I forget that fool? No telling how many dope boys he robbed.

"Riding the bus and train all around town, going into projects he had no business in, robbing dope boys with a toy pistol in his coat and getting away clean. God sure had his back."

"Until one of Red's boys shot him in the face," Sunny said.

"You have to admit Sunny, if Cornbread had been laying on some note-taking psychiatrist's couch, he might not be lying six feet under in a casket."

"Yeah, I guess you right," Sunny said. "The late 80's was stupid crazy."

"That's what I'm saying, girl. Black folks see crazy every day, but we just blow it off as if crazy just supposed to get sane over time. You always hear about rich white folks lying on someone's couch telling all they business. They even done gone to calling them therapists, life coaches, and support systems, instead of psychologists. Hell, I bet Tupac and Biggie woulda' been alive today, if they would've gotten some help."

"What make you think Tupac and Biggie had a few screws loose?" Sunny asked.

"As much money and poo-tang as they was getting, and they acted like crabs in a barrel instead of kings on a throne…"

"I know where you goin' with this Assata and I don't like it."

"I'm your best friend, hell, I'm your only real friend. We go back to middle school. We've screwed and have gotten screwed together. I even lied on the stand to help get Raynelle put away."

"What does all of that have to do with the price of tea in China?"

"Huh?" Assata asked.

"It's a saying. Means what does all that you are saying have to do with anything?"

"It means I love you unconditionally and I want for you what I want for myself. You know I love my goddaughter as much as anyone. I just think we should consider getting her tested."

"Tested! Tested for what?"

"I don't know. She's been having these dreams about this little boy for years. What about the way she sneaks up on people. She moves like a ghost. And last month –"

Sunny interrupted, "The way she makes things do what they aren't supposed to do from time to time has nothing to do with her mental stability. Last month was just some freak power surge."

"Freak power surge." Assata crossed her arms. "We came here after we rocked Macy's for three grand in clothing to find your lights had been cut off. Apartment darker than night. The cut-off notice was still on the knob. We go in Mira's room and she's at her desk doing homework – homework sitting under a brightly lit desk light that was plugged in to one of your plugs that had no power. A desk light that cut off when Mira realized that we were in the room."

"Assata, you are my girl to the end of the end, but Miracle is my child and I will not waste money I don't have and time that I can't afford to take my daughter to some note-taking, dumb question-asking stranger. And what you think they gon' say when I ask if my baby is touched. You know good and damn well they gon' say my baby's nuttier than a peanut factory. That way they can keep seeing her, getting more money that I don't have. So, now that you done killed my high," Sunny handed Assata her cut from the wallets, "I'm going to bed."

Assata rose to her feet. "One last question."

Sunny shook her head. "Not if it's about my baby's sanity."

"Nah, I've said my piece on that. I was just thinking about you and Mr. Stokes."

"What about me and Mr. Stokes?"

"Well, remember when we went down to the free clinic the first time."

"Yeah, I thought I was pregnant with his baby."

"You weren't," Assata said.

"Right."

"The doctor said you couldn't be, because your uterus was abnormal," Assata said.

"He also said I could never have children and less than four months later, I became pregnant. Only reason I didn't have an abortion was because Dr. Polski had said I was never going to be able to conceive."

"Ole Dr. Polski, don't even know he really the one that named Mira," Assata said.

"Yep. Miracle Joy Brown." Sunny smiled. "The brown miracle that brought me joy by coming into being."

"You ain't never been pregnant but the one time, girl, you never know."

"Know what," Sunny said.

"Might not have been Raynelle."

"Assata, why you suddenly all up in mine. Damn."

"I'm just saying. You should have them do a DNA test."

"Who is them? No, never mind. I done told you, Assata. It don't make no difference who the father is. Raynelle shouldn't have left me alone for one minute in that big ass house. Bottom line, I was raped and somebody got me pregnant."

"You said my daddy was dead." Miracle stood in front of the patio door.

"Shit." Assata put a hand over her heart. "Good Lord, girl you 'bout scared me to death. I didn't even hear the door slide open."

"I knew he wasn't dead. I just knew it." She patted her chest. "I feel him in here."

Chapter 9

November 21, 2005
THREE YEARS LATER: **Langley, Virginia**

At his father's prodding, forty years ago, Gerald Bush went to work for J. Edgar Hoover at the FBI as a senior field agent, a position that usually took at least ten years to earn. All his life he was pushed to the front and almost every promotion and accolade he'd received was because of his father. Senator Bradley Bush was a big brash bull that wielded his political power like a sword, cutting down anyone that stood in his path. Gerald's father was known by friend and foe as the Bull. Bull was short for bulldozer, although most thought Bully was a better moniker for the overbearing huge man that always seemed to have a cigar in his mouth or between his fingers.

Gerald was the complete opposite of his father. He'd avoided hard work like the plague his entire life. While bullying wasn't Gerald's way, finding ways to manipulate others to bend to his will was. He'd never been in a physical fight, nor had he ever actually shot someone. His rise in the CIA was partly due to his father's unique way of collecting on favors he was owed, but it was mostly in part due to his success after recruiting Treble 'XR13' Frazier. It was in the FBI that Gerald met Treble Frazier.

*****

Then, the director of the FBI, J. Edgar Hoover did not like anyone who interfered with his FBI, as he put it. Gerald's father had done just that. As head of FRAC, the Federal Resources Appropriations Committee, the Senator had threatened to cut the FBI fiscal budget in half unless Gerald was promoted to Senior Field Agent. Although Dr. King had just been declared an enemy of the government, Gerald's father had become an enemy of Hoover, which trumped an enemy of the state. That's why with less than a week's notice and absolutely no field experience, thirty-eight years ago, back in '67, Gerald's first assignment as a Senior Field Agent was to appropriate a sniper and take out Dr. King before he publicly took a stand on the Vietnam War at the huge multi ethnic, interdenominational Riverside Church in Upper Manhattan. Hoover often equivocated his success to others failures, and Gerald's monumental impending failure would force Hoover's hand to rescind Gerald's promotion.

The day had been sunny and cloudless. It was a mild sixty-degrees on this New York, early Spring April day. The wind and visual conditions were almost perfect, Gerald thought as he watched people from all races, creeds, and colors file into the church. The people were dressed in their finest clothes. It was as if they were expecting royalty.

Although Gerald was on the eighth floor of an abandoned building, one city block away from the church, he had a great view of the front entrance where Dr. Martin Luther King Jr. was due to enter once he arrived. Hoover's orders had been to make sure King never made it into the church.

The sniper Gerald appropriated was said to be one of the best. Gerald was somewhat nervous being that this was his first time being a spotter on a real hit. He'd only been a spotter in training exercises at the academy. He was actually more nervous at failing his father than failing to manage a kill shot. The high-powered spotter's one-eyed scope and the cool clear day helped to alleviate some of the young agent's trepidation.

A bright light momentarily blinded Gerald when Dr. King's entourage pulled in front of the colossal interdenominational church. It was the light of another spotter's scope. There was another sniper. Gerald could have had his guy take out the sniper but he figured the other sniper was a friendly sent by Hoover to make sure there were no screw-ups. If everything went as planned, Gerald knew that if he got King then he would be the future king of the FBI. Hoover was too eccentric and even more controlling than his father.

After measuring the breeze Gerald gave the sniper the coordinates. King stepped out of the vehicle. Gerald gave the order. A muffled pop went off as the sniper squeezed the trigger.

Gerald and his sniper were at a loss for words. Their mouths dropped open. If they hadn't seen it for themselves they wouldn't have believed it. Shooting like this was unheard of. It was almost impossible to purposely do what they had just witnessed. Two bullets colliding in mid air, a hundred yards away from Dr. King.

Gerald immediately saw this as an opportunity instead of a failure. Gerald promised the sniper fifty thousand dollars, the same amount the government was giving the hired killer after King was assassinated. In return, the sniper would collect the shell casings from the street below and blame his failure on a rifle malfunction. Gerald trained his high-powered scope on where the other sniper fired the shot. Soon, he spotted a young, tall, medium built dark skinned professionally dressed black male leaving the Chemical Bank building on the opposite end of the church with a suitcase just large enough to carry a broken down sniper's rifle. The man moved with absolutely no urgency. This gave Gerald time to get in position to follow him. Gerald did just that, all the way from New York City to Ebenezer Baptist Church located in the well-to-do Auburn Avenue area in downtown Atlanta, Georgia.

Gerald had always followed orders and had never strayed. But, this time was different. He just couldn't bear to face his father in light of his recent failure. He could care less about Hoover and the Bureau. Now was his chance to redeem himself and he wouldn't let protocol stand in the way.

On that first day of the surveillance, Gerald saw Treble shaking hands with an older distinguished looking black gentleman wearing a white clergy collar outside of Dr. King's home church. Gerald immediately knew that the pastor was a man of means. Even affluent Blacks didn't drive convertible Mercedes Benz's in the 60's. After running the plates on the pastor's year-old 220E Mercedes, he found out that Dr. John Boyce was a famed archaeologist who specialized in Sub-Saharan artifacts and African religions. Bush was also surprised to learn that Dr. Boyce had earned a PhD from Morehouse in theology and was even occasionally called to preach at Dr. King's Ebenezer Baptist Church, as well as other Black churches around the nation.

Over the next week, Treble was seen coming to the lavish estate home of Dr. John Boyce. It was really odd that Treble was never seen leaving. After a week of discovering nothing about Treble Frazier, Gerald decided to move in and arrest him.

Since the Bureau had not sanctioned the arrest, Gerald had to use the basement in a foreclosed metro Atlanta home for the interrogation. After two days of nothing, the interrogation ended with an opportunity for Treble.

Gerald had confirmed that Treble was a former Army Ranger, one of the first African-Americans to be accepted into the rigorous military unit. He couldn't believe that racism prevented the government from recruiting him as a federal agent. Treble Frazier's skill set scores were the highest ever recorded. Marksmanship, archery, hand to hand combat, strategic planning, no one could come close to his skill set. After studying Treble's dossier, Gerald was even more in awe of the man he saw split a bullet from over three hundred yards away.

Even under interrogation, torture, and the threat of death, Treble hadn't acted like a man taking his last few breaths. Calm and stoic, Treble fluidly and articulately answered all of Gerald's questions – some even honestly. Afraid of killing the man that he intended on recruiting, Gerald ended the weeklong interrogation and torture. As long as Gerald could convince Treble to work for and with him, then how he knew about the King assassination plot was irrelevant and he told Treble as much and agreed to cover it up as long as Treble acquiesced. Seeing that he didn't have much of a chance to see another tomorrow Treble accepted Gerald's offer to join him once he obtained a position in the CIA.

After botching the hit on King, and going AWOL the week after, Gerald knew he would have too much of a hard way to go at the Bureau with Hoover at the helm. The CIA was going through a restructuring phase because of the way the agency had mishandled the situation on the Indochina peninsula – the situation that had led to the Vietnam War. Hoover would see it as the ultimate revenge for the Senator's intervention on Gerald's behalf. Gerald just had to make it seem like it was Hoover's idea to have him transferred to the F.B.I.'s troubled stepbrother agency. Once there, he would use his father's resources and Treble to help turn the agency around.

Orphaned at three, Treble had been raised on a farm in Gary, Indiana by a distant relative, a widow named Hattie Mae Frazier. Gerald learned that Treble joined the Army straight out of high school. Hattie Mae was a church-going woman. Her and Treble had very few friends. It was just the two of them living on a forty-acre farm, raising livestock and vegetables. So what was the connection between a Midwestern farm boy and a world-renowned archaeologist and popular theologian? What part did the Reverend Dr. John Boyce play in the life of Treble Lee Frazier? Gerald planned to get answers soon to those, and so many other questions. Soon would constitute and consist of two things: One, Gerald establishing himself as a power-player in the CIA and secondly, a visit to Dr. Boyce, one where Gerald would get the answers he wanted. In exchange, he would either allow the archaeologist to remain among the living, or he would make Dr. Boyce's death instant.

*****

TODAY: November 21, 2005

Gerald and the agency had known about the bomb shelter and the underground tunnel a couple weeks after XR13's house exploded. It had taken almost two years before probate issues were resolved before the land was put back on the market. To the best of the agency's knowledge, no one knew about the elaborate bomb shelter and the quarter mile tunnel that led to a public sewer. As instructed, the city had informed the FBI, who had in turn informed the CIA when an offer came in on the land.

The land had only been listed a few hours when the Focus Holdings offer came over the fax. It was a full price offer at two-hundred and fifty thousand, a hundred thousand more than the land was worth. Gerald had known that if someone offered anywhere near the asking price that they were probably linked to Treble "XR13" Frazier.

Upon further investigation and a lot of shell-company digging, Gerald found what he was searching for. Greenway Financial owned Focus Holdings, the name on the offer. Greenway Financial was owned by Quality Essential imports. Beatrice Foods owned Quality Essential Imports, and TLC

owned Beatrice Foods and TLC was owned by the Reginald
Lewis Foundation, and the Chair and CEO of the Reginald
Lewis Foundation was Dr. John Boyce.

"Low and behold, the winner or shall I say the loser is
the esteemed Reverend Dr. John Boyce," the director said,
spinning around in his seat.

"Sir, are you all right?" Gerald's secretary, asked as she
cracked the office door and stepped in.

He looked up from his computer with a mile-wide smile
on his face. "I'm fine, Judy. I am
supercalifragilisticsespialidocious fine."

"Ooookay then." She smiled. "I will just close your
door and leave you to spinning around in your chair."

Gerald thought back to something his dad used to say.
Junior, sometimes it's better to be lucky than good. It wasn't
all luck, he surmised. He had followed Treble back in '67. He
was the only one that knew that a connection between Treble
and Dr. Boyce existed. Despite not being able to explain away
the DNA lab results that confirmed XR13's demise, the director
never truly believed that XR13 was dead. Covering up his own
death would be child's play to someone as accomplished as
XR13. And now, all he had to do was send a team in to sit on
Dr. Boyce. He wouldn't risk planting bugs. If XR13 were still
alive, he'd detect the bugs or he could have taught Dr. Boyce
how. No, he'd wait. He'd waited almost forty years to
interrogate the retired archaeologist and church leader, a little
while longer wouldn't hurt.

Chapter 10

Thanksgiving, 2005
Lithonia, Georgia

"Miracle?" Sunny called out.

After thirteen years, Edmond Dantes was finally escaping from prison. Raynelle had been in prison the same amount of time as Edmond Dantes. I wonder what he was doing? Did they serve turkey to inmates on Thanksgiving? Heck, why should I even care? He raped Momma. But, what if Auntie Assata was right? What if Raynelle didn't touch Momma at all? What if he was innocent like Edmond Dantes?

"Miracle? I know you hear me calling you."

Dang. Miracle marked her page before putting her book "The Count of Monte Cristo" down beside her on the bed. "Why can't she just leave me alone?" Miracle muttered. *I hate being around her and any of her boyfriends, especially this new one. The way he stares at me gives me the willies.* Her whole body shook thinking about the man. *And why did her boyfriends have to be so young?*

"Miracle!"

"Huh?"

"Don't huh me. Come see what I want, girl?"

"Coming." Miracle rolled her eyes as she got up from her four-poster queen size bed, slipped on some jeans over her gym shorts before pulling the Florida A&M hoodie over her head. After slipping on her all white Jordan's, she put a rubberband around her dreads and headed downstairs.

*****

"Stop, boy!" Sunny said as she playfully stuck her behind out, pushing the young man away. "My baby will be down here any minute."

"Your baby is down here now, momma," Miracle said, hoping her mother would be embarrassed by her sudden entry.

Sunny turned around. "Miracle Joy Brown."

Oh Lord, what did I do now?

"I told you about sneaking up on folks."

Miracle shook her head in disgust, as she eyeballed the man wearing a wife beater and some beige Dickies that were way too big for his skinny behind. *No way momma woulda' even gave this wanna be young thug the time of day if she was in her right mind.*

"Stop staring at the man, Miracle." Sunny looked at her boyfriend, as he stared at the contents inside of the sub zero refrigerator. "Excuse us a minute, Rodney."

"Handle your business, sweet pea," the man said, taking out a Heineken.

"Come with me, young lady," Sunny said as she ushered Miracle into the first floor guest bedroom.

After closing the door Sunny began, "Mira, you are thirteen. How many times do I have to tell you, that you are a young lady? And a young lady carries herself with respect and doesn't go anywhere looking like anything but a young lady."

"I ain't going nowhere."

"I am not going anywhere," Sunny corrected her daughter.

"I am not going anywhere, mother."

Sunny pointed a finger in her daughters face. "Don't get smart, Mira."

"I thought that was the whole point."

"What are you talking about girl?"

"Getting smart. Isn't that why you corrected my English, so I can get smart?"

"You lucky we got company."

"Lucky that we *have* company, mom."

"You must think I'm something to play with." Sunny raised her arm in the air, "So help me God, girl, I will –"

"Knock me into next week?"

"What's wrong with you, girl? Did you come on your cycle early?"

"No, mom. I'm tired of pretending like I'm your little angel. I like wearing jeans, sneakers and big T-shirts. I like hanging out at the Pointe with Yum-Yum. I ain't never played, I mean, I have never played with dolls and girls are too giggly and stupid. You should be glad I'm not like what's-his-name out there."

"What do you mean by that?"

"At least I wear my pants above my behind. I wish you would apply your How-to-be-a-young-lady-rules to yourself."

Pop! Sunny slapped Miracle.

"First, young lady," Sunny waved a finger in Miracle's face, "you will do as I say, not as I do. And second, don't nobody care what you like to wear and what you like to do. I am the mother and you are the child. I am not raising you to be no bulldyker, nor am I raising you to be a thug. I moved you away from the Pointe into a nice house and a respectable neighborhood to get you away from all that madness." Sunny pointed at the bedroom door. "Now take your behind back up them stairs, do something with that mop on your head and put on some ladylike clothes. As long as I pay the bills around here, you will do as I say."

"OMG. Are you even hearing yourself?"

"They're my words, aren't they?" Sunny crossed her arms.

"Mom, you pay the bills around here but I make the money, been making it ever since Auntie went to jail two years ago. It's you and me at the dice games, but I'm the one the dice listen to. This house, your car, our Thanksgiving dinner, even that boy out there," Mira pointed in the direction of the kitchen, "my work paid for all of …"

Pop! Sunny slapped Mira with much more ferocity than last time.

This only made Mira angrier. This was her first time really standing up to Sunny. She held a palm to her stinging cheek. "You talk about me dressing like a boy, you insinuate that I'm gay but you messing around with these young boys that are closer to my age than yours. You got me out here in back alleys and pool halls, controlling the dice in games all around town. How ladylike is that, mom?"

"You don't like the way I run things, then you know where the door is," Sunny said.

Mira turned and ran out of the room and up the stairs into her room. A few minutes later, Mira came down the stairs with hat, coat, gloves, and her school backpack strapped around her shoulders.

Sunny had her hands on her hips, blocking Mira's path.

"Where do you think you're going, young lady?"

Mira turned and ran to the back door. "I don't know, but anywhere is better than here," she said before slamming the back door.

It was Thanksgiving and the city bus wasn't running. It was cold out but Mira was so heated she could barely feel the chill as she walked. *None of this woulda' happened if Auntie Assata was here. I knew momma wasn't in her right mind, but I couldn't continue watching as she killed herself with that crack. That's the only reason she even let me help her work dice games all around the city. It seemed like soon as Auntie got locked up, momma started to unravel. I tried to put momma back together several times, but there's only so much I can do.*

After walking for about ten minutes, Mira wished that her mother had come looking for her. She took out her iPhone. Not even a phone call. "She cares more about them drugs and that man than she does about me," Mira mumbled.

She continued staring at the iPhone screen, willing it to ring. When it didn't, she turned onto Evans Mill Road and continued down the main street. She hadn't even given any thought to where she would go. She was too far away from the Pointe to walk. She didn't have cab fare and the 86 bus didn't run on Thanksgiving.

Her thoughts turned to her best friend. Yum-Yum was probably enjoying his Thanksgiving dinner with his mom and two sisters. *No need to ruin his day,* Mira thought. One thing about Yum-Yum, he was always cracking jokes and making fun of people, but he never made fun of or judged Mira. Never. *Hmm, I bet if I knew who my daddy was, I bet he would love me no matter what I wore and no matter what my hair looked like. I bet Momma wasn't even raped. She probably did it with somebody that didn't have any earning potential. That's what she called men that she thought was worth dating.*

The Spinners began singing, *It takes a fool to learn, yes sir, that love don't love nobody.* It was her ringtone. Mira pressed the Send button.

"What it do, Boo-Boo?"

"Dang, it's only you, Yum-Yum." Mira sighed.

"Don't sound so happy to hear from me on this day that we commemorate the mass murder of the real O.G. Americans."

"OMG, Yum-Yum, you doin' too much."

"I ain't doin' enough. Besides, didn't I ask you to stop calling me Yum-Yum?"

"I ain't about to call you Early X."

"Okay, forget Early X. I will give you the distinct honor of calling me Big Daddy Jook 'Em Good or if you prefer, Big Daddy Jook 'Em Long Time."

"Boy, I ain't calling you no dang-on Big Daddy nothing. Yo' momma named you Early, and I'm gon' call you Yum-Yum, like I always have."

"Technically, my mother named me Early, because she say I came a week early. Either people make my name two words and call me Earl Lee or they call me Yum-Yum. Either way, both have to go. We teenagers and I'm getting too old to be going upside people's heads and getting my head busted over my name."

"Seriously, Yum-Yum, what you want to be called?"

"Hmmm… How about Hannibal?"

"As in 'Silence of the Lambs'," Mira asked.

"Nah, dummy, Hannibal as in Hannibal of Carthage."

"Who's he?" she asked.

"He was the greatest warrior that ever lived. He used African elephants to help whip Alexander the Great's behind," Yum-Yum said with authority. "And guess what else?"

"What?" she asked.

"He was a black man, blacker than you, Mira."

"If he's all that, why haven't I ever heard of him?"

"Because white folks scared to teach the truth."

"What they scared of? They own everything," Mira said.

"They know that if we knew who we were and what we've accomplished throughout history we'd take over corporate America just like we've taken over professional sports."

"Where you been getting all this black stuff from, Yum-Yum?"

"Call me, Hannibal!" he shouted in the phone. "Remember, the church I told you about?"

"The one my Aunt Assata used to go to?" Mira asked.

"Yeah. First Afrikan," he said. "Momma joined and she made me go to Bible Study a few weeks ago."

"What that got ta' do with your new found blackness?"

"That's what I'm trying to tell you. First Afrikan teaches us our history in the bible and outside of the bible. You oughta' come check out Black Study next Wednesday."

"You mean Bible study?"

"Nah, I meant Black Study. The bible is full of stories about people who look like me and you, so we call it Black Study."

"I can't think that far ahead, Yum-Yum. I don't even know where I'm going to sleep tonight."

"You and Sunny got into it again?"

"Yep, this time was different though. She clowned on me in front of the current flavor of the month."

"It ain't her, Mira. You know what crack does to folks."

"I know, that's' the only reason I stayed this long," Mira said. "I am so confused. I'm worried about momma, but I can't stay there anymore. I don't know what to do?"

"Where you at right now?"

"The Citgo on Evans Mill across the street from the Waffle House."

"You got any money on you?" he asked.

"I got a couple dollars."

"Okay, go on over to the Waffle House, I'm on my way."

"How you gon' get here and why did you ask if I had money?"

"Because, I might be a minute and if you don't order something, they might put you out."

"How you gon' come get me?"

"You worried about the wrong thing, Mira. I ain't about to leave my best homie out in the wind."

She was sitting in the back booth by the doors leading to the restroom sipping on her second cup of hot cocoa.

"Can I get you anything else, darlin'?" the three-toothed, leather-faced Waffle House waitress asked.

"No, thank you. I'm okay, just waiting for my dad to pull up."

I had no idea why I'd said that. But, then again, maybe I was waiting for my dad to pull up. Maybe I had always been waiting for him. He might be able to help me understand how I could move small things around by only imagining them moving to where my mind said. I bet he could explain the boy in my dreams. I bet he had the same gifts I did.

Mira pulled out her wallet, this time she retrieved a piece of paper.

Raynelle James Tolliver. Inmate # 027841632.
Hwy. 36 West PO Box 3877
Jackson, GA. 30233

Chapter 11

Thanksgiving, 2005
Sahara Dessert, North Africa

While the larger part of American society was feasting or preparing to feast on Thanksgiving turkey and other fixings, Zion Uhuru Jones was in the middle of a summer sandstorm in the North African Sahara Desert. While being pelted with a million granules of sand in the one hundred and twenty degree heat, Zion reflected back to a couple years ago, when Baba took him back to the late sixteenth century. It was one thing to read history, but to actually watch how Thanksgiving came about was horrifying. His spirit cried for the original Americans – men, women, and children, shot down, stabbed, and bludgeoned to death like rabid dogs, Native American men's heads impaled on their own spears and displayed throughout the murdering white town during the elaborate Thanksgiving feasts held after each massacre.

Zion witnessed first hand the evil that men were capable of and he still had a hard time believing that human beings were capable of such savagery against their fellow man. And what was even more unbelievable was people in America had turned the mass slaughter of the original Americans into a holy day, and worse, the ones that knew the history made excuses why they still celebrated the occasion on the very day the descendants of the murderers ascribed. It was like celebrating the mass murder of Jews during the Holocaust, or choosing a day to celebrate the beginning of Chattel slavery. But now, Zion had more pressing matters to attend to than to keep reflecting on why people made excuses for the backward things they did.

Although the sandstorm had just ended, Zion still couldn't see two feet in front of him. No worries, he'd been taught to rely on his mind's eye as Baba had called it. His mind's eye was a combination of using the other six senses to make up for the sense that was lacking.

He closed his eyes and began a slow, barely audible hum. He used his mind to block out the sun's intense one hundred nineteen degree sweltering heat, the sand swirling in the air, and the distant hawking sound of hungry vultures circling in the air, waiting – waiting for the unlucky trespasser that dared cross the path of one of the Sahara's many hungry and dangerous animals – waiting for whatever spoils the victor left behind.

For thirty-four days, Zion had walked across the burning hot Sahara desert sands, stopping only for nourishment, to relieve himself, sleep, and to pray. Spending forty days and nights alone in the Sahara was the second part of the ancient priesthood initiation process. Over the last three years, he had learned to unlock doors with his mind that he had no idea existed. Discipline had proven to be the most difficult virtue to conquer. The situation he was currently in called the strictest of discipline. One wrong move and his earthly existence would be over.

Zion closed his eyes and raised both arms to the sky. He willed the fear he felt away as he walked toward the slight vibration he felt in his toes. He felt the sand stir in a spiral direction only a few feet away from him. As he moved closer he heard another heart beat, he listened as it sped up. Zion was on alert as he realized the animal he was stalking knew of his presence. Visibility was still zero, but neither Zion nor the rattlesnake that waited rarely used their eyesight to help them ensnare their prey.

Zion was less than three steps away from the coiled serpent. Without preamble, the snake lunged its five-foot long body through the sandy air. Its' mouth was open wide, its' venom dripping, fangs only inches from Zion's throat when he bent over backward and grabbed the snake one-inch too low.

The snake dug its fangs into Zion's hand, between his thumb and index finger. He fought the urge to drop the snake and scream, knowing that if he did, his meal would get away and he would be forced to go another day without food. He called upon the strength of his father and the strength of his mighty ancestors to give him the mite to strangle the life force from the squirming serpent.

A warm sensation coarsed down Zion's arm as the snake went limp. The sensation did not come from the snake's blood that ran the length of his arm; it was the life force draining from Zion. It was a culmination of the sun's intense heat, and Zion's thirst and hunger that caused the venom to take affect much quicker then it would have on a strong healthy boy.

As Zion dropped to his knees, snake still in hand, he recalled something that Baba had said repeatedly, "Six is your number. After six, there is either a beginning or an ending."

Fighting for the life force he felt draining from his own body, he realized that the snake he held in his hand was the seventh snake. He'd killed and had eaten six rattlesnakes over the last five weeks and had never gotten bitten. And now the seventh would be the end of him in this stage of life unless he fought. He could have reached in his pouch, pulled out the only weapon he was allowed, a pearl handled six-inch hunting knife. The way his body was quickly weakening, he knew that it was too late to use the titanium blade to open up the wound. At this point, trying to suck the poison out would be futile; as the poison was already slithering through his system. His feet and hands were growing numb. He had just enough strength to get to a praying position or so he thought, before falling over in the sand. With his face lying in the sand, he prayed.

"Mother of my father, Mother of my ancestors, Mother of Shango and all the gods that serve you, make this body whole, this vessel you have placed my spirit in, fortify it to withstand the poison that coarses through it's veins, as you have fortified my heart, my spirit, my soul. We have come so far, Lord. I have been your servant and have listened to you as you led me through Kenyan rainforests, where you taught me to conquer the snake, my greatest fear. After overcoming my fear of the serpent you caste me into a den of hungry lions and allowed me to emerge without a scratch, but as a valued friend to the king of beasts. I listened as you taught me humility in the Kenyan jungles. You gave me the choice to starve or share the carcass of a rhinoceros with a pack of hyenas. I listened as you taught me the power of faith when you left me with the decision to swim across the violent crocodile infested waters of Lake Victoria. Although I couldn't swim, it was my faith and love for you that pushed me off that cliff. Just like it was my faith that carried me across the Lake.

"Now as I am six days from completing the initiation into the ancient priesthood, I call on you once again. Save this body that I have grown comfortable in."

"Come!" a voice said.

Zion tried to open his eyes, but he was too weak.

"Come!" he heard the deep baritone voice repeat.

His eyes were closed but he could see his surroundings just as if his eyes were wide open. Better as a matter of fact. He saw straight through the cloud of sand that surrounded him.

"Come!" the voice called out.

He tried to rise but his body wouldn't respond.

Two huge muscled legs appeared. A loincloth was the only thing covering his almond shell brown skin. His tribal masquerade mask revealed his identity.

"Shango," Zion heard himself say.

"Come!" the voice called again.

A huge hand reached out.

With ease, Zion rose up and stepped onto the hand.

While Shango's hand and arm rose, Zion looked down at his dying body.

The sun was suddenly clouded by darkness. Bolts of lightning streaked through the sky.

Zion stood atop the world in Shango's hand. The rain washed over the young man as he looked into Shango's beaded mask.

Shango's voice thundered forth, "Son of my sons, light from the light I brought forth, flame of the fire that I lit, your story has been written in the blood of our ancestors, since the day that evil came into being. Zion, you are the sun, the light of mankind. This time you will not die for the sins of man, you will kill death and rid the world of sin or sin will destroy mankind. Sun, you have to do what I could not."

Zion was listening but he couldn't help but hope that Shango saved his body before his heart stopped.

"I was given the task of ridding this world of evil several thousand years ago," Shango continued, "My failure to do so caused the Supreme One to send several messengers to mankind. Vanity and pride were my downfall. I was the envy of man and woman. I had three wives. My first wife, Oba was the most beautiful woman in the kingdom. Out of envy, my wife Oshun fooled Oba into maiming herself in the name of love. At the time, I didn't have a clue to what was going on in my own household. Over time I began noticing the gele that Oba started wearing over her ears.

"My deceitful wife, Oshun had the patience of Job. It was months after my wife maimed herself before Oshun came back and told me that she was more beautiful and pure than Oba. Of course, I came to Oba's defense. I called Oshun a liar. And when she told me that Oba had cut off her ear, I burst into laughter. 'My wife was perfect and would never do something so misguided I had said'.

"Later that evening over dinner, I asked Oba to remove the gele. My heart dropped when I saw that Oshun had been right. I no longer had the perfect mate. I was incensed. I looked down into my food, and there was her ear. I was so disgusted that I threw Oba out and banished her from my kingdom. I didn't give her a chance to speak. A while after being banished, Oba gave up on me. I was her everything and I didn't give her an opportunity to explain. I treated her like an object instead of my queen."

The tears that cascaded down his face dropped to the sandy desert and formed a lake.

"I am telling you this, young Zion, because you have to do what I wasn't strong enough

to do. You will need the love of the last descendant of Oba to stand any chance at defeating Evil. You and her must become one in order for your powers to unite. Together, yours and her power will have the ability to re-light the world and destroy evil.

"Who is she, this last descendant of Oba? How do I find her?"

"She's not lost, sun."

"What do I say to her?"

"What's more important is what you will do for her." Shango smiled. "When she calls, go to her."

Shango disappeared and like a feather, Zion floated back down into the body that the Lord gave him.

His eyes opened. The swelling in his right hand was gone. So were the two puncture wounds that the snake's fangs had made. Zion still had a vice-like grip around his next meal. The sun had returned and so had the vultures above. He placed the snake down on the sand beside him. He couldn't resist the desert lake that Shango's tears had just made.

He cupped his hands together and was about to drink when the lake began to stir into a whirlpool. Zion closed his eyes and concentrated on calming the water, instead, Dr. Boyce's image rose from the lake along with other images. He was being followed.

Zion kept concentrating but he couldn't see who was following the reverend-doctor. Suddenly, the water rose and transformed the watery images into a huge hypodermic needle.

Zion's eyes popped open. "Uncle John!"

Chapter 12

October 20, 2007
TWO YEARS LATER: **New York, New York**

FBI director, J. Edgar Hoover ran a government sanctioned silencing program from 1965 to 1971. The program was established to eliminate anyone that was deemed a threat to the American government's domestic and foreign policies. This program's code name was Cointelpro, short for the counterintelligence protection program. The program's success was due to J. Edgar Hoover. Ultimately, so was its downfall.

Over time, Hoover became drunk with power as he used Cointelpro as his own hit squad, ruining lives and even killing those he deemed a threat to national security. Having JFK assassinated was what began as Cointelpro's and Hoover's downfall – a downfall that experienced some high points; such as successfully dividing the Black Muslims and orchestrating the assassination of Malcolm X. He was a hero in the eyes of his bosses and peers after pulling off his greatest coup. Bernard Schwartz had called it the grand finale, Hoover's coup de grace. Hoover could do no wrong after successfully having Dr. Martin Luther King Jr. shot at a Memphis hotel, at least that was until he had Bobby Kennedy killed a couple months later. That is when the proverbial cookie began to crumble.

With all the others except for JFK, Hoover had followed Cointelpro protocol – protocol established by then, the most powerful men in the world, Trilateral Commission leaders, Rockefeller, Carnegie, Schwartz, and Swift. The protocol was simple – gather and manipulate information on the target, assassinate the target's character through the media with created and manipulated realistic information, and then silence the target for good.

Despite the public's outrage and near catastrophic disaster, Hoover almost caused by circumventing the first two steps before taking out JFK, he did the exact same thing five years later with RFK. Schwartz had then passed the death sentence on Cointelpro. But before he allowed due process to take its course, records and recordings had to be altered and destroyed – records indicating any involvement by the architects of Cointelpro. It wasn't until three years after the RFK assassination fiasco that the Senate dismantled Cointelpro.

Schwartz had always thought it was Hoover who had leaked the name of the Trilateral Commission. Whether it was Hoover or not, the Trilateral Commission went public in 1973. The Commission members all played a part in creating fantastic conspiracy stories for the media to cover up their plans and who they really were. Over fifty conspiracy theory stories were created – stories that put the Trilateral Commission at the head or in the middle of scandal and world domination plots. Ironically, a third of the stories had some truth to them, but at the time the Trilateral Commission went public the American people were too consumed with the White House and the Watergate scandal to be concerned with far-fetched One World Government conspiracy stories.

At seventy-seven, Bernard Schwartz was the last surviving founding member of the Trilateral Commission. His body was failing him, but his mind was as sharp as it was fifty years ago when Senator McCarthy proposed the One World Order concept to him.

Both men had different ideas on how to implement a program dedicated to creating a One World Government controlled by a handful of European and Euro-American men. Not being able to come to a compromise, Schwartz had the outspoken Senator from Wisconsin assassinated. The death certificate read, *'natural causes'*. Although Senator McCarthy was an alcoholic, there was nothing natural about consuming a gallon of 100 proof whiskey in five minutes. Before he decided to have the Senator killed, Schwartz had considered planting stories in his fifty-two national and international newspaper publications, but he didn't want to risk the chance of McCarthy taking the idea to anyone else.

Now, fifty years after the covered-up McCarthy assassination, Bernard Aryeh Schwartz's own mortality lay in the balance of the seven men that sat in the Trilateral Commission's underground headquarters, fifty feet below Schwartz's New York five star Waldorf Astoria hotel.

Shwartz used his cane to help him stand. The World's most powerful men that sat in front of him didn't dare meet his ocean blue-eyed stare. They couldn't.

"I made you seven men rich beyond any fantasy or dream you ever had." Schwartz walked around his desk. He stood in front of them, his platinum handled cane dangling at his side.

Media mogul Rupert Cain decided to take the lead. "Bernie, we all know and are in your debt for all the money and power you've helped us acquire over the years."

"Helped you acquire? I virtually delivered Iraq's oil reserves to the Commission. Half, if not all of you, doubted me, when I laid out the plan to take out the towers in 2001. As I told you they would, virtually overnight my news presses turned America's interest away from Bin Laden to Hussein. My news presses invented the stories of WMD's in Iraq." The chairman briefly turned his attention to media mogul Rupert Cain. "My news presses and yours, Cain, put the fear of God in the American people. And when the UN forbid us from going into Iraq, I'm the one that said fuck the United Nations."

"We know, Bernie." Connie Greenspan attempted to calm the chairman. "We respect all that you have done."

"Respect?" the chairman spat. "Son, I been playing chess with the government's money since before you were even a thought in your mothers mind. So, don't tell me about respect. But, you can tell me about loyalty."

"Bernie?" Greenspan said in a tone that suggested that he was hurt by the chairman's blanket accusations.

"I'm your superior, address me as such, Mr. Greenspan."

The young man squirmed inside before re-addressing his uncle. "Chairman Schwartz, no one is pushing you out. We just feel that the Commission's ultimate goal would be best served at this time by someone else at the helm."

"Someone younger – someone like you?"

"I'm your nephew, Uncle Bernie. You provided for me after mother passed."

"I'm glad you remembered."

"You've been preparing me for this day since I was five," Greenspan pleaded. "And now that it's come you talk of loyalty and respect, like, like I've betrayed you."

Director Bush leaned forward. "Look, Bernie the housing crisis has blown up in our faces. The people are calling for your head on a platter."

He pointed a liver-spotted finger at his godson, Gerald Bush. "Just because your Uncle GB Sr., stepped down due to health conditions doesn't mean I am ready to step down, and it does not mean you can interrupt me when I am speaking." The chairman turned his attention back toward the others that sat in front of him. "The people will believe whatever stories I create for the media. The American people are Goyim, cattle waiting to be herded wherever I lead them." He switched his attention from the men to his nephew. "So, do not tell me what the people are calling for. Besides, we knew the economy would collapse before I changed banking's home loan restrictions. This nation thrives on greed and greed has caused this crisis, not me, not us." Bernie waved an arm around the room. "All we are doing with this so-called mortgage crisis is eliminating the middle class. They are proving to have way too much power."

"Chairman Schwartz," his nephew addressed him, "the decision has already been made for you."

Bernie smiled before lifting and waving his cane around the room. "None of you gentlemen have any idea how far my arm reaches. If you knew what I am truly capable of, you would not have made this decision without my input." His cane-waving stopped at his sister's only son."

A loud pop ensued.

Smoke came from the end of Bernie's Cane.

A tear rose up and fell from his nephew's eye. "Why?" the thirty-six-year-old man muttered as he crumbled to the hardwood floor.

Before the others realized that the chairman had shot his nephew in the heart, he'd turned the cane on himself, put it in his mouth and used the edge of the desk to pull the trigger.

Pow!

Blood and brain matter splattered onto the world's most powerful men, and onto the four walls of books that surrounded them.

Gerald rushed over to Greenspan. Before he could administer CPR, Greenspan coughed, then he started breathing.

The day after Bernie's private funeral, Constance Aryeh Greenspan not only inherited his uncle's entire empire of banks, news presses and media outlets, but he also unofficially inherited the role as Trilateral Commission Chairman, which made him the single most powerful man in the world.

The Trilateral Commission created an elaborate cover story to explain the bullet that passed through Greenspan's chest and back – a story that made Greenspan an instant American hero. The story went viral and a week after the funeral, Director Bush, Greenspan, and the nation's President were a mile in the air on Air Force One.

"Connie," the president began, "your recovery is nothing short of remarkable. I don't know anyone that has ever survived after being shot in the chest with a rifle at close range," the President said.

"I don't remember much of the incident myself Mr. President. Last thing I can recall was a black bag being thrown over my head and being lifted into a vehicle. I don't know if they knew that I could understand Arabic. When I heard them say in Arabic that my beheading would be broadcast over the web, I knew I had nothing to lose and that the element of surprise was on my side. God spoke to me and I responded with fists. Teeth, legs, everything I had," he lied.

"And you managed to kill four Al-Qaeda operatives inside a nineteen foot U-Haul truck." The president turned his attention to the director. "Any Intel on the U-Haul's driver?"

The director shook his head. "Not yet, Mr. President, but we have every available man on it."

"Goes to show, you can come out on top bringing a pocket knife to a gun fight." The President leaned forward. "Mr. Chairman, I asked you here, because of John McNeil."

"The Republican party's candidate for your job, sir?" Greenspan asked.

"Yes." The president nodded. "We're in trouble. We don't think the longtime Arizona Senator can win against the Junior Senator out of Illinois."

"He's black," Gerald interjected. "No way, America will elect him. He's inexperienced, he has Islamic family ties, and he's... black."

The nation's forty-third president held a hand up in a stopping gesture. "Please, Gerald, we are aware of the Junior Senator's ethnic background?"

The president crossed his legs. "Have you met Michael Metal?"

"The majority Whip in the House?"

The president swallowed the hundred-year-old Brandy before placing the glass in the chairs cup holder and then responding. "Metal and I agree that you would be a shoo-in, in oh-eight. Now I know we have only days to announce, but we will throw the full backing of the Republican Party behind you."

"I have no political experience. I wouldn't know the first thing –"

"You're a war hero, Connie. And now, you're the people's hero. You come from a long line of politicians and world changers. You're young, but not too young. Next year at thirty-seven, you will be the forty-forth president of the United States."

"I'm honored, Mr. President, but with all due respect, I have to decline. I have a huge responsibility as the Trilateral Commission Chairman."

"Trilateral Commission. Son, you can play with your rich friends anytime. What's more important than running the country?" the president asked.

"Making sure that the country's financial resources are secure so that the country can run, that's why I'd like to be appointed as my uncles' successor as the Chair of the Federal Reserve."

"I'm already having someone vetted for the Chair position. Besides, I think you'd make a better CEO of this country than you would as Federal Reserve Chair."

"Excuse me, gentlemen," the CIA director rose from his seat, "nature calls."

After the director was out of earshot, Greenspan leaned forward in his chair so the Secret Service agents behind and in front of them couldn't hear. Greenspan looked in the President's eyes. "Once I finish speaking you will get on the phone and stop the vetting process. Once we land, you will formally introduce me as my uncle's successor."

Moments later when Gerald returned, the President was on the phone ordering that the vetting process be stopped and that a new one for Constance Greenspan be started.

Director Bush took his seat. "What's going on?"

"The president has reconsidered and has offered me the Chair position," Greenspan said.

"I figured as much," the director said while looking at the President's animated gestures as he spoke on the government satellite phone. "Looks like he's having a hard time selling you."

"That's not my or your problem," Greenspan said. "Speaking of problems, where are we at on the Boyce, investigation?"

The director stammered as he was caught completely off guard. "I, well we've not been able to get anything on him, not yet."

Greenspan opened a manila file folder and stared at the contents inside. "It says here that you've had the target under investigation for almost two years. In that time you've spent upwards to a million dollars in man-hours and surveillance equipment. Surely a million dollars has netted something to facilitate a reason for us to allocate more taxpayer's money to your investigation"

The director gathered his thoughts. "Well, actually, we've developed Intel that suggests that Boyce is working with a network of Christian pastors around the country and –"

"One month," the chairman interrupted.

"Sir?" the director said.

"You have exactly one month to tie Boyce to terrorist activity, Gerald."

"How am I supposed to wrap up –?"

"Take the gloves off, man. Remember Cointelpro."

"What do you know about Cointelpro?" the director asked. "You were in diapers when it was disbanded."

Greenspan smiled. "My uncle told me all I need to know." Connie looked at the time on his uncle's favorite Rolex. "The clock is ticking Gerald, you have one month to nail Boyce, or we might have to sit down and have a conversation about your future."

Chapter 13

October 27, 2007
SEVEN DAYS LATER: Jackson, Georgia

It was unseasonably warm for late October. The Georgia sunshine kissed everyone that crossed its path – innocent, guilty, free, and incarcerated. Behind the twenty-foot, fourteen-inch thick dull gray concrete walls of the Jackson Georgia State Penitentiary, shirtless men of all ages, shapes, and sizes were taking advantage of the seventy-five degree cloudless Autumn Saturday morning.

In one area, men were grunting and growling as they pushed, pulled, squatted, and curled, outdated metal bars with round, thick, iron gray and black plates attached; in another area, men were running up and down an eighty-four foot cracked-up slab of concrete chasing a bouncing ball and trying to prevent it from being shot into a rusty, netless, eighteen-inch cylinder. In yet another area, men sweated like pigs in a blanket as they chased and used the palm of their hands to smack a small hard rubber ball against a chipping concrete wall.

Raynelle James Tolliver watched as he walked around the quarter-mile walking track that surrounded the rec yard, chow hall, and the recreation, religion, and education building. He had been sentenced to serve his time at the Jackson Diagnostic and Classification Prison fifteen years ago. All inmates sentenced in Georgia came through Jackson. It was a ginormous military-like dull gray processing center with bars, prison guards, and restrictive movement – a hustler's prison paradise as far as Raynelle was concerned. With the exception of inmates on Death Row and the inmates that were sentenced to serve their time at Jackson, the others were semi quarantined in prison pods – pods that had only eighty beds for the hundred plus men. The beds were first come first serve, leaving the others to sleep on the floor in the pods common area.

Fifteen years ago upon arriving at Jackson, Raynelle was assigned to work in the prison kitchen. It had taken him two months to start his restaurant and delivery service. Inmates, especially those housed in the diagnostic pods, had no problem having their families and friends deposit money in a designated Paypal account to pay for Raynelles plates.

Twenty-dollars for a four-piece fried chicken snack that included a plate of fries and an eight ounce carton of orange juice or milk was a steal considering Raynelle's food was the bomb and besides the dog food the prison served in the chow hall, there wasn't another restaurant around. As time went on, prison cafeteria food got progressively worse due to Raynelle explaining to the warden how good for business it was to serve more processed and water-based foods, while he sold chicken, steak, hamburger and pork chop meals at a premium. Everyone benefitted – the warden, the captain, the kitchen guards, the runners, and the hungry inmates that could afford to pay.

Each month after everyone received their cut, Raynelle still pocketed an upscale house note. By his tenth year on the inside Raynelle had his hand in every prison hustler's pocket – everyone but Saul Grotolli's.

Saul was serving three life sentences for multiple counts of murder. The only reason the fifty-three-year-old, mob hit man wasn't sentenced to death was because of the long arms of his Uncle Frank. Although Frank Grotolli was the Capo of the Grotolli crime family in Jersey, the old man had well-placed political connections all over the country, including Georgia.

Raynelle was walking over to a sitting area near the chow hall where a buddy of his stood watch over the comings and goings of men that had been caste out of society for one crime or another.

Standing with his legs spread, arms crossed, and a frown on his face, Raynelle resembled an angry Greek God in blackface. His gaze was fixated on the little short fat man leaving the chow hall with his two middle aged, much taller pals. Their weekend daily schedule never changed, Raynelle thought as he shook his head from side to side. "You know, Ofodile," Raynelle waved an arm in Saul's direction, "A man that follows a routine is an easy target."

"I don't know how easy a target Saul is with two bodyguards always at his side."

Raynelle looked over at his friend. "Is that what you call them?" He turned his attention to the averaged built, middle-aged Italian men that walked with the former mob hitman. "Ofodile, those two can't guard traffic in a ghost town."

"If those three would have used the same undertaker for all of their hits," Ofodile directed his attention toward Saul and his cronies, "then that undertaker would be near the top of the Forbes 500 list."

"Have killed," Raynelle pointed out, "are the key words, Ofodile."

"You sure you want this to happen?" Ofodile asked.

"Too late for it not to happen," Raynelle said as he watched the short, fat man wobble over to the rec room with his lackeys on his left and his right.

"It's never too late," Ofodile said.

"It is when I've already paid out fifty-stacks to you and everyone involved."

"Its just money, Ray. Chalk it off to a bad decision."

"If it's *just money*, give me your *just money* cut back. Matter of fact, how about when I'm making all the *just money* in here, you forfeit your *just money* cut?"

"I get your point, Ray."

"As to what you refer to as a bad decision?" Raynelle looked up at his friend. "It was a business decision and the right one at the time that I made it."

"That was a year ago," Ofodile said. "Back then, you didn't know that the Appellate Court was even going to hear your appeal, not only did they hear it, they granted it. Now, thanks to modern technology your DNA is being tested. And when the results prove your innocence you'll be a memory behind these walls. Do you really wanna risk your freedom by having Saul killed?"

"I paid you and the others, so, what would I be risking?"

An inmate walking to the chow hall shouted, "Ray-Ray, I'm 'bout to bring out the bones, hope you ain't ate up all your commissary."

"Dog, you ain't got a domino idea. If my babygirl wasn't coming to visit, I'd gladly take what little commissary you and your boys have in your lockers."

The inmate shouted, "Ofodile, you see Ray-Ray's delirious. You need to take him to the infirmary." The inmate laughed with some other buddies while walking into G building, which housed the rec room, and doubled as Grotolli's gambling operation headquarters.

"As I was saying before that clown interrupted," Raynelle turned back to Ofodile, "I been down fifteen years for some shit I didn't do. How much faith do you really think I have in the legal system? That bitch and her girlfriend's lies was all they needed to lock me in this cage."

"Stop being such a pessimist, Ray. It seems like every month I hear of someone getting their case overturned due to DNA."

"I'm not being pessimistic, I'm keeping it 100. The same way they locked me away for damn near half my life without any evidence, is the same way they can keep me 'til I parole out in 2011, or 2015. Sooo, just in case the wind don't blow my way when the judge rules, the money will. With Saul out of the picture, I'll have the gambling on lock in here."

Ofodile shook his head. "If you say so."

"Cheer up, Ofodile, we're about to add another zero to our net worth."

"What about Frank Grotolli? You don't think he's going to find it odd that right after his nephew is killed, you take over the gambling? At the least, Frank is going to want a cut."

"Why do you think I coughed up fifty-grand?" Raynelle asked. "That money was long distance money."

Ofodile looked confused. "Long distance money?"

"Yeah, long distance money. I would've stuck the sharp end of a reshaped toothbrush in that fat Wop's neck five years ago when he laughed at my offer of twenty-five grand for a piece of his gambling operation. Only reason I didn't do it then or have some flunky do it, was because of Frank. Now, that I've paid you and you paid who you needed to, I am a long distance away from the hit."

"So, you're not the least bit concerned that Frank Grotolli may put two and two together?"

"And I should be concerned for what, again?" Raynelle looked squarely in the eyes of his friend before continuing. "We know Frank can make the streets run red with blood, but in here, I'm the Capo. I don't want war, but I'm sure Frank is a smart man. I'm sure he'll realize that my little prison operation is not worth the time and money that a state prison war will cost him."

Raynelle stood up. "I need to go shave."

"That's right, you did say your daughter was coming to see you this morning?" Ofodile said.

"My babygirl, not my daughter."

"You think you two will be as close when the DNA results prove that you're not her father?"

He shrugged. "Who knows, but I will tell you this. I'm sure enjoying the ride now."

"Why, because she does everything you say?"

"Everything I ask," Raynelle corrected, "not say. You just make sure Saul stops breathing before visitation hours end."

Ofodile's radio beeped. "Code red! Code red! Multiple inmate confrontation in indoor rec area."

Lieutenant Orlando Ofodile removed his nightstick and took off toward the building that housed the prison library where Raynelle worked, the education department, religious services, and the indoor rec room.

*****

As he had done every day over the past two years since her first visit, Raynelle placed the wallet photo of Miracle on the metal mirror. He wanted her close to him as he meticulously shaved and groomed himself. She looked just like her mother did at that age.

He closed his eyes and imagined each hair being cut down at the roots – each hair that would grow back in a few days time. He tried not to smile at the irony of his situation.

Fifteen years ago, a woman put him in jail for fathering the daughter that he didn't. Now, if he did get his case overturned, it would be because of the same daughter that he didn't father.

Over the last couple of years, he'd actually grown fond of the young lady. He even looked forward to the weekly letters and the monthly visits. He didn't want to hurt her, but his need to hurt Sunny in the worst way superseded his not wanting to hurt Miracle.

Chapter 14

October 27, 2007
SAME DAY: **Atlanta, Georgia**

YUM-YUM WHER U AT? U NO THIS MY DAY 2
GO C MY POP. CALL ME 911.
She looked up. Right as she sent the text, a polished
black Lincoln Town car pulled up to the hotel entrance.
The impeccably dressed blonde haired driver got out
and looked around until his blue eyes landed on Miracle. "Are
you," he looked down at his cell phone, "Mrs. Paul Robinson?"
"Huh." Miracle frowned. "Who me?"
The young man attempted to block the glare of the
Saturday morning sunlight by pulling his black chauffeur's cap
down on his head before looking down at his phone again.
Next, he casually walked over to Miracle and reached out his
arm. "This is you, isn't it?"
She looked down at the screen. She couldn't help but
smile. She remembered as if she took the picture yesterday. It
was actually taken three days ago on Wednesday evening
during Black Study. All the teens were asked to come to church
dressed as an African or African-American freedom fighter

from the past. Yum-Yum was Paul Robeson and Miracle came as Ida B. Wells Barnett.

Miracle looked up. "Okay, where is Yum-Yum?"

A puzzled expression appeared on the young man's face. "Who?"

Miracle tried to downplay her embarrassment. The driver was young, maybe twenty-one, twenty-two, only six, seven years older than her and Yum-Yum. And Yum-Yum, the king of practical jokes is why she thought the driver and Yum-Yum were in cahoots. But of course her thought process did an instant one-eighty when the look on the driver's face suggested that he had no idea who or what a Yum-Yum was. And there was no way that she was going to explain that Yum-Yum was her best friend. Suddenly, she felt bad about being embarrassed over using her friend's nickname. Worse, she didn't understand the way she was feeling. At school and around the hood, she'd never been embarrassed about using Early's nickname, so why the embarrassment now? Why did she feel dumb around this white guy that she had never met, but she didn't feel any kind of way around blacks when she mentioned Yum-Yum's nickname.

"So, you're not Mrs. Robinson?" the young man asked. "It doesn't make me a difference either way." His black suit jacket rose as he shrugged his shoulders. "Executive Limousine service has already been paid to pick up a Mrs. Ida B. Robinson and take her to the Jackson Diagnostic and Classification Prison."

Miracle looked up and met the driver's stare head on. "Robeson," she said, slowly enunciating the word. "Mrs. Ida B. Wells Robeson."

The driver looked at the teenage girl like he could care less who she was.

"Well?" Miracle said with a sudden air of entitlement in her voice.

"Excuse me?"

"Are you going to open the door for me or does that not come with the service?"

"Yes ma'am, I'm just a little –"

"Confused?" Miracle interrupted. "Don't be. I'm sixteen," she lied. "It's normal and quite natural for Muslim women to marry as early as fourteen." She doubted that the white man knew anything about Islam.

A half hour later, Mira's phone rang while travelling down the interstate.

"Husband," she said after answering.

"Mira, I know you hot, but I can explain."

"I'm all ears, my love," she said through gritted teeth.

"Well, last night after I dropped you off at the Courtyard, I accidentally ended up in the Pointe."

She held the phone close and spoke in a low tone. "Negro, how did you accidentally end up in the hood, twenty miles away? You were just going to get something to eat. And besides, you knew I was going to see Ray this morning. Only reason I let you push the whip is cause you got the fake driver's license."

"I know. But, it ain't my fault. I was minding mine, going through Mickey Dee's drive thru right around the corner of the hotel when my phone rings. It's dark in the car and I couldn't reach my phone to check the caller ID, so I answered with my earpiece. Guess who was on my other line?"

"Boy, don't play with me."

"Okay. Okay. It was Drop-it-like-it's-hot-Dreanna."

"What?"

"Drop-it-like-it's-hot-Dreanna…"

"I heard you he first time." She shook her head. "Tell me you didn't…"

"I couldn't help it. You don't understand Mira.

"OMG. Help me understand."

"Okay, you know how long I been trying to get at her."

"And every other female that has a pulse."

"You got jokes." He said. "But for real, for real, Dreanna said and I quote, bring the bud and the Bacardi and we can party."

"You don't even drink fool."

"I know I don't, but she know I got ID to buy booze, and she know a brotha be holdin' a few dollars. And she know I've been trying to get at her since her top came off in the pool last summer."

Miracle whispered. "You about the smartest dummy I've ever met. Only thing she needs to know is that you a horny little toad that she can call when no one else will come. But, sho' nuff, the Captain save-a-slut that you are, proved her right." Miracle looked up and into the driver's rearview mirror. Satisfied that he wasn't paying attention to her conversation, she continued. "That being said, it still don't explain why you couldn't call, text, or communicate with me. You know how important my monthly visits with Ray are."

"You see, it's like this. But before I fully explain, I just wanna tell you how much I love you, Mira. I don't know where I'd be if I didn't have you as a friend."

"Save it for the toilet, cause I am not trying to hear it, Early Earnest Morning. Just tell me the deal."

"Uhm, while being devirginized by Dreanna, Sunny started banging on the vacant apartment door we'd broken into."

"How did my mom know where you were?"

"I think Dreanna, might have sort of set me up," Yum-Yum said.

"Where's my car?"

"I got my wallet. That's how I paid for the limo. I used one of the pre-paid credit cards."

"Where is my car, Early?"

"Sunny took it."

"How did momma get my damn keys?"

"Dreanna."

"I'm gon' beat that tramp's ass. I should beat yours, for being so stupid. Just wait 'til I see her. Giving my keys to my mother. She done lost her damn mind. That's okay, I'm gon' sho' nuff help her find it. Uhm-hmm I got something for Dreanna alright." Miracle nodded. "Negro, I hoped you at least used three condoms. No telling what viruses are breeding up in her cooter."

"Come on, Mira, it ain't that serious?"

"When you wake up with disease and bacteria dripping from your thing, we'll see how serious it is."

The Towncar exited the expressway.

Miracle looked out the window. The line of cars entering the prison grounds looked like a funeral procession.

"I gotta go. We're almost there."

"What do you want me to do about the car?"

"Go to the room, get the spare key out of the safe and go get my damn car. I'll deal with Dreanna and momma later. And, be here at three in my car, no limo. I ain't playin' Yum-Yum. Visiting hours are over at three, you better not leave me hanging." She hung up before he even had the chance to respond.

Chapter 15

October 27, 2007
SAME DAY: **McLean, Virginia**

Director Bush's eyes went from one thirty-two inch screen to another as Blackhawk Special Ops Agent Hodges filled him in from his ground location. He was in his home office, drinking his breakfast while watching the scene unfold.

"We have the unsub in view now. He is about one mile north, heading this way."

"Hodges, every camera, every image you see, I see in HD," the director said to the head of the operation. "You are absolutely positive that Boyce has no plans today. No one's expecting him to be anywhere, Mr. Hodges."

"Sir, I understand your trepidation, and I'm sure you already know that in the last ten years the government has used my services twelve times and out of those –"

Gerald interrupted. "As you said, I know the numbers. Your success rate is one hundred percent. If you weren't as efficient as your record states I wouldn't have contracted you. But, remember at this particular time, you work for me, Mr.

Hodges and despite how redundant or idiotic my questions may seem, I need you to answer them."

"Yes sir," Hodges replied. "We have been monitoring all of the unsubs incoming and outgoing calls and text messages for months, as you know, sir. Forty-eight hours ago, before flying out of Ankure Airport in Ondo, Nigeria, the unsub started clearing his schedule for today, he finished while laying over in London's Heathrow Airport."

Director Bush watched the long white limousine pull up to the newly installed security gates. "Hodges, be very careful. Boyce may not look it, but he's eighty-three. There is no way to tell how much his heart can take, and I need him alive until I'm satisfied that he's given us all the information he knows."

"That's why I have an anesthesiologist and a heart specialist in his master bedroom now. Sir, I have to stop all verbal communication."

"Do not administer the drugs until I give the word," the director said into a dead phone.

Chapter 16

October 27, 2007
SAME DAY: **Jackson, Georgia**

As Mira walked up to the penitentiary steel doors, thoughts of Sunny invaded her consciousness. *Momma was everything, until Auntie Assata went to prison for shooting Man-Man. Back then, I was young, but I was old enough to know that momma blamed herself for Aunties downfall. Just because she's the one that told Man-Man to go sell drugs somewhere else besides the Pointe ain't cause for blaming yourself when that fool was the one that hit Auntie in the mouth.*

Man-Man was a grown man, what was she supposed to do? Besides Man-Man attacked Auntie six months after momma busted him and his boys out for having my dumb butt best friend running crack while they stayed in the cut smoking weed. Heck, all she was trying to do was get Yum-Yum away from them fools. Man-Man didn't even live in the Pointe. He had no idea how Auntie got down until he buried his fist in her face. I didn't see it myself but word on the streets was that Auntie had pulled a .380 out of her purse and blasted Man-Man in the face three times. Not only was that not momma's fault, but Auntie shouldn't have even gone to prison. She was just a woman defending herself.

A few minutes later, Miracle was inside the prison waiting in the long visitation line. At least it was warm, she thought as the line slowly moved. It was amazing what a wig, some makeup, a pair of bra socks, and heels did for a woman, she thought. She'd been playing dress up since she began coming to see Raynelle a couple years ago. The first time, she came with Yum-Yum and was turned away because an adult didn't accompany her and she wasn't on Raynelle's visitation list.

Around 9:30, thirty minutes after visitation hours began and thirty minutes after Miracle had been in line, the line started moving pretty fast. Miracle was lost in thought when the woman behind gave her a little nudge.

"Honey, you're next," the woman said.

Miracle Joy Brown still had the dimples and the teenaged babyface, but her hair, makeup and body said that she was a grown woman. Her Georgia I.D. did, too. According to the laminated card, Miracle was twenty-one and her name was Nigeria Hunter.

"Go on in, Ms. Hunter," the female guard said before winking an eye at Miracle.

After being patted down by another guard, Miracle walked in to the large visitation area. She walked past several inmates and their families. Some were huddled up to the round tables in deep conversation, while others were eating snacks or just relaxing while enjoying family time. As always, Raynelle was at a table in the back of the cafeteria-like room, and he already had snacks and drinks waiting.

He stood up from the metal stool and held out his tree-trunk thick arms. "Babygirl."

One lady was staring so hard that Miracle licked her tongue out at the woman. As always, she floated into his strong arms. He planted a kiss on her forehead before they sat across from one another.

"What was that all about?" Raynelle asked.

"That woman." Miracle nodded in the direction of the lady.

Raynelle turned around in his chair.

"No, don't look at her, Ray."

He turned back to Miracle.

"You know she saw you looking, Ray. Now, I bet she thinks she has your attention." Miracle shook her head. "That's a dog-gone shame. She supposed to be visiting her man and she out here sweating you," Miracle said.

"Babygirl," Ray put a large calloused hand over hers, "you are a princess, you're above her and everyone else in this piece. Don't let anyone bring you down to their level."

"I understand whachu' saying, Ray, but you been in here fifteen years. These women out here on these streets are straight scandalous, they ain't like the women," she paused to think about what she was saying, but she'd already put her foot in her mouth, "that were around before you got jammed."

"What do you know about scandalous women?" Ray asked.

She wanted to disappear. At that moment she'd just realized that her own mother was the queen of scandalous. Miracle had no doubt that the DNA test would prove just how scandalous Sunny really was. Miracle didn't care if her and Raynelle did not share the same DNA. As far as she was concerned he was her dad. He needed her and she needed him.

Raynelle leaned back in his chair with his arms behind his head. He patiently waited for Miracle's response.

Miracle waited until thoughts of Yum-Yum popped into her head. "Yum-Yum got my car jacked last night, messing with some scandalous female."

"The Impala?"

"Don't trip, Ray. Mom took it."

"Dammit!" he said before leaning back in his chair and taking a deep breath. "Babygirl, I paid for that car. She has no right."

"I know, Dad, but she don't know that you paid for it."

He leaned forward. "What did you just call me?"

"You know she think I hustled some dice games on the side to pay for it. Anyway, Yum-Yum is gon' take my spare key and steal it back."

"First, what did I tell you about calling that man, Yum-Yum? That's the most ghetto mess I have ever heard. He's a young man, babygirl. He's not one of these loose booty pants-under-they-behind-punks. Second, you can't steal what's already yours." He held a palm out. "Now, most important, did you just call me dad?"

"Huh?" she frowned.

"A minute ago, you said, or I thought you said, I know, dad, but she doesn't know that you paid for it."

"I don't know." Mira shrugged her shoulders. "Is it okay if I did?"

He wore the biggest smile on his face. "I'm just honored that you think of me as a father figure."

"Well, you are. You've taken care of me since I met you two years ago."

"We've taken care of each other, babygirl. If it weren't for you and Early, I'd be serving three more years at least. All I've done was buy you a car and some clothes. Your dice hustle pays your momma's rent, bills, your needs, and up until recently, paid for her drugs. But don't worry, babygirl," he patted the back of her hand, "when I hit the streets, I'm really going to show you how to get paid with your talents. And for the record, babygirl, I tell everyone in here that you are my daughter." He shook his head and sighed.

"What's wrong, Dad?"

He looked up. "Ain't no need in beating a dead horse, but I will never understand why Sunny lied on me."

"Get in line. You know how strong momma was, well maybe you didn't, but momma was a soldier, and to see her now. . ." A tear escaped Miracle's eye as she shook her head, "I can't stand to be around her. She's mean, and all she care about is the man she's sleeping with and that crack."

Raynelle stood up, walked around the table and sat next to Miracle. While rubbing her back he said, "Babygirl, I love you and I am so proud of the young lady you are becoming, despite the fact that you look like a little too grown with your fake boobs, hair, and that party dress."

She hit Ray in the chest.

"Owww."

"This *fakeness* has been fooling the guards and getting me in to see you since I was thirteen."

He smiled, "I know babygirl. You a boss hustler just like your pops." He leaned in, "You think Early's sister will hook me up with a Georgia driver's license if I get out?"

"Not if. When," Miracle said. "And I'm sure she will."

"Tell her I'll pay whatever." He shook his head. "I ain't looking for no free ride, Babygirl."

"I'll take care of it. Consider it a coming home gift, Ray."

"Fifteen," Raynelle had an approving look on his face, "and you handling grown woman business, better than most grown women would. Say what you want about Sunny, but you can't say she didn't raise a priceless jewel."

"If she only appreciated me half as much as you." Mira looked off into space as her mood turned dark.

"Come on babygirl, your momma loves you, she's just lost. Hey, maybe I can help."

"Help, doing what?"

"I don't know." He shrugged. "I read somewhere that sometimes it's better to release your frustration instead of keeping it all bottled in."

"I got enough frustration built up in me to destroy a small country."

Raynelle rubbed her back again. "Talk to me babygirl, tell me how it all started. Your momma's downfall."

"I don't know." She turned to face Ray. "You got your own problems."

"Yeah, I do. My most pressing problem right now is that my babygirl ain't right cause something weighing her down. And, please believe I'll swim across the Sahara and walk across the Pacific to take the weight off of my princess. Talk to me babygirl."

Miracle took a deep breath. "A few months after Auntie Assata got locked up, stuff started disappearing."

"What kind of stuff?"

"The flat screen TV in mommas bedroom, and then both DVD players, stuff like that. When I asked what happened, momma said we was struggling cause she no longer had a point person to watch her back."

"What did she mean by that?"

"I don't know and I didn't ask. I was just anxious to help."

"You were only twelve, babygirl. How could you help?"

"Well, I already told you about the marbles, right."

"The marbles you controlled with your mind?"

She nodded. "Yeah, the ones I made move when I was six. All I had to do was think about them long enough. Watch this."

Mira focused her concentration on the empty can of coke on the side were Ray sat a few minutes ago.

The can slid across the table and fell over onto Ray's arm.

"What did I tell you about that?" Ray looked around nervously. "I know what you can do babygirl, but we can't let anyone else know. That'll ruin everything."

"I know, I'm sorry."

"Get back to the story."

"Okay, so long story short, me and Yum, I mean Early were playing Monopoly a few days after Auntie got busted. Early was killing me and talking big trash in the process. So, anyway I had just landed on Park Place, which I bought. Next, I shook the dice and concentrated on two. That's what I needed to get Boardwalk. When I rolled the dice, it was like they were turning around in slow motion. Once one popped up on one dice, I dropped my concentration on that one and when the other landed on one I did the same."

"That's cheating, babygirl?"

"You told me a crime is only a crime if you got caught." She smiled.

"I did say that, didn't I?"

"Yes, you did."

"Well, did you get caught cheating?"

"Nope." She shook her head.

"Did you win the game?"

"Yep. He couldn't stop landing on Park Place and Boardwalk."

"So how did Sunny come to know what you could do with the dice?"

A few months after Auntie got locked up Momma was sitting at the kitchen table drinking coffee while I was getting ready for school. I sat across from her. I said something like Mom watch this, she looked up and I rolled the dice. I said two before the dice stopped. They landed on two. I reached across the table, grabbed the dice again rolled them and said three before they came to a stop on three."

"I bet you had Sunnys full attention then."

"You know it. I went all the way up to twelve before I left for school that morning. That afternoon momma sat me down and explained the rules to shooting craps. We practiced for about an hour before we left. Before midnight we were back home ten thousand dollars richer. In less than a month we moved out of the Pointe. We didn't take anything but the clothes on our backs and my book collection."

"Is that when you two moved into that big fine house in the subdivision where Bishop TJ Money used to live?"

"Yep. We're paying three thousand a month for it."

"You mean you are paying three thousand a month for your mother and her friends to live in it, while you use prepaid credit cards to live out of hotels."

She shrugged her shoulders. "Yeah, I guess."

"You guess? Babygirl, I know Sunny's your mother, and I have never spoken ill of her, but exploiting her own daughter just ain't right."

"I know, but I can't just leave momma out there. She won't get help. She won't even admit that she has a problem."

"I take it she sleeps during the day and get's high at night?"

"Pretty much," Miracle said.

An alarm went off somewhere in the prison.

Everyone looked up to where the source of the noisy alarm came from.

The intercom came to life. "Attention in the visitation area, attention in the visitation area. Due to circumstances beyond our control visitation is terminated for the rest of the weekend. All inmates will immediately move to the inmate processing area and stand in a single file line. Any inmate caught lingering will lose their visitation privileges for six months.

"Visitors please stay seated in the visitation area. I repeat visitors stay seated in the visitation area until further instructed."

After a hug, a kiss on the cheek, and a promise to call her next week, Raynelle got up and made his way to the long line forming on the other side of the visitation room.

"Say, Ray," an older man standing in front of Raynelle got his attention.

"Whachu want old head?"

"A hotel suite at the Ritz, a few butt naked honeys, and a bottle of Viagra, but since I can't get none of that in here, I'll settle for a smoke." The older inmate reached a weathered hand out.

"Nah, old head. I don't smoke."

"You know they 'bout to lock the whole prison down. Some fools done killed two of Grotolli's men, and they say Grotolli just about got himself killed too. Word is, it was a hit. I sure feel sorry for the folks that have to answer for this," the old man said.

Chapter 17

October 27, 2007
SAME DAY: Ile-Ife, Nigeria

As far as any one in the Nigerian palace was concerned, Zion was just one of Baba's seventy royal servants. Over the five years he's lived in and below the palace, he'd acquired five times the knowledge and understanding of an American university PhD graduate. While the average adult used less than ten percent of their brain capacity, Baba had taught Zion to use over sixty percent of his. That would explain his computer memory, his athletic prowess, his mental manipulation of matter, and so much more.

Zion was underground in his bedchambers doing his two favorite things, eating chocolate dipped in peanut butter and reading street novels. It was around 9 pm and Zion was in the middle of a Donald Goines classic. Ronald was just about to lure Daddy Cool's teenage daughter into a life of prostitution when Baba entered his thoughts. He tried to block his mentor and teacher from entering his subconscious world, but Zion knew he had about as much luck of blocking out Baba as a two-month old baby had at blocking a seasoned NFL linebacker.

"Zion?"

He shoved the book inside the couch he was sitting on. "Yes, Baba."

"Why don't you come up top for the celebration? It'll be fun."

I don't know. I'm kind of busy. You know, the forty-three painfully boring books by Charles Darwin that you assigned me to read by Monday."

"Do you mean the same books that you haven't touched since you put them on the floor in the corner under your flat screen TV yesterday morning?" Baba asked. "You're not doing anything significant, Zion. Come on up and enjoy the party."

"We have the celebration of life every month. I can miss out on one, Baba."

"What's wrong, Zion?"

"You should know."

"No, I shouldn't," Baba said. "I communicate with you telepathically because it's private and the more we communicate this way, the stronger your mind and your senses become. Although, you are right, I can invade your thoughts and discover what's bothering you, but I don't and I won't. Once you completed the journey into priesthood-manhood Zion, you also took sole ownership of your thoughts, beliefs and actions. You are a man, and I will respect you, as a man should another. So, you wanna tell me what's on your mind?"

"Around three this afternoon, an eerie feeling washed over me and I can't seem to shake it."

"Do you feel nauseated?"

Zion shook his head as if Baba were right in front of him. "No, nothing physical. I feel that something bad is going to happen, kind of like in a horror movie when the creepy background music gets louder and speeds up before someone gets killed."

"I could go inside your mind and tell you what the feeling is about."

"Nah, because if something bad is about to happen I can't do anything to alter the outcome."

"Technically, you could," Baba said, "but it would be another two-thousand years before the Creator would send you back to battle Evil."

"I know. If it's fine by you, I'm just going to hang out down here in my man cave."

"Fine by me, I'll just leave you to your thoughts and your Donald Goines novels that you have hidden inside the couch you are sitting on."

"Hey, you just said –"

Baba corrected Zion before he could even finish his incorrect thought. "I said, I wasn't going to invade your private thoughts. I said nothing about your actions. You know, once I am in your mind I see through your eyes, yet you still try and hide books from me."

"Why didn't you ever say anything?"

"Why should I have? I wasn't the one ashamed of what I was doing."

"Are you disappointed in me?"

"Some, but not for reasons you may think."

"Well then, why are you? Zion asked.

"When the Archangel tricked the first man and woman into committing sin, they felt shame – shame of their entire being. The first thing their eyes witnessed after eating what the Creator forbid was their own nakedness. Upon seeing their nakedness as their shame instead of their glory, they covered up God's greatest masterpiece."

"So, you're disappointed because I am ashamed of what I am reading?"

"If what you say is true, tell me why your shame is my problem?" Baba replied.

"Because I am a part of you and you are a part of me just as every man woman and child are a part of everyone living and everyone that has ever lived. And as long as I am not dishonoring man, the gods, and the Creator, I shouldn't be ashamed of my actions, such as reading street novels."

"There is nothing I love more than wisdom exemplified." Baba said. "You make my job so fulfilling, young Zion. I can't imagine how strong you will be in two years when you obtain the three hundred and sixty degrees of knowledge. Then, you will have the wisdom of the gods. And with wisdom, you'll have immense power – immense power to change, immense power to create, and immense power to destroy," Baba said. "On that note, I will leave you to your thoughts, but remember if you wanna open up, just send me a mental text and I'll be there, goodnight."

The only downside to telepathy was that there was no physical privacy. But then again, if it weren't for the first two people on Earth, then there wouldn't be any need for physical privacy.

Two hours went by like it was two minutes. Zion had just completed Donald Goines's sixteen-book collection. It had taken two hours but he read them straight through.

That eerie feeling suddenly became much more intense. The hair on his arms, chest and lips were standing at attention. Now, the foreboding feeling manifested itself in a physical sense – in the form of a dull pounding in Zion's head. It was like thunder exploding the air before a storm. Zion looked straight ahead at the black sixty-inch flat screen television that he rarely watched, before turning his attention to the forty-three books stacked up in the corner next to the television.

He dreaded his weekend homework – reading forty-three books by the godfather of racism. But, he knew that sometimes it took understanding someone else's culture to help further the understanding of your own. Baba had taught Zion some time back that the most important history is the history that you don't know. He said that people have manipulated others throughout history with one thing – knowledge. So as bad as he hated to read them, he knew he would begin in the morning. It would take all day probably, but they would be read and memorized. But now, he could hardly keep his eyes open and that dull pounding was rapidly turning into a migraine. He decided to lie down; maybe he would get up a little later and read the notoriously racist, rambling theories that Darwin wrote in his book *The Origin of Species.*

Dr. Boyce's image entered his mind. *Hmph, wonder what Uncle John would say about Charles Darwin's "Survival of the Fittest" theory. If Uncle John lived in the 1800's when Charles Darwin was around, he would have made Darwin's theories look so irrational, that the English government would have probably locked Darwin in a white jacket and put him away in a padded room.* The sleepier Zion got, the clearer his vision of Dr. Boyce's surroundings became.

*****

The sun was disappearing into the sky as darkness began to creep in. The street sign read Northside Drive. Million dollar homes on five-acre lots lined the street. Huge older estate homes. Old money. Homes that had been in families for generations. The next street sign read Conway Drive. Five houses down Conway was Uncle John's house. It sat atop a hill as if it were too good for the other estate homes on the street. The sixteen-foot white metal pillars accentuated the twelve-foot black wrought iron fence and gate that surrounded the property. The black asphalt driveway leading to the White antebellum plantation style home had to be the largest horseshoe driveway in the city. The huge white Roman pillars that lined the front of the home made it look like a governor's mansion. The black shutters on each side of the second floor windows were decorative eyelashes on the forty-five hundred square foot two-story, while huge, stained glass picture windows accentuated the ground level. The house was dark. The lights that helped guide vehicles up and around the driveway weren't even on

As the darkness came closer to blocking out all light, Zion's senses became keener. Although no cars were visible in the driveway, he could feel several life-forces close by. Just as he was about to walk in the house one of the four garage doors began to open.

First, he saw two bright red eyes. As the vehicle backed out, he realized that the red eyes were the taillights on a government tagged black Suburban. Although the darkness consumed most of the night's natural light and the windows on the large SUV were tinted, Zion was able to get a clear look at all its inhabitants. The years of reading, studying, and moving in total darkness had taught him to see with his mind and his eyes.

Five men, all white, all were armed. He had to make a choice. It was either follow them, or go inside and see if Uncle John was all right. Rationale told him to follow the SUV, his heart told him to go inside. He knew Uncle John was still alive, because he could hear his heartbeat. After memorizing the license plate, the SUV, and everything about the five men inside of it, he hurried into the house. He followed the sound of Uncle Johns heart.

He took the winding staircase to the second floor. An unnatural light was visible at the end of the hall were Uncle Johns bedroom was. In an instant, Zion went through the door.

"Uncle John! No!" The bedroom chandelier rattled as Zion belched out screams of anguish.

The esteemed Reverend Dr. John Boyce sat strapped into something that closely resembled an electric chair. There was minimal bruising on his eighty-three-year-old face, but his naked body told another story. The hair on his legs and chest were singed as if someone set him on fire repeatedly and put it out quickly.

Zion didn't understand how he could love someone so much without even really knowing them. Sitting at Uncle John's feet, he cried. It had taken five years, but he cried. He cried for his mother. He cried for his father. He cried for his Uncle John, and for everyone throughout antiquity whose lives were prematurely ended at the hands of men that devoured other men in order to elevate their social and economic standing in the world.

He felt fingers – fingers on his baldhead.

"Zion Uhuru Jones."

The Reverend Doctor's voice was faint.

Zion looked up into the face of the man that saved his life and started him on the journey to conquer evil.

"My work is done here. It's time I go home and be with our Heavenly Mother."

"Nooo. I need you. I can't defeat evil on my own, Uncle John."

"You won't have to."

"Baba can't help me. He can't even leave the Palace, I mean physically. You can't just bring me this far and leave me."

"Sun, I am not leaving you. My death will bring life."

"I don't understand?"

"You will, when it's time. You will. In the meantime, I need you to remember this."

"Okay." Zion nodded.

"At the end of this existence, we only have three things that matter – two numbers and a dash. The numbers represents when God released us from his bosom and sent us to this earthly plain. The second represents God calling us home or casting us into the depths of hell. Although these two numbers do matter, as they are a point of reference, the dash that separates these numbers is what makes all the difference in the world. You see, Zion, the dash represents everything you have done to spread love, life, and God consciousness to community. The dash is the legacy of that person. It's the determining factor whether their spirit will live forever free to create whatever reality they desire, or whether their spirit will die with the evil that you will annihilate."

Chapter 18

October 31, 2007
FOUR DAYS LATER: **Manhattan**

The doormen at one of the most prestigious hotels in America were wearing fire red pants, shiny black button down shirts, matching red ties, and red suit jackets. Both men had red glitter on their faces and two red horns on their heads, as they greeted patrons coming in and out of the Waldorf. The rain had abated some, but not enough for the director of the nations international spy network. It was rainy, cloudy, and windy when one of the doormen opened the rear door to the limousine that the man stepped out of.

"Great costume, Mickey." The director of National Intelligence greeted the doorman.

"Thank you, Mr. Bush, but I hate it."

"I bet the kids love it," the director said.

"That's the only upside to wearing this monkey suit in the rain, well, that and people tip much better when you're dressed as the devil on Halloween."

The director walked through the five star hotel's busy lobby. He blended right in with the multitude of patrons that were checking in and registering for the annual Haunter's Convention held at the hotel. There were people waiting to get on every single elevator. The director walked up to the elevator where only two people stood. The door opened. The man and woman waiting before him got on first.

"Sorry, pal," the man dressed as Thor said to the director after pushing ahead to get on the elevator.

The door closed.

Thor continued. "Hey, great costume, pal. But, where is your white pointy hat." He pointed to the man's head. "It would have been more authentic if you would have had the initials and the emblem sewn in on the front of your sheet."

No matter where you went, there was always at least one idiot who thought someone really cared about what they had to say, the director surmised.

"He's dressed as Jesus Christ," the man's wife said.

"Well, I'll be damned to hell in a hand basket. Thought you was the Ku Klux," Thor said.

Husband and wife got off at the third floor.

The director waved a finger at Thor. "I know you from somewhere, young man."

"They say I have one of those familiar faces." Thor shrugged. "But, who knows." The elevator stopped on six.

"Well, enjoy the convention, the director said while getting off the elevator."

"I sure will. You have a bullet splitting time yourself," the man said.

The director spun on his heels only to see a huge smile fading as the elevator doors closed.

"XR13!" he said aloud, before shaking his head. Impossible. That man was clearly a white man. His face was still familiar. Why would he say bullet splitting? Out of the three men that saw XR13 split a bullet, only the director was still alive or so he thought.

He racked his mind for answers until he got to the room on the sixth floor. He never truly believed that XR13 died in that explosion. Even after forensics confirmed XR13's charred remains, he still didn't quite believe that the super agent was dead. The director inserted the credit card key before entering. After closing the room door, he flipped what looked like an ordinary light switch and waited. Moments later, a bell rang. He opened the mirrored closet doors and walked onto another elevator. The elevator had only two buttons, up and down. He pressed the down button. Moments later, he exited the elevator into a conference room sized private library. Director Bush looked around at the floor, and the four walls that were surrounded by floor to ceiling, wall-to-wall books. There wasn't a speck of blood or brain matter anywhere. It was like Bernie had never shot his nephew or himself a few weeks ago at the beginning of the month.

"Gerald," Constance Greenspan held out his hand.

The two men shook.

"Congratulations on your confirmation," the director said.

"Thank you, but as we all know the deal was done before my uncle ate that bullet, we just had to convince the President to sign off on my appointment." Greenspan was referring to his new appointment as Chairman of the Federal Reserve Bank.

The chairman's' jovial tone and the way he spoke of his recently deceased uncle unnerved the director.

The chairman was impeccably dressed, in very similar fashion to his uncle, which was weird. On the few occasions that the director met Constance, he couldn't help but think that his taste in clothing had a lot to be desired. On one occasion, the director was in Big Sky, Montana at the Yellowstone Ski & Golf Resort Private Country Club meeting with Bernie, when Constance walked up wearing white linen pants and a matching sports jacket. The jacket not only had a zipper but under it,

Constance wore a colorful argyle sweater. The worst part about his ensemble was not the zipper on the sports suit, nor the 80's argyle sweater, but the fact that he had the audacity to wear it at one of the world's top country club's in Winter-white January.

The chairman waved for the director to take a seat in front of his desk. "So, tell me what Mr. Boyce had to say." Constance crossed his legs while awaiting a response.

The director was tempted to rewrite the story in his mind before giving voice to what John Boyce had really said. The only reason he decided on the truth was that four other men had heard Boyce's far-fetched bedroom confession.

"Gerald, is there a problem?" the chairman asked. "Do you need some water to loosen your tongue?"

"No, I'm fine, sir." The director retrieved a manila file folder from his briefcase. "Everything is transcribed in here, sir."

"Thank you, Gerald. Now brief me on what he said after you administered the Sodium-Pentothal."

"His answers were short and somewhat incomprehensible, until we administered an experimental truth serum drug."

The chairman uncrossed his legs. "Look, Gerald, I don't mean to be crass, but I earn over one hundred dollars a minute. Each minute I'm down here, I can't monitor my money. So, spare me the details about how you got him to talk. Just tell me what was said."

Chapter 19

October 31, 2007
SAME DAY: **Jackson, Georgia**

Raynelle sucked in all the air he could before blowing it out. He turned to look at the twenty-foot gray walls one last time – the gray walls that he'd spent fifteen precious years behind. The hate began to boil to the surface, as he thought of the woman responsible for the time he had lost.

He'd received the letter yesterday, but wasn't released until this morning. It took a couple hours for Raynelle to be processed out and another hour for the prison to issue a check for the two thousand dollars he had on his books. Money was the least of his worries. One thing was for sure, he was dead broke when he was arrested and now he had turned nothing into two hundred and seventy eight thousand dollars. He would have had more if his attorney didn't take twenty percent of his earnings for setting up the prison kitchen Paypal account and laundering the money through different offshore accounts.

Each time Raynelles Paypal account had accumulated a thousand dollars it was electronically transferred into an offshore account. Then it was divided up and transferred to an account that the Warden's sister had, a trust account for Lieutenant Ofodiles grandchildren, and then three other accounts.

Raynelle had a smile on his face as the yellow taxi pulled up to the prison's front entrance.

"The dispatcher did tell you that it would be a flat rate of two hundred dollars to take you all the way to Stone Mountain?"

Raynelle leaned forward. "Take me to the closest Bank of America first."

"I'm not trying to get in your business," the older black cabbie said. "But, if you trying to cash a prison check, you have to go to the Ivy Wesley Check Cashing center over on Main, unless you have two forms of ID on ya."

"Take me there first then," Raynelle said. "Appreciate the 411, old man."

"Don't thank me yet. Once the Wesley's take out twenty percent of whatever you have, I don't think you gon' be in a thanking mood."

"Twenty percent! Hell nah!"

"I know. But, what can you do. The Wesley's are the only one's that will cash them checks with just a prison ID," the cabbie said while he drove.

Raynelle leaned forward. "The Wesley's that own the check cashing spot, are they related to Bill Wesley?"

The cabbie nodded. "Yep, Warden Bill owns the place."

Raynelle snickered. "I should have known. Warden Bill "Crooked" Wesley was a bigger criminal than most of the cons in his prison."

Thirty minutes later, Raynelle was relaxing in the back seat of the yellow cab after cashing the prison check, and buying a minute phone from Walmart.

By next week this time, he would be a millionaire. Miracle didn't even realize her earning potential. Raynelle definitely planned to show her. Las Vegas would not soon forget the teenage girl that cost them millions at the dice table. But, first things first. He had some urgent business to attend to – a debt that had to be settled.

If his plans went smoothly, Miracle wouldn't suspect a thing. And he would be right back in front of the prison Friday morning awaiting her arrival. That's when he told her that he'd be released.

The sun was still smiling at 6 pm, when the cabbie got off on the Memorial Drive exit in Stone Mountain. Four turns later, the yellow cab slowed as it pulled up to the small gray two story with the pink shutters on the windows. An older pink Cadillac Deville with Mary Kay stenciled in the back window was in the driveway.

"Don't stop. Keep driving," Raynelle said to the cab driver.

"Where to?"

"Anywhere, we just need to drive around for about thirty minutes."

He didn't want anyone to know he was out, not even his mother. But, it was Wednesday and he knew she'd be leaving for Bible Study soon.

Thirty-three minutes later, the cab dropped Raynelle off at the Ingles grocery store around the corner from where his mother lived.

After handing the cabbie some cash, he said, "I have another fifty if you're here when I get back."

"'Bout how long you gon' be?"

"Fifteen, twenty minutes tops, old man. And I'll give you another fifty to take me fifteen minutes up the road to Lithonia."

"I'll be right here," the cabbie said.

Ten minutes later, Raynelle had broken a rear window and was in the house he grew up in. He ran up the stairs and pulled down the attic door before unfolding the wooden stairs that led up. After climbing to the top, he lifted a heap of pink insulation and retrieved a black Glock nine-millimeter handgun. Next, he popped the clip out and checked it for ammunition. Satisfied, he inserted the clip and left the same way he'd come.

He jogged back to the Ingles, hoping the cabbie hadn't left. He had said twenty minutes tops. It took almost thirty. As he got closer he saw that the cab hadn't moved. He checked his watch. It was almost seven. He'd be at Sunny's house near the same time Miracle walked into Bible Study with Early.

Chapter 20

October 31, 2007
SAME DAY: Ile-Ife, Nigeria

Every morning, Zion took at least an hour to commune with nature, and God. This morning he was still in his meditative state when Baba entered his space. Baba knelt down on the underground concrete floor and sat on his legs next to Zion.

"Baba?" Zion said as mentor and teacher entered the subconscious world that Zion had created. "I have to go back."

Baba chose to ignore Zion's last statement for the moment. "Good morning, sun," Baba said, while marveling at the scenery around him. "This space is absolutely breathtaking."

"Thank you." Zion pointed to the crystal clear waterfall that ran down the snow-capped mountain into the lake they sat on top of.

"What are those?" Baba asked while pointing to all the colorful flowers surrounding the lake.

"I call them Dancing Rolips," Zion said, admiring the hybrid flowers that moved in sync with the wind.

"Rolips?"

"Yes. I visualized a tulip - rose hybrid moving to the beat of the wind and," he pointed to the millions of flowers that provided ground cover for the paradise he and Baba were in, "and these are what manifested from my vision."

"So, this is where you come to commune with nature and the gods?"

Zion stared at all the colorful exotic looking fish that were swimming in the clear water below him as he answered. "Not so much with the gods, but with nature and the Creator."

Baba turned to Zion. "Sun, do you know why I call you sun?"

Zion shook his head before a red and yellow striped fish jumped into his lap. He placed the fish back into the water before answering. "No, sir."

"The word son is a derivative of the word sun. It simply means 'light.'" Baba took Zion's hand. "You are the light, Zion – the light of the Mother, the light of the gods. The light is the truth," Baba smiled, "it is the path back to the Creator. Life anywhere cannot exist without light. 20,000 leagues below the sea, if there is a single plant living, there is light. All of the Creator's messengers were illuminated above others so they could be walking, breathing examples of how man was supposed to reign over creation. Zion, you cannot ever forget or forsake the ancestors, the gods, or the people. The same way you have created your own heaven, you must free the people from evil so they can see and create as you do."

"I accept the calling and I will be that beacon of light that will emancipate the people from Evil," Zion said. "If God be for me, who can be against me."

"No one and nothing," Baba said. "Two more years with me and Evil won't stand a chance. Leave now and Evil will quickly see what you don't know. Your ignorance will be used against you, sun. Are you sure you wanna go back into the world now, at such a disadvantage?"

"No, I don't want to," Zion shook his head, " but I have to in order to save Oba's last descendant?"

"At the beginning of this journey, I told you that you needed her love in order to defeat Evil. Do you remember?"

Zion nodded.

"If she transitions from this world to the next, you can still commune with her. You can still win her love, as you have been doing your whole life through the dreams you two share."

"So, you're saying that if I stay here for two more years and she transitions in that time, that I can still win her over and defeat Evil?"

"That is exactly what I am saying, sun. If she transitions, it will be easier for you to come together as one and in two years you will have the strength and the wisdom of the gods. Evil won't be able to withstand your wrath."

Zion returned to conscious reality. He was back in his bedchambers. The lake he sat on top of was now gray concrete. He rose from his knees, as did Baba.

"I have to go. I am not going to let Evil take her from this Earth, like it did my mother."

"You're taking a huge risk, sun." Baba said. "Mankind is at stake here."

"So is the physical life of an innocent girl."

"You love her, don't you?"

"With everything in my being," Zion said.

"You're willing to risk your life and the eternal life of mankind."

"I am. But, Baba I don't see it as a risk."

"How do you see it?"

"I see it as something I was born to do. Something that has to happen. Miracle's life is just as important as the three-hundred and twelve million lives on American soil."

Baba smiled. "How do you know her name?"

153

Zion looked confused. "I don't know. Her name just popped into my head. Up until now I had no idea who she was."

"You know more than you think you know about her. Close your eyes, sun; consciously reach down into your dreams. Tell me when you see her," Baba said.

Zion's eyelids fluttered as an encyclopedia of images raced through his mind. "I see her." His eyes popped open.

"Miracle Joy Brown. She lives in the Atlanta area," Zion said as he grabbed Baba's arms. "I know who she is and where she is. How, I don't know, but I know that I know that I know who and where she is." Zion sang and danced around Baba.

"Sun, stop dancing and look at me."

Zion instantly did as he was told.

"You know who Miracle is," Baba said, "but she doesn't know who she is just like she has no idea that she was immaculately conceived."

"So, she's half human, half god?" Zion asked.

"No half anything. Using Christian terminology, she's an angel. Under the African Centered Vodun spirituality, she is a god," Baba explained. "She has the power of Oba but she doesn't know how to use it. Don't get me wrong, she knows a little about her power but it's such a precious little."

"Should I bring her here? Will you show her, like you did me? I'll wait five years for her to catch up to where I am and we can finish the last two years together."

Baba shook his head. "Sun, there is no here. Here exists in your mind."

"No, I've been here for five years. Up top, the palace the servants, the animals."

"Just like the paradise you created in your subconscious, I created this reality," Baba said, before clapping his hands together.

*****

Zion woke up.

He sat up and focused his eyes. Wherever he was, it was black dark. All he knew is that he was in a bed under some white sheets that he discarded while swinging his legs over to the floor. It was cold and hard.

By the time he stood up his eyes had completely adjusted to the darkness. There was a dresser to his left and a TV stand with a flat screen TV on it to his right. The walls were gray and the floor was gray concrete. He looked down at his legs and midsection and was astonished at what his eyes registered.

For the first time since he went away, he realized that he was no longer a skinny ten-year-old kid. He made his muscles jump in his Olympic sprinter-like legs. He ran an index finger down the lines and waves on his muscled stomach. Finally, he looked into the mirror and nodded, before holding his hands in a prayer position. "Thank you."

He walked to the first door he saw. After opening it, he walked inside. It was a small bathroom. After relieving himself, he washed his hands and looked into the bathroom mirror. He hardly recognized the man that stared back at him. Gone was the fat cheek baby face. Now, he stared at a man with accents and strong pronounced cheekbones. The only thing that seemed the same was his bubble gum shaped bald head.

There was another door inside the small bathroom. He opened it and walked out. A gentle breeze rubbed up against his skin as he easily navigated his way down the hallway. It opened up into what looked like a den. Light coming from under a gray metal door illuminated the large room. The floor was still gray concrete, but the walls, all four of them were lined from floor to ceiling with books. With catlike stealth, Zion walked to the door. He closed his eyes and concentrated on sound.

He heard male voices. Singing.

155

"Wake up all the teachers, time to teach a new way. Maybe then they'll listen to whatcha' have to say."

A flood of relief washed over his soul.

"The world has changed so very much, from what it used to be."

His dad had always told him, that he could trust anyone that sings Harold Melvin and the Bluenotes old school hit, "Wake Up Everybody." Treble had referred to certain songs as safe code songs and this was one of them.

"There's so much hatred, war and poverty."

He recognized the distinct golden calypso voice of a man he'd studied extensively while under Baba's tutelage. Even if they weren't singing the safe code song, Zion knew the four voices singing behind the door where men to be trusted, men of God. He put his hand on the knob and turned before opening the door.

Zion was almost as shocked as the four men that sent the black and white dominoes flying into the air. Zion stared, not believing the assembly of men that had almost jumped out of their skin. Zion had studied these men and the movements they were a part of. He knew as much as an outsider could know about the four men seated at and under the wooden round table.

The pastor with the graying red dreads was the first to take his gun's site off of Zion. He came from under the table and stood up.

"Dr. Fast?" Zion recognized the Muslim cleric that had saved him five years ago.

Two others put their handguns away as they, too, came from under the table.

"Good Lord," Reverend Jeremiah White said. "Boy, you done took ten years off my life – hell," he looked around at his peers, "off all of our lives."

The men put their guns down and started getting to their feet.

"Say, Jeremiah why aren't you down here with us?" the Honorable Minister Louis Muhammad asked while getting to his feet? "What if Zion had been the enemy?"

"I would have tried to be his friend. I can't help that these old knees have a delayed reaction," Reverend White said, rubbing his knees. "By the time my knees woke up, I'd already recognized the young Lion of Judah."

Dr. Fast was the first to welcome Zion with a handshake, one that rapidly turned into a prolonged hug. Zion held the Imam. He couldn't stop thinking about his mother and all of the innocent lives that the American government's top spy agency had taken. Like a movie, hundreds, thousands of images raced through his mind's eye – images of men, women, and children that had been casualties of the covert spy, entrap, and kill Agency. This year marked the agency's sixtieth year. It was in 1947 that President Truman had signed the National Security Act that paved the way for the Central Intelligence Agency's formation.

The tears came. Zion pressed his face into the Imam's shoulder. He didn't want the other men to see him crying.

"It's okay, sun. We're all family," Dr. Fast said.

The lone white man in the group, Reverend Joel Naison gently placed a hand on Zion's broad back. "Release, son. Let it out. You are holding way too much pain inside." He rubbed Zion's back. "That's it. Release the pain. You'll feel better," Reverend Naison said. "Sun, eight years ago in '99, I lost my father. It was sudden. Heart attack. He passed the same week I gave my first sermon. My dad was my hero – is my hero." The Houston, Texas mega pastor teared up as he spoke. "My dad wasn't taken like Treble was, but he was taken suddenly and I miss him all the same."

Zion looked up from the shelter of Dr. Fast's shoulder. His face contorted in an unnatural position, his mouth opened so wide that his eyes became slits and then the deep, howling gut wrenching sobs spewed forth. The Honorable Minister

Louis Muhammad, Reverend Jeremiah White and Joel Naison formed a cocoon around the young lion.

The four men held him while he released his pain. The long hand had almost completely circled the clock before Zion was calm and seated at the rickety wooden table with the four clerics.

Dr. Fast began, "Zion, the four of us and eight other spiritual leaders have set up a sort of Underground railroad in twelve major cities across the nation. Los Angeles, Houston, Atlanta, Chicago, DC, New York, Indianapolis, Detroit, Nashville, Miami, L.A., and Jackson."

Zion listened intently, committing every city and every address to memory. Joel Naison handed Zion a file folder. Naison began, "In there," he pointed, "you will find ten phone numbers, they will change weekly. Every Sunday you will log onto craigslist.org and go to the Atlanta area postings. You will look under the farm & garden section. You will then type in the craigslist search engine the words Dark Horse Army. You will click on each item and take down the ten digit phone numbers, write down the sixth number of each set of numbers in sequence that they are listed. The finished product will be the phone number you need to reach one of us. Only call if it's an absolute emergency, otherwise, if you need refuge just come to any of the addresses in the file folder night or day, someone will be there to receive you. Make sure you're not followed and there is no tracking device on or around you. You will be safe in any one of these safe houses."

"I wanna thank you all for everything you have done. I don't know how or exactly who I must fight, but fight I will. Unless any of you have a better idea, I am going after the Evil in men and the Evil that is manifested in the American government's systems."

Minister Muhammad spoke. "Zion, we are not here to question or advise, your wisdom vastly outweighs ours. Our mission is to support you in every and any way you deem fit."

The minister waved an arm around the others. "We are followers of the Creator and in Quran it is written, 'be conscious of the day on which you shall be brought back unto God, whereupon every human being shall be repaid in full for what he has earned, and none shall be wronged.'" The Minister quoted. "Sun, we are here to help you rid the world of Evil, so we can save mankind from Allah's condemnation."

Reverend White chimed in, "I couldn't have said it better." He looked at his old friend, Minister Muhammad, "Well, maybe a little better if I quoted from the Gospel, just joking, Louis."

Joel Naison spoke. "But if we judge ourselves truly, we will not be judged."

Dr. Fast said, "Corinthians 1, 11:31."

"You know your bible, Hakim?" Reverend White said to the Islamic scholar and cleric.

"I'm supposed to, Reverend," Dr. Fast replied. "Quran tells us that its mission is to verify the truths that are in the Torah and the Gospel. And I can't confirm truth or falsehood unless I first know the bible."

"Maybe you four should go on television and show your solidarity," Zion said. He pointed in Dr. Fast's direction. "One of the most respected leaders in the American orthodox Muslim community," he looked in Minister Muhammad's direction, "the leader of the Nation of Islam,' he placed a hand on Reverend Naison's shoulder, "one of the most pragmatic and prolific *White* Christian ministers in America," Zion looked to his right at Reverend White, "and a black Christian leader and spiritual mentor to quite possibly the next and first African-American president."

"Yeah, and the day after we went on television, we'd all be delivering the Word of God to the seals in Siberia," Reverend White said.

"Or Guantanamo Bay," Dr. Fast replied.

Zion was the only one not sharing in the laughter.

Reverend Naison looked over at Zion. "You're serious."

"As the truth on Judgment day," Zion said. "But, we'll revisit this when the time comes, but now I have to get to Atlanta in a hurry."

"I'll take you. Haven't seen Dr. Lomax in a minute." Reverend White said, while rising from the wooden chair. "I'll introduce you two. He's your underground contact over at First Afrikan in Lithonia."

"Lithonia? That's where I need to go."

Chapter 21

October 31, 2007
SAME DAY: **Lithonia, Georgia**

Fifteen years, eleven months and twenty-nine days. That's how long Raynelle had lived inside a cage. And it was fifteen years, eleven months and twenty-nine days that he'd been consumed with thoughts of a woman he barely knew, a woman he had never taken to bed, a woman that had sat on a witness stand and tearfully accused him of raping her. The muscles in Raynelle's huge arms contracted as the darkness threatened to consume what little reason he had left.

He'd spent weeks, months, years, anticipating this day. He took a deep breath as he stared at the three-sided light gray brick newer home. There was no porch light on to welcome the neighborhood trick-or-treaters.

The front yard was meticulously manicured like every other front yard on the street. The grass was an evenly cut shade of brown. A sprinkling of colorful autumn leaves gave the grass some color, as did the purple and gold fall perennials blooming around the brick mailbox. He walked down the driveway. No cars were parked outside. Seconds later, he cupped his hand over a garage window. No cars inside.

Good. Maybe she was alone.

He had planned this moment over and over again in his head for weeks, months, years. He knew exactly what to do... up until now. His anger didn't allow him to think clearly. He was on autopilot. He didn't care who saw him as he opened the white picket fence door and walked around to the back of the house.

The shirtless young man sitting at the kitchen table was focused on evenly distributing marijuana in an emptied out cigar. He didn't even notice Raynelle looking through a rear window next to the back door.

Sunny walked into Raynelle's line of view. As soon as they locked eyes, she dropped the glass of wine that she had been sipping from. Shock registered on her face. Glass and the red liquid scattered along the kitchen floor.

Out of instinct, Sunny's boyfriend jumped up from the table, dropping the cigar scattering the marijuana on the floor.

The maniacal smile on Raynelle's face caused Sunny to release a blood-curdling scream. The back door came off of its hinges as Raynelle walked through it as if it weren't even there. Glass from the French door went flying, several shards protruded from Raynelle's body.

The boyfriend reached for the gun in his back pocket and would have gotten it if his sagging jeans weren't hanging so low.

Raynelle's nine-millimeter barked once. The bullet left smoke and a powder burn stain in the middle of the boyfriend's forehead. The boyfriend's mouth hung open and his eyes and facial expression seemed to ask the question, why?

Sunny's shock quickly faded when she realized that her very existence was at stake. Just ten minutes ago, little white rocks sizzled on top of her pipe as she inhaled the sweet aroma of ecstasy. Every nerve ending of her body danced as the drug took effect. And now those same nerve endings were standing at rapt attention as Sunny looked on in horror. Seeing her boyfriend's brains all over her gray granite countertops and stainless steel appliances had an instant sobering affect.

"Why?" was all she could think of to say.

Raynelle placed the gun on the kitchen table and took two long determined strides toward her. He was in the face of his accuser. "Why? What the hell you mean, why?"

She met his stare head on.

"You don't even know who I am do you?"

She didn't reply. There was none needed. The look on her face told him that she knew exactly who he was.

He took off his gloves. He was no longer concerned about leaving prints. His anger only exacerbated when she failed to apologize or show any remorse for what she had done to him. In an instant, his hand was around her neck. Her clawing and fighting didn't move or change the intent expression on his face. "DNA tests proved that I did not father Miracle."

Her eyes threatened to jump out of her head. "Raynelle!"

He turned his head to the side. "Did you miss me honey?"

She struggled to breathe. His hand was a boa constrictor squeezing the life from his prey. Her fingernails drew blood as she clawed his choking arm.

With very little effort, he lifted Sunny by the neck and slung her into the den. Slowly and methodically, he took measured steps over to her cowering frame. She wheezed and coughed, fighting to get air into her lungs, as she scooted back into the fireplace.

"Fifteen years, eleven months, and twenty-nine days. You can't even begin to imagine how it feels to be falsely accused and convicted of rape." He slapped his chest. "Well, take a good look at me, Sunny."

She continued coughing.

"Look at me!" he screamed.

Her head rose.

He held his arms out. "This is what you created. To survive in the caged jungle you sent me to, I had to become a monster. It wasn't enough to simply beat my enemies. I had to devour them. Enemies that never would have been," he pointed, "if you hadn't lied."

He took another step.

"Please believe I had many enemies."

He took another step.

"Rapists and child molesters are the lowest kind of convict – often sodomized with mop bucket handles, broken broomsticks, and even knives and razors. All of which you will have the distinct horror of experiencing."

"I'm sorry," she pleaded. "I didn't know. How was I to know that you didn't rape me?"

"The same way you knew that I did. No worries, though, we will have a couple of days to get to know each other." He smiled. "I'm going to give you fair warning. The next forty-eight hours are going to be real intense. I'm going to make you feel sixteen years of pain in those forty-eight hours." He shrugged his shoulders. "Give or take a few hours. And right before you die…"

Black Jesus with dreads hanging from a cross that hung directly above the fireplace caught his eye, distracting him but only for a minute. His attention returned to the woman cowering inside her own fireplace. A sinister smile creased his lips. A circular stain began to form on her white tights as a stream of urine ran down the length of her legs and came to rest in a pool on the brick fireplace floor.

He grabbed her arm and yanked. "Get your ass up out of there."

Chapter 22

November 1, 2007
NEXT DAY: **Atlanta, Georgia**

Early was leaning so hard you'd think he would fall onto the student parking lot ground any moment. Miracle's cherry red Impala was the only thing preventing him from falling over.

"Just cause you have a cute smile and a car, I'm just supposed to go to a hotel with you?" the Northside High school cheerleader asked.

"Of course not, gorgeous."

"I don't even know you like that." She looked him up and down. "For real."

"When do you ever know some one?"

"Uhmm, when you have been acquainted with them for at least ninety days."

He licked his lips. "Did you really just put a time frame on love?"

"Your name may be Early, but that lame shit that just came out your mouth, was way too late."

"Nah, gorgeous, what I'm saying is right on time." He smiled. "How many dudes you done known for one, two, three years and you still didn't really know them. And then you have us, you and I who have known each other a short time, but you know way more about me and I know way more about you than probably most do." He used his hand to lift her chin up. "Time don't have nothing to do with how two people feel about each other. Does that make sense?"

She shrugged. "I don't know. I guess," she thought for a moment, "maybe you're right."

"I know I'm right. We been kickin' it out here for two weeks now. I don't usually move this fast, but I feel like," he stood up and put a hand over his heart, "I just wanna show you a greater tomorrow every day."

"Ahhhh, that's so sweet," the cheerleader said before gently taking his hand.

"I mean, we place so much emphasis on time. But, what is time?" Early paused for dramatic affect. "It can't be measured but yet, people still measure it. You can't measure the way two people feel about each other. And gorgeous, love don't wear a watch. If it did I wouldn't feel the way I do about you this soon."

She blinked a few times, trying to prevent the tears from coming. "Soooooo," she dragged the word out, "what are you saying?"

"He's saying whatever it takes to get under your skirt," Miracle said as she walked up. "I bet he gave you the quantity versus quality bit, or did he do the time measuring thing. And my favorite, love don't wear a watch, gets them all the time."

The girl turned to Early.

"Come on, gorgeous, don't feed into the hate. What we have is bigger than the words of man."

"The words of a wo-man, fool," Miracle said. "Now, wrap it on up with Sponge Betty."

The girl put her hands on her hips and looked at Miracle. "You need to teach your sister some manners, Early."

"Now see," Miracle said, looking at Early while waving her arm in the cheerleader's direction, "she is what happens when you don't use protection." Miracle shook her head. "Such a waste of sperm and an egg."

"Early, you just gon' let that," she pointed at Miracle, "that wanna be man insult me?"

"I'm sorry," he said. "She's my fam."

After the cheerleader stormed off, Early and Miracle got into the car.

"Why you had to go and do that, Mira. Dang. Shorty was done, well done and ready to be devoured."

"Uhm-hmm. I told you that you was gone pay for sending that limo to take me to see Ray. You know what they say about payback."

"Nah, Mira. What you did was way beyond what I didn't do. You know I been workin' on that for a couple weeks now. She woulda' been my first snow bunny."

"The female that you call '*That*' has a name. A name that I didn't hear you use one time. Early, I bet you don't even know her name."

"Come on, Mira. You doin' too much. Of course I know Shorty's name."

"What is it?"

He smiled. "It's Gorgeous."

They both laughed.

"Yum-Yum, I mean Early, you are so full of it."

"And thanks to you, I won't be giving Shorty any of it."

"I need you to run me by mom's house right quick."

"I thought we was hittin' the mall so you could pick up some clothes for Ray."

"We are, but you know it's the first. I gotta take mom the rent, bill, and the get high money."

"Yo, Mira, you ever think about getting your mom's some help?"

"All the time. But, you know how she is," Miracle said.

"Yeah, she ain't ready. Oh yeah, I'm taking the GED Monday."

She sat up in her seat. "You passed the pre-test?"

"Come on now, Mira, you already know."

"I'm so proud of you. Dang, I almost feel bad for busting your groove with Sponge Betty. But, seriously, Early, I wish you would show the same respect for other girls as you do me."

He laughed. "You ain't no girl."

The expression on her face immediately told him that he'd said the wrong thing.

"I mean you ain't like no regular girl."

"You better quit before you choke on the foot I'm about to put in your mouth."

He put the car in park while Miracle took out her door key.

"You want me to wait out here?" he asked.

"Yeah, but if I'm not out in ten minutes, come get me. Sunny might be in one of her rare motherly love moods. And I don't have time. I have a lot to do in two days. Ray is going to be so surprised."

Chapter 23

November 1, 2007
SAME DAY: **Pine Mountain, Kentucky**

Pine Mountain was in Eastern Kentucky, just west of the Appalachians about an hour from Tennessee. The twenty-four inch all-terrain tires rolled over the snow and dirt, crushing any and everything in their path. A Huey helicopter awaited instructions at the small Tri-Cities regional airport in Blountville, Tennessee, ninety miles Southeast.

Gerald Bush, General Lesure, and Constance Greenspan watched the action from the one hundred twenty inch computer screen in the situation room at CIA headquarters.

"I do not like this," the NSA chief said. "This is not the way we operate. I still say we should have farmed the job out to the Patriot Act or one of our other Black Op contractors."

"And we would have done just that, Maurice, if we had had the time," the red haired, pale late thirty something, chairman said. "We don't know how long the pastors will be there. Our Intel is already forty-eight hours old."

The NSA chief shook his head. "I'm sorry you two, it's just incredibly hard to believe that Joel Naison, Louis

Muhammad, Hakim Fast, and Jeremiah White are part of a grand conspiracy to take down the government. If you were to tell me that Muhammad or Fast were involved, I could almost wrap my mind around that, but Naison? And I'm not just saying that because he's white. Naison has too much too lose. How would he benefit?"

"That's the sixty-four thousand dollar question," Chairman Greenspan said while watching the Hummers slowly navigate the snow and muddy wooded mountain terrain.

"I've reviewed the test results from all nine subjects that were injected with the 5E1G truth serum before we injected Boyce," General Lesure remarked. "I know all of them answered the five hundred polygraph questions truthfully, but do either of you think it's even remotely possible that Boyce lied about some of what he said. I mean some of the things that came out of the old man's mouth were so far fetched, they bordered on fantasy."

"Such as?" Connie interrupted.

The NSA chief thought a second before responding. "Well, Boyce rambled on about XR13's son being the last descendant of some Herculean god. The old man could have been in the early stages of dementia, I guess. Hell, I don't know any other way of explaining why someone as sharp as him would rattle off the nonsense that he did. I mean, come on. The old man sounded like he really believed that nonsense about XR13's boy being the second coming of Christ."

Gerald pointed. "Look!"

The words RADIO SILENCE flashed across the screen. That meant absolute silence from there on out. The Bluetooth transmitter in their ears allowed the chief to command them from seven hundred miles away at CIA headquarters, not even he was to break radio silence.

In the spring and summer, the cabin would have been completely hidden in the dense vegetation that surrounded it. But thanks to Jack Frost freezing the greenery, naked trees and the snow covered mountain terrain made the cabin much easier to see.

Less than forty-eight hours had passed since the NSA chief had convinced Vice President Haney that the cabin was a suspected terrorist cell and that he needed seven of the military's best killers to take down the cell. And now, seven American trained killers had fully automatic AK-47's strapped to their backs as they tiptoed in two inches of melting snow and muddy forest. They used hand signals to communicate as they closed in on all four sides of the cabin. Once they were about eight feet away, they unstrapped their rifles and pointed them at the cabin.

"I do not feel good about this." The NSA chief bit his bottom lip. "No. I've done a lot of things, but this," he crossed his arms over his large chest, "I can't do it."

Chairman Greenspan shot up from his seat. "Give the friggin' order now, Maurice!"

Director Bush didn't give the chief a chance to act. Before the words were out of the chairman's mouth the director leaned over and pressed the command button and shouted, "Fire!"

All seven guns went off. The screen turned a wavy orangish red before going black.

"Son of a . . . " The General's face was beet red. His eyes bulged before he jumped to his feet, turned and swung.

His fists were in tight large balls as his arms hung to his side. NSA chief, General Lesure stared at his fallen superior with pure hate before turning to the chairman. He stabbed a finger in the chairman's direction. "I told you I didn't feel right abut this." Next, he turned his attention back to the floor where he just laid the CIA director out. "He had no friggin' right." He turned and pointed at the chairman again. "You had no right. Those were my men." The General's teeth were clenched as he took a step toward the chairman.

The thirty something, lanky, red headed chairman stopped swiveling in his chair and looked directly into the NSA chief's eyes. Below a whisper he said, "I have every right. I make the right and the wrong." Greenspan stood up, straightened out one of the sleeves of his navy blue and coral pinstriped tailored suit jacket before taking a step forward. The two men stood face to neck, glaring at each other. The scene looked like a modern day David and Goliath.

The director had to look up to make eye contact with the much larger NSA chief. Calm and his voice barely above a whisper, Greenspan said, "Those men that died just now, if that is what actually happened, they weren't your men, Maurice. My money, my influence allows for secret military Special Forces to even exist. Do you really think Dickey Haney did all of this in less than two days notice? The briefings, the blueprints, the drone that took pictures from the sky and those," the director waved an arm toward the hundred and twenty-inch screen. "If those men did in fact die, they died a heroes' death. They died while serving their country. I don't like what may have happened to those men, but at the end of the day life goes on."

"Life goes on. What kind of frigging mess is that? Those men are dead. Their families will be – "

"Fine. Their families will be fine, Maurice. You didn't make any noise about all the lives that were lost on nine-eleven. But, seven agents die in the line of duty and you're ready to abandon the ship."

"I didn't know that the planes would cause so much loss of life. Besides, this is different."

"Bullshit. What we did on nine-eleven..." Chairman Greenspan paused to collect his thoughts. "Maurice, I am not even going to explain how idiotic your last comment was. Let me tell you something General. Since the Korean War, I have broken, split, destroyed, and rebuilt entire countries, imagine what I could do to one man that got into my path."

"That was your uncle, and you are not him," the NSA chief barked.

"You're correct. I'm not my uncle, but let me give you a sample of what my money, and my influence has allowed me to acquire." The chairman paused, before a sinister smile creased his lips. "Luscious, that sweet twenty-two year old call girl. At first, it was once a month and now that your Jessica, poor Jessica. Your beloved wife, Jessica of thirty-two years. Stage three Lung Cancer." The director shook his head from side to side. "Uhm-Uhm-Uhm! A shame! Damn shame!"

The General took a step back and turned trying to avoid the chairman's touch. But it was to no avail. Like a heat sinking missile that had locked onto its target, the chairman followed the chief's movements until the chairman's freckled hand patted the huge NSA chief on the shoulder. "Don't worry Maurice, I'll make sure that Jessica nor her family or the media or anyone ever finds out about your little black whore."

It was hard to tell if the General was trembling from fear or anger. His complexion was getting closer to the color of hot sauce, but his usually penetrating blue eyes had a dull look. And when he opened his mouth to reply, nothing came out.

"By the way, Maurice, in case you did not know, Luscious is really the birth name of the ghetto garbage you're banging."

His teeth were locked together. "I could kill you," the general growled.

"You could try. But," Greenspan took a step closer to the retreating General and pointed a finger in the air, "if you fail, I will surely kill you."

"My men, the men, they didn't have to die today."

The chairman took a couple steps back and sat back down. After crossing his legs, he said, "Obviously, they did."

"Did what?" the General asked.

"They had to die. Nothing happens by accident. There is a purpose for everything. Just because we aren't aware of that purpose doesn't mean there isn't one. Those men died protecting the freedoms of 312 million Americans," the chairman said. "Sometimes our intelligence is flawed, but our hearts and intentions are pure."

"Flawed?" Maurice pointed to the black picture on the theatre-sized computer screen. "My men were just blown to hell. The pastors knew that we were coming and the only ones that knew our plan were the seven agents, you, Gerald and me."

The chairman crossed his legs before looking the chief directly in his eyes. "You don't necessarily know for sure that it was a bomb."

"What?" the NSA chief's face twisted up. "Sir, no disrespect intended, but what in the Sam Hell else do you think that orange bright light was right before the screen went black?"

Chapter 24

November 1, 2007
SAME DAY: **Somewhere, Georgia**

Zion bolted upright, bumping his head on the ceiling of the Camry.

Reverend White looked over at the fifteen-year-old man-child. "Bad dream?"

"You didn't hear that?" Zion looked out of the window at the rain.

"Hear what?"

"The explosion."

"Sun, the only thing exploding around here is this heavy rain in my line of view."

Zion looked behind him. "Where are the pastors?"

"Zion, what is wrong with you?"

"Reverend White, please tell me where the Minister and the others are?"

He looked at his watch. "It's quarter of five. They should be at the airport in Blountsville, Tennessee." He passed his cell phone to Zion. "Look in my contacts and pull up Louis M."

Zion looked at the phone. He turned it on its' back. He pressed a couple buttons but the phone's three-inch screen didn't change.

Reverend White looked over at Zion. "You have to be the only kid in America that doesn't know how to work a cell phone."

"I know how to operate a cell phone. I just don't know how to work this one," he said, handing it back to the reverend.

"This is the new IPhone. I'm generally a technology dummy, but this thing," he held up his cellphone, "is my personal assistant. I just had it for a couple months and I can't remember how I ever operated without it." The reverend demonstrated. "Just press this button like so, and slide your finger across the screen."

The black screen turned blue and several icons appeared.

"Here." He handed the phone back to Zion. "Press the icon that reads contacts and you can figure it out from there."

A minute later, Zion had the Minister on speakerphone.

"A-salaam alaikum," Zion greeted the minister in the Arabic greeting words of peace.

"Wa-alaikum-salaam," the Minister returned the greeting.

"You're alive," Zion said.

"You sound surprised," the leader of the Nation of Islam replied.

"So, everybody is fine, Reverend Naison, Imam Fast?"

"Everyone is fine. We are all about to board a charter jet. What has you so concerned?"

"The cabin just exploded," Zion said.

"What?" Reverend White said.

He heard the minister repeating his exact words to the others.

There was an awkward moment of silence inside the rental and over the phone.

"What happened?" the Minister asked.

Zion closed his eyes and concentrated. "Seven of them. All men. White and brown camouflage snow suits. Assault rifles." He opened his eyes. "They shot up the cabin with assault rifles before the explosion."

"Which one of the government's alphabet boys were behind this?" Reverend White asked.

"Does it really make a difference, Reverend?" the Minister asked. "Malcolm referred to Kennedy's death as chickens coming home to roost. I think this phrase is much more appropriately used in referring to what happened to the government's men back at the cabin."

Reverend White followed up with, "While referring to JFK, Malcolm also said, 'Being an old farm boy myself, chickens coming home to roost never did make me sad; they always made me glad.'"

"Thank you, Zion. We will monitor the situation at the cabin," the minister said. "Jeremiah, please fill in the blanks for our young lion. We're walking out to get on board the plane. Call me anytime Zion, and I mean anytime you want to talk," Minister Muhammed said before disconnecting.

"What was all that chickens coming home to roost business?" Zion asked.

"First, let me explain what probably happened at the cabin," Reverend White said. "We had a weapons expert rig the cabin to explode upon being fired on."

"You mean, the only way the bomb could have gone off is if a bullet hit it?" Zion asked.

"Not a bullet, but several bullets had to hit the bombs, not bomb. Hate those men died, but serves the government right. Sending assassins in to kill men of the cloth."

"How do you know that they were government assassins?" Zion asked.

"How do you know that the sun is going to come out tomorrow?" Reverend White asked.

"I…"

"It's the nature of the sun right?"

Zion nodded his head.

"It's their nature as well. We've been watching the CIA, NSA, FBI and Homeland Security for five years."

"Since they killed my – "

"Yes," the reverend interrupted. "We don't know a lot, but what little we know is enough to figure out that the chance of a sanctioned hit would be probable, being that all of us have a voice and are spreading a different message than what the government is preaching."

"You expected the government to send assassins to the cabin?" Zion asked.

"Anticipated, is a better term," Reverend White said. "You know, sun, there's a Yoruba proverb that goes something like, 'One going to take a pointed stick to pinch a baby bird should first try it on himself to feel how it hurts.'"

"Okay, I get it now," Zion said. "The evil that men do sometimes comes back to bite them quicker than expected. Instead of doing the killing, the government hit men at the cabin ended up killing themselves in the process of trying to kill you four."

"Us five," the reverend said, glancing over at Zion. "You were at the cabin, too."

Just that fast Zion had drifted off with his eyes wide open.

"Zion?" the reverend called out.

Fifteen-twenty seconds lapsed before Zion turned his head to the Reverend. Tears began to stain his cheeks. "It's bad. It's very bad." Zion shook his head from side to side.

"What's bad?" the Reverend asked.

Zion squeezed his fists into a ball, "How much longer? Please. Reverend, please hurry. I have to get to Lithonia before something happens to Miracle."

Chapter 25

November 1, 2007
SAME DAY: **Lithonia, Georgia**

In the past she'd tried to see through the stained glass a million times and each time, she saw blurred images of the hardwood foyer and the edge of the wrap around stairwell. And this time was no different. After she was satisfied with what she didn't see, Miracle put the key in the nickel-plated lock.

The lock's tumblers turned as the one-inch rectangular bar slid back into the cavity of the oak wood door.

As soon a she stepped across the threshold, a tidal wave of dread washed over her.

Fear had a stranglehold on the teenager's heart, making it hard for her to breathe. She hadn't referred to Sunny as mom in years. The crack, the men, the dice games; this behavior was not that of a loving mother, and therefore Mom became Sunny. But this time, the words she spoke were that of a scared child seeking the comfort and protection of her mother. She didn't understand the feeling she was experiencing, nor did she understand the dark cloud of dread she felt. It wasn't visible to the naked eye, but the cloud was real, and it was in the house.

The dark cloud was a living, breathing animal. Miracle didn't know how she knew this, and she didn't know what the cloud's purpose was, but she knew it wasn't good. Her eyes unconsciously began to search the front room for clues in to the dark cloud mystery. The black hand-stitched leather furniture, the peanut butter colored couch pillows, the picture of Black Jesus hanging over the fireplace, nothing seemed out of place. She looked up. Beyond the second floor wrought iron stair railings, she could see that the bedroom, bathroom, and laundry room doors were closed. She walked over to the bottom stair. That's where she saw it. Blood. It was only a couple of drops, until she looked up the stairs and saw several more.

"Mooommmm?" Miracle shouted.

"Run!" Sunny shouted.

A whooshing sound came from the master bedroom and then a snapping sound followed by a gurgly blood-curdling scream. "Ahhhhhhh - ghhhh!"

Before she realized what she was doing, Miracle sprinted up the steps. She opened her mother's bedroom door. Her mouth fell open. Shock registered on her face.

The man she came to love, the man that had become her father over the last two years was right there. A twisted smile shrouded his sweaty face. He was naked with the exception of the black high tech boots he wore on his feet. An extension cord with blood soaked exposed copper wires at the end was in his right hand.

The shock on Miracle's face was interrupted by something dropping onto her head. She looked up just in time for another drop of blood to dot her forehead.

"I'm sorry," Sunny said.

"Moommmmmmm!" Miracle shouted as tears raced down her face and cheeks.

Sunny's body was nailed to a huge wooden cross that was attached to the bedroom ceiling. Wet and dried blood covered her naked, pale, pecan skin.

A primal scream bellowed up from somewhere deep inside Miracle before her fear turned to anger and her anger transformed in to a hate so fierce that Miracle no longer cared for her own safety. Annihilating the cause of her hate was the only thing on her mind.

She lunged at Raynelle. "Ahhhhhhh!"

Raynelle balled up his fist and swung. He caught Miracle on the side of her temple. She was unconscious before she crumbled to the gray carpet beside Sunny's bed.

"My baby! No! Please. Please. Please God. Please let my baby be okay," Sunny pleaded.

Raynelle dropped the extension cord, bent down and lifted Miracle up and placed her on the bed. Slow and meticulous, he untied Miracle's Timberland boot shoelaces, removed her boots and unbuckled her belt. He looked up at Sunny and smiled.

Sunny shook her head. "No, Ray. No. She didn't have anything to with what I did to you. Please, no. Don't do this."

He looked up. "You're right. She didn't have anything do with what you did to me. But, taking the child you blamed me for fathering would hurt you more than all the times I took you, and beat you over the last day and a half." He looked down at his rising manhood. "And just when I thought I had no more energy left."

"Noooooooooooooo!" Sunny screamed.

Raynelle rolled Miracle over on her back before getting on top of the queen-sized bed. His legs were between Miracles fifteen year old knees when Raynelle felt a presence behind him. He turned his head.

Early swung one of Miracle's boots.

Raynelle fell over on to the floor after the boot cracked him in the face. Early didn't hesitate to pick up the flat screen TV that was already lying face down on the floor. The fifty-two inch flat screen took a minute to lift. It wasn't as heavy as it was awkward.

Those extra seconds gave Raynelle time to recuperate. Early came down with all the force his weight and momentum could bring. Raynelle rolled over allowing his back to absorb the impact.

Early's neck and eyes darted around the room. He was looking for something else to use for a weapon. Anything.

"The dresser," Sunny words were barely decipherable. Blood was being coughed up each time she spoke.

Early either didn't hear her words or he was in too much of a panic to comprehend. Frantically, he continued his roaming eye search. He didn't see anything that would hurt the man that had arms larger than his legs.

Early knew that if he allowed Raynelle to grab any part of his body it would be over. Not seeing anything to hurt the huge muscled man, Early ran up to Raynelle's head, lifted his foot up and started coming down.

Raynelle's arm shot up and his huge hand grabbed Early's ankle and twisted.

"Ahhhhhhh! Oh - God! Oh - God!" Early shouted as his body came crashing down on the gray carpet floor.

Just that fast, Raynelle and Early had reversed positions. Now, Raynelle was standing over the chubby, baby-faced sixteen-year-old boy.

"You never stomp a guy, especially wearing soft rubber soled shoes." Raynelle pointed to the latest Air Jordan's that Early had on his feet. "You get so much more momentum from kicking a person than stomping them." Raynelle drew his leg back and kicked Early in the jaw as if he were trying to kick a fifty-yard field goal.

"Shittttt!" Early shouted after losing a tooth.

"Ah, hell, that was just a pooch kick. Let me show you how to kick a home run. One kick and I guarantee, you will never wake up.

Early's jaw hung at an odd angle. His eyes and outstretched arms pleaded for Raynelle to show mercy. "Please!"

"Don't beg now. You shoulda' used your head before coming up in here playing Billy Bad Ass, with a grown ass man." Raynelle cracked his neck to the left and then to the right before taking two steps back. "Gotta get a running start."

Raynelle hadn't paid attention to Sunny or Miracle the last three minutes since Early came onto the scene.

Miracle was in deep concentration. There was no room, no bed, no Early. No Sunny, No Raynelle, No Miracle. There were no walls, no floor, no air. There was only space, two boards fashioned into a six foot cross, and eight six inch metal nails, hammered into her mother's arms and legs. Nothing else existed, nothing else mattered but the images she concentrated on. The space began to expand under the nails.

Sunny's eyes pleaded for Miracle to hurry.

Raynelle had stepped back to the door. He was determined to kill Early with one kick to the head. He took off.

Early's arms covered his head.

Sunny's body followed the six-inch nails that dropped from the ceiling. Sunny crashed on top of Raynelle stopping his momentum and toppling both of them in a heap on the floor. Sunny summoned what little strength she had left and bit down on Raynelles left ear.

"Ahhhhh. Funky tramp," he shouted before throwing her off of him.

A piece of Raynelle's ear flew out of her mouth as she landed on the carpet next to the dresser.

Disoriented, Raynelle stumbled while getting to his feet.

A small bottle of nail remover hit him in the face, followed by make up and jewelry. Miracle was sitting up in the bed while every small item from her mother's bathroom flew at Raynelle.

By the time he took the few steps to get to Miracle, he had various cuts and bruises on his face and torso.

"He grabbed her arms, yanked her close before head butting her, instantly rendering her unconscious."

"I really didn't want to hurt you Miracle. That was never my plan, but my wanting to hurt your mother more is the only reason I am doing this." He grabbed her legs and spread them apart. He was on his knees on top of the bed when a strong wind blew through the room.

Raynelle turned his head.

Zion stood right outside the door.

"Damn, another kid." He shrugged. "Oh, well." Raynelle dropped Miracle's legs and got to his feet.

"You don't want this, young buck," Raynelle said, sizing up the kid that stood right inside the door. Raynelle stepped to the boy with fire raging in his dark brown eyes. "Now, normally I wouldn't give you the opportunity to see another day, but being that I have enough on my plate I am going to give you a chance to live."

The young man's eyes were on Miracle's unmoving frame. He still had not moved or said a word.

Once Raynelle was within striking distance, he swung a haymaker while he thought the kid wasn't looking. The young man ducked. Raynelle's fist connected with the bedroom door. At least one knuckle was broke but Raynelle didn't have time to nurse his injury. A second later, Raynelle was in even more pain, having just pulled a groin muscle trying to knee the boy. Raynelle couldn't understand how someone moved as fast as the teen-age boy now standing in front of the dresser. It was like the young man was toying with him. This time, the boy had to turn his head at an awkward angle to see Miracle. It was like the kid was obsessed. That was fine with Raynelle, who took the distraction as an opportunity. He charged forward. At the last possible moment, the young man stepped to his right. Raynelle's fist and head crashed in to the dresser's mirror.

Shards of glass went flying, most of it landed in some part of Raynelle's skin. Raynelle's body was leaking blood like a broken faucet.

Early was sitting up against the wall next to the bed.

Sunny's eyes still had life to them but her body seemed dead. She laid on her back in a semi-spread eagle position.

Raynelle had a fist wrapped around a nice size piece of mirrored glass. The glass had apparently cut into Raynelle's hand as blood dripped from his wrist. "Playtime's over, young buck. I'm gon' fillet that ass."

Raynelle charged, slicing the air in wide arcs.

Zion ducked, and side stepped Raynelle's Boa constrictor-like arms like a young Floyd Mayweather Jr.

"Son of a…" Raynelle shouted after accidentally gashing himself in the arm. Raynelle used his free arm to grab the kid's jacket collar. With all the force Raynelle could muster, he yanked. Zion used Raynelle's momentum to spin out of the jacket.

"Sunny lifted her knee. Raynelle tripped. He stumbled a few seconds before swiveling his body just enough to catch his balance. Just as he stood upright, Sunny kicked him in his ankle. This time, he came crashing down on top of her.

"Noooo," Miracle screamed as the pointy side of the glass shard Raynelle was holding embedded itself into Sunny's neck sending a geyser of blood spurting everywhere.

The violence, the blood, all of it had Early trying to back up into the wall.

Raynelle, slowly rose to his feet. Blood was everywhere, his blood and Sunny's blood.

Raynelle turned back and smiled at the dead stare Sunny's eyes held. "Bitch!" He spat before turning back to the boy. The young man slowly backed up while Raynelle stalked forward.

Suddenly, Raynelle moved to his left and opened the dresser's top left drawer. That's where he had put the gun yesterday before nailing Sunny to the cross that he'd screwed to the bedroom ceiling while she was tied up.

He smiled as his arm came out with the black nine-millimeter handgun. Raynelle continued stalking forward. Zion backed up against the two-story stairwell railing.

"It ain't no fun when Ray got the gun," Raynelle said standing five feet away at the bedroom entryway. He raised the gun, pointed and....

Click! Click! Click!

Nothing happened.

Raynelle turned the gun upside down. The clip wasn't even in it. Out of sheer rage, he ran at the boy with the gun raised above his head like a club.

Zion leaped into the air and dove right over Raynelle, who simultaneously flew head first over the second floor stair railing.

Chapter 26

November 6, 2008
A YEAR LATER: **Manhattan**

People from all walks of life, all creeds, colors and religions, folks all around the world were somewhere tuned in to see if history was going to be made. When Bakari Hussein Osama first announced his candidacy, most world leaders and it's citizens gave the African-American Junior Senator about as much chance as a snowball in Hell. But as the year leading up to the election progressed, something happened – something that only God and the seven men in the secret meeting room twenty feet below the Waldorf Astoria foresaw.

People in power, political leaders, media moguls, famous actors, and musicians overtly made public racist statements and published racist caricatures of the Junior Senator from Illinois. The statements and the caricatures didn't surprise the world, what left so many slack jawed and scratching their heads was the reaction of the American greater White community.

Black folk have endured the most horrendous conditions that a people have ever suffered; two-hundred and forty-six years as slaves, and another hundred and forty three of being treated like slaves, and never in America's history has there been such an outpouring of support – White American support against racism. They were incensed. White celebrities such as Bill Mahrer, Sean Penn, Keith Olbermann, and a host of others attacked the Republican Party with fervor, charging them with being ignorant and racist.

Earlier, CNN top news pundit and political analyst, Paula Burkes stood outside different polling spots around Manhattan interviewing African-Americans. When asked who he was voting for, a middle class Ford motor company retiree answered, "Osama, of course." He spoke and gestured as if her question had been the dumbest in the world for an African-American journalist to ask.

When asked what was the deciding factor in his decision, the older gentleman simply replied, "Because he's black, and before you ask me to elaborate, let me tell you this. Ever since the first person of color ran against a White American, White folks been voting white just cause they couldn't stomach the idea of a person other than white folk running any aspect of the American government, so why not vote black, you see how far voting white has gotten us."

She pulled the microphone back to her chin. "But sir, you don't think that voting for the most qualified candidate that represents your party's interests is more important than the color of a candidate's skin?"

"I certainly do." He nodded while speaking. "If Osama does not do one thing to advance the plight of people of color in America, just him being elected to the highest office in the land does more for the future of African-Americans than any of the prior presidents."

Paula pulled the microphone away from the well-dressed older man. "How do you mean?"

"Little black kids all over America overwhelmingly aspire to be rappers, singers, actors, and professional athletes because that's what they see. These images look like them so they can relate. Based on greater society's understanding of respect and success, our youth see these roles as achieving the highest level of respect and success."

Paula nodded; acknowledging the signal her cameraman gave her. She had thirty seconds to wrap it up.

The distinguished gentleman continued. "Now for the first time in history, children of color will be able to realistically visualize themselves as president. Although most won't ever become president, many will end up in political positions that effect change and growth, and the future of our children to me embodies what the democratic party represents."

"In ten seconds, tell our viewers what you mean by respect and success," she said.

"The true measure of success is how the community respects…"

Without provocation the picture on the theatre screen in the Trilateral Commission underground meeting room jumped back to the newsroom.

CNN anchor Campbell Brown's face appeared. "We've just received word that seventy nine percent of the polling stations have reported in. The McClain camp is due to make an announcement conceding the election and congratulating what looks to be the next President elect, Bakari Hussein Osama."

The chairman of the Federal Reserve muted the theatre screen and slowly rose to his feet. "Gentlemen." He tapped a spoon against his wine glass to get the attention of the seven impeccably dressed white men. Collectively, these men earned more in a year than two hundred and fifty of the three hundred and twelve million American citizens combined.

Chairman Greenspan was glowing. "They say the biggest trick the devil ever pulled was convincing the world that he didn't exist."

He briefly studied the expressions of every man in the room before lifting his glass. "I am honored to say that we have outdone the myth. Greater than convincing the world that Islamic terrorists orchestrated Nine-Eleven, we have convinced the American people to elect a black man with an Islamic name to the highest office in the land." He smiled, "Just as we have done throughout the campaign, we will continue secretly promoting Osama as a beacon of hope, while we continue our campaign against Islam." Constance looked up at the ceiling the same way his uncle used to when he was in the middle of a thought. "Twenty-years ago, my uncle stood before you all and told you that the key to creating a universal world order is oil, and to gain control of the world's largest oil reserves he said that we have to start an international smear campaign unlike the world has ever known. Bernie said, no need to re-invent the wheel, make it a religious war. As you all know, people have died and killed for their religious beliefs since the beginning of organized religion. Bernie said use the news *we* create to steer the sheep into hating the oil rich regions people and their religion. Now, twenty-years later we control Kuwait, Iraq, and most of Afghanistan, and once we decimate Libya and Syria, we'll go after Nigeria and once we have them, we will drive the petroleum market up to ridiculous prices. Anarchy will erupt throughout the world as people will become desperate, and everywhere, where a middle class exists will quickly be eliminated."

He pointed a finger in the air. "That's when we come in and use FEMA to declare martial law over America and the world. China will be forced to capitulate or we cut off their oil and watch as they return to the dark ages."

The chairman searched the men's eyes for any sign of indecision, when he found none, he continued. "A toast," he raised his glass, "to the men in this room who tricked the world into thinking that the American people elected the first black President of their own free will."

Chapter 27

November 7, 2008
THE NEXT DAY: **Covington, Georgia**

The three of them sat on the couch watching the election coverage.

"We did it!" Early shouted. "Miracle," he grabbed her hand, "look." Early pointed to the small television they were all watching.

"What did you two do?" Zion asked.

Early stood up, put his thumbs in his front jeans pockets, puffed out his chest and said, "We got the first black man elected President."

"*We*?" Zion looked at Early with question marks in his eyes. "When did *we* become eligible to vote at sixteen and seventeen?" Zion asked.

"We did more than just vote." Early looked over at Miracle. "We were the first team of volunteers at First Afrikan to go out and register one hundred new voters.

"Really?" Zion replied.

"You don't believe me, read my thoughts." Early challenged him.

Zion looked around at the naked walls that surrounded them before returning his gaze to Early. "I could've sworn *we* have been behind these walls together for a year now."

"You got jokes," Early said. "The church started a get out and vote campaign last March, a month after the president announced his candidacy. I told you to read my thoughts if you didn't believe me."

"I won't intrude on yours or anyone else's privacy unless it's absolutely necessary."

Early's expression turned to one of confusion. "Zee Money, I don't get it."

"You don't get what?"

"I mean, you can jump in folk's heads, read and drive they thoughts, why waste time asking them questions? I mean if I was you, I'd read everyone's minds and when I saw crazy thoughts, I'd just erase them from they minds and keep it moving. Seems to me that, *absolutely necessary* would be when anyone is planning to do wrong."

"First," Zion held a finger in the air, "if you could read minds, Early, it would be *absolutely necessary* for you to have every beautiful sista that crossed your path."

Early smiled before replying. "And every woman that had the pleasure of crossing my path would leave crying because their time with me would be over."

"And how do you know this?" Zion asked.

"Because, I'd put the *need me* thoughts in they heads," Early said.

Zion shook his head. "You need help."

Early turned his head sideways. "I'm just joking."

"No, you're not."

"You just said you wouldn't read my mind?"

Zion laughed. "I don't have to read your mind to know when you're full of it. I've lived with you for over a year now."

"That's another thing. Seems to me like that it is *absolutely necessary* for you to bring Miracle out of her condition so we can go out and kick some *absolutely necessary* Evil butt."

Both young men looked at Miracle who sat between them on the couch. She faced the thirty-two-inch flat screen, slightly rocking back and forth to a rhythm that she could only hear. A dead man had more life in his eyes then Miracle had in hers. Behind her dull expression and those dead man's eyes, Miracles conscious mind had taken residence inside of her subconscious.

Zion took one of Miracle's hands in his. "I love her too much to bring her back into this world without her wanting to come back. Have faith Early. She'll come back to us when she's ready."

"I love her, too, Zion, but we been in here a year. A year that the world done got even more messed up. Only real good I see is that we got a brotha in the White House. Zee Money, we gotta get outta here and do something. These cops are killing our brothas at will, and the brothas the cops ain't killing are killing each other."

Zion nodded his head before getting up from the couch. "I'm going to carry her to bed." He turned to Early, "You should get some rest."

"Why? It ain't like I'm going anywhere anytime soon."

"So, you're not taking me to the Pointe later this evening?"

Early's eyes lit up with the prospect of moving beyond the four gray walls and the few wooded acres that surrounded the property they'd been on for over a year.

"The Pointe. Whachu know about the hood, Zee Money?" Early asked.

"Not much. But I don't need to. I know about my people and who they really are."

"Knowing who yo' people is, ain't gon' save you from a desperate man's pistol."

"You don't think so?"

"Zee Money, you may be the Second Coming, but if a fool draw down on us, I'll be the first running."

"Early, you ain't got no sense," Zion laughed.

"Oh, you'd be surprised how much good sense I have once I see any sign of someone pulling out a gun." Early's expression changed. "Real talk though, Zee, I was born and raised in the Pointe. It ain't like nowhere else. It's a war zone. You've been watching the news. They don't call it Iraq for nothing. Why you wanna go to the hood anyway? We need to roll up on five-oh, the feds; real talk, Zee Money, we need to bust some heads, let 'em know you here."

"I'll keep that in mind," Zion said before walking off with Miracle in his arms.

Chapter 28

November 7, 2008
SAME DAY: **Covington, Georgia**

Zion sat in a metal fold-up chair next to the bed Miracle was resting in. If an angel or a goddess had a definitive look, Zion figured Miracle fit it. Her orangish bronze skin even glowed in the darkness. In the year that they'd been in the safe house, Zion noticed that Mira's hair had grown seven and a third inches. Every day since they'd been at the safe house, Zion had twisted her hair daily, making sure that when she did decide to come back that she would be as physically perfect as she was when she retreated into her subconscious.

Her eyes were closed but Zion sensed that she wasn't dreaming. When she finally did begin to drift into a dream state, Zion closed his eyes and entered her subconscious.

*****

He heard music, Erykah Badu was singing, "Next Lifetime." Zion did a three-sixty trying to locate where the music was coming from.

"See, it ain't nothing wrong with dreaming. Boy don't get me wrong."

Miracle had been busy since the last time he'd visited. As far as the eye could see there were upscale women's clothing stores, The Limited, Donna Karan, Ralph Lauren, Jill St. John, there were so many.

As he walked, he noticed that the ground felt a little soft. He looked down for the first time. The streets were dark brown. He knelt down and swiped a finger across the road before putting it in his mouth. "Chocolate."

Over the past year, Zion had learned from Early that Miracle had a serious love affair with Hershey's chocolate, and sure enough, as far as the eye could see, the roads were paved with Hershey's chocolate. He knew he was getting close to Miracle, because the music got louder as he walked down the chocolate road.

"Cause every time I see you. Every single time. It just let's me know just how strong that my love is for my baby."

Zion came to a four-way stop. Even the stop signs were made of chocolate. Willy Wonka would've been thoroughly impressed, Zion thought as he turned left and continued following the music.

"Well, I know I'm a lot of woman."

"Yes, you are," Zion spoke his thoughts aloud after hearing the lyrics. The chocolate street that he'd just turned on was full of beauty salons and nail shops. He was busy gazing at the three dark red suns that lit up the land and the sky, when he bumped into an Asian woman. "Excuse me, ma'am."

"Pedicure, manicure?" The lady spoke in choppy English. "Come," she took his arm. "I give you pedicure. Make feet feel good."

"No thanks, another time possibly," Zion said as he continued walking toward the source of the music.

"But not enough to divide the pie."

At the next street he found what he was looking for. There were at least five hundred red lights that looked exactly like cherry Charm Pops, another of Miracle's favorites. The Charm Pops were shaped into three words, THE APOLLO THEATRE. There were no doors, only a dark red carpet leading inside.

"Ticket, sir," a familiar looking man materialized at the door.

"I don't have –"

"What, you don't have a ticket?" the usher asked.

Zion shook his head.

"I guess your confession was an honest one, and since I can see that you got it bad, I'm going to show you some love in this club," the usher moved to the side. "Now, you take it nice and slow," he said before spinning around and doing a back flip.

"O-kay," Zion said, before turning and walking toward the huge double wide red curtain that the usher pointed to... "Usher," Zion said aloud as he just realized that the usher was Usher Raymond the Grammy award-winning recording artist. When he didn't see him Zion turned back toward the curtains.

As soon as he parted the curtains, Zion looked to the stage. His breath caught in his throat and before he could breathe a bunch of headless somethings with little brown stubby arms and legs wearing a Black t-shirt with the word WIND stenciled in white ran past him. And although the theatre and the stage were pitch dark, there was not enough darkness in empty space to hide the infinite beauty that graced the stage.

Suddenly, three lights shaped like small suns came together as one, illuminating the angel that graced the shiny red wood stage floor. "Wow?" was all he could think to say.

All of a sudden, Zion had to turn to the side in order to move out of the way. A cavalry of two-foot high, hardcover dictionaries with little chubby brown baby legs and chubby brown baby arms ran past him and out of the theatre.

197

Was Mira reading his thoughts, Zion wondered?

Before the dictionaries got up and ran out, he had just been thinking that there were no words or sounds that have ever been uttered by man or animal that could even begin to describe Miracle's beauty.

She sounded even better than Erykah Badu. So much emotion, so much passion, so much soul.

Miracle's red and brown dreads were streaked with gold – the same color of her glowing complexion. Zion was in the dark and at least fifty feet away from the stage and he could clearly see the heart-shaped indentions in her chipmunk cheeks – indentions that most people referred to as dimples. The sparkling miniature red and glitter gold pillowy lips creased, bent and opened as she formed the words that came out as song. The red silk dress wrapped around her body had just the right amount of sex appeal. And those three inch heels. The way she moved. Class.

Who would've thought that Miracle had legs that a young Tina Turner would envy?

Miracle had Zion so deep in a trance he didn't even notice that she had stopped singing. A thousand sets of eyes turned to the top of the theatre were Zion was standing. The spotlight shown on him before he realized that she had caught him in her world.

The music stopped.

"How long have you been standing there?" Miracle asked.

"Forever, and that still wasn't long enough."

A thousand eyes turned to whoever was speaking.

"You were amazing," Zion said.

"I was, wasn't I?"

"Bakari Osama won the election," Zion said.

"Good for him."

"Early and I are going to visit the Pointe later today."

"That's nice."

"I don't know how nice that will be. The police are still looking for you and Early, of course."

"Zion, I appreciate what you have done and what you are trying to do, but this is my world now. Here." She looked around. "No one can hurt me or anyone I love in here."

"Maybe not, but you are God's Miracle. There are people all over the earth that need a Miracle."

"They need to believe, pray and create," she said.

"How can people believe in what they have no understanding of?"

"They understand something," Miracle said. "Have you seen how crowded church is on Sunday morning?"

"They go to church because evil has tricked the masses into believing that if they don't go, they'll burn. Since sin began, man has tried to mold God into an image that best helps them subjugate other groups, and like sheep, the masses have followed the path of corrupt leaders and a corrupt system instead of following the path of the just Creator."

"After all of the corruption, destruction, and decimation of life, all the chances that God has given mankind, why does She keep sending messengers to save a people that don't wanna be saved?" Miracle asked.

He smiled before saying, "Love."

"Love?" Miracle questioned.

"If you had children, Miracle – children that you nurtured and watched grow into adulthood, you would do anything for them."

Zion began walking to the stage. The thousand eyes followed his movements.

"The Creator loves Her children wholly and unconditionally."

Miracle's face was clouded with doubt. "Shoot, if I was God, I woulda' made the oceans swallow up mankind as soon as the first slave ship lifted its anchor to cross the Atlantic."

"Thank God you are not Her," Zion said as he proceeded forward.

"You think Man is going to respond any different to you than they have done with Moses, Jesus or any of God's prophets?" Miracle asked. "Once your physical presence fades, what makes you think that man won't forget you like he's forgotten God and His messengers?"

Zion walked up the stairs to the stage.

"Man's view has been manipulated and clouded by Evil." He smiled. "Miracle, I'm here to remind them and to remove the Evil that has blinded mankind since the serpent tempted Eve."

The thousand brown eyes blinked several times.

"Miracle, so many great men and women have perpetuated acts of Evil simply because of a twisted psychosis brought on by greed and envy. This psychosis has mankind loving man made objects while committing crimes against their own brothers and sisters."

"Psychosis or no psychosis, man is jacked up." Tears escaped her eyes. "Man got my mother strung out on crack. Man crucified my mother from her own bedroom ceiling. Man sends other men thousands of miles across the ocean to kill men, women, children, old and young for what, Zion?" She crossed her arms and uncrossed them. "Oil! You hear me Zion. I said dirty, black, stank, oil. Hmmph." She crossed her arms again. "It may be a psychosis, Zion, but man has no respect for other human or any other life. It would be better to destroy them all, so no child will ever have to witness the evil that men do."

The eyes turned to Zion.

He reached for Miracle's hand.

She just stared at the appendage.

When she didn't put her hand in his, Zion said, "You can't even begin to imagine how much man has hurt God, with all the Evil that they have perpetuated against their brothers and sisters, just like you can't imagine how Man has pleased God with selfless acts of resisting Evil. Malcolm, Martin, Marcus, L'Ouverture, Delaney, Chin, there are so many stories of selfless acts of resistance and self-determination against the powers of Evil. Miracle," he used two fingers to lift her chin so she would be looking into his dark brown eyes, "with your unconditional love, we can fight and rid the world of Evil so no child will ever have to witness Evil in any of it's various forms. Stand with me, Miracle, so the righteous can live in peace in the land that the Creator promised them."

"I can't, Zion. I'm not the me you think you see," she said.

"Oh, but you are, Miracle." He used a finger to wipe the tear from her cheek.

"How do you mean?" she asked.

"The only reality is what has always been. There is nothing that the *Seeing Eye* can see that is, was, and always will be. Everything seen is a manipulation of fast moving matter held together by this thing called gravity. You see, Miracle, you can't see your soul, you can't see love, you can't see God, but without a doubt in your mind you know that they all exist and if you close your eyes and concentrate on any of the above you will see them more clearly than you could ever see anything with the physical eye. Just like . . . " He closed his eyes and grabbed her hand. "Just like, I can see so much more in you than you can see in yourself.

"I hear you, Zion, truly I do, but I can't be who you say I am." She cried out. "I can't love. I've lost the capacity to love. I don't wanna love. Loving is what causes the pain of loss." She shook her head. "I just can't."

Chapter 29

November 7, 2008
SAME DAY: Atlanta, Georgia

The late Wednesday afternoon sky was a cloudy grayish blue. The rusted hinges on the old barn doors squeaked as Zion and Early pried them open.

"Zee, you gon' learn to listen to me," Early said as he removed the plastic trash bags from around his legs and shoes."

"You're right," Zion said as he wiped mud and grass off of his beige Timberland boots. "I'm just glad the rain stopped."

Early stood up. Admiration sparkled in his eyes as his gaze fell on to Miracle's stoplight red '96 SS Impala. "There she is, Red Cherry," Early said. "Baby, did you miss daddy?" Early rubbed his hand over the dusty hood.

"Don't talk to me, leaving me locked up in here for a year."

"Shit!" Early jumped back.

Zion laughed.

"Man." Early put a hand over his heart. " You can't be doing that, Zee, you 'bout scared me half to death."

"I couldn't resist. You should have seen your face, when I projected my voice over to the car." Zion continued laughing while Early disarmed the alarm and unlocked the doors with the remote.

"What are you doing?" Zion asked while wiping tears from his eyes

"Uhhhh, getting in the car so we can ride out."

Zion shook his head. "You know we can't take that."

"Why not?"

"Because the police are looking for the car and you, or did you forget?"

"So what, you a god. The Second Coming, the last descendant of Shango, Black Tarzan, ruler of the concrete jungle. What the police gon' do to me as long as I'm riding out with you, big homie," Early replied. "God said if I had the faith of a mustard seed I'd be good or something like that." Early put an arm around Zion's broad shoulders. "Zee money, after seeing your work firsthand, I got the faith of a virgin saint in church on communion Sunday."

"You are a natural fool, Early. Boy, you need help." Zion laughed.

"You keep saying' that," Early said. "If you really wanna help a brotha, you'd give me this Tuesday's winning mega millions lottery numbers."

"That's it?" Zion asked.

"Yeah." Early nodded. "That's all.

"Okay, consider it done."

"You ain't lyin' to me, right?"

"Early, I don't lie." Zion crossed his arms. "First thing Wednesday morning, I'll write the winning numbers down for you."

The excitement in the seventeen-year-old young man's eyes was gone. "Dang, Zee, you done got my mind all ready to ball out on some millions, and you snatch the dream right out of my mind. You know that ain't even right."

"I know that after we crush Evil it'll be like everyone left standing will win the lottery of everlasting peace, which morphs any amount of money you could win," Zion said, walking over to the battered old pick-up on the other side of the Impala.

"I know you don't expect me to ride in that," Early said, looking over at the 1970 something rusted out, beat-up old pick-up.

"We'll be a driving billboard if we take that red, chromed out, limo tinted thing. And the wrong attention is what I'm trying not to attract, at least not yet." Zion said, pointing to the Impala. "And those truck sized chrome wheels are screaming, 'look at me'."

"Soooo, what are you saying Zee?"

Zion turned around and pitched a set of keys in the air. "Think fast."

Early caught the keys. "What are these for?"

Zion opened the rusty passengers door of the old truck. "Kick dust, Early. Let's ride out."

"Oh, hell no." Early shook his head. "Hell to the double N-O. Ain't no way I'm gon' be seen riding in that rust bucket. Come on, Zee, I ain't been seen in over a year. You can't be serious?"

Zion smiled before getting into the passenger's seat.

*****

Fifteen minutes after tinkering with the carburetor, the truck lurched forward. Early looked over at Zion. "I can't believe you got me driving this junkyard reject."

"Early, it's just a means to get us from one point to another. It isn't that serious."

"Says the man that can read minds."

Twenty minutes later, Early pulled into an apartment complex.

"This isn't the Pointe."

Early smiled. "I know. I just have one little stop to make first."

"Early?"

"Trust me." He put the truck in park and jumped out. "I'll be right, right back."

A few minutes passed before Early climbed back into the passengers seat. He pulled a black handgun from under his red and black Miami Heat hoodie. "Here." He handed the gun to Zion.

"Did you get one for yourself," Zion asked.

Early pulled out a chrome .38 police special. "Now you know I got your back, Zee money."

"Can I hold yours?"

Early proudly handed his gun over.

Zion closed his eyes as he held the guns in both hands.

"You alright, Zee?" Early asked while watching Zion zone out.

Early's eyes were drawn to the guns in Zion's open palms. The guns began to melt and transform themselves into a black, toy fire truck.

"How did you . . .?" Early asked before looking up at Zion. "Why?"

"You see what I just did, right?" Zion asked.

Early nodded.

"If I can do what you just witnessed, why would we need guns?"

"Good point big homie." Early nodded. "It's your world, squirrel, I'm just trying to get a nut."

"You'll have all the nuts you want once we destroy Evil."

Early looked over at Zion. "We?"

"That's what I just said."

"So, you putting me down with the movement?"

"Early, you've been down with the movement, since before you were a thought in your mother's mind."

"Yeah, yeah that's right." Early nodded. "I'm all the way down."

"You are so down, that you fear nothing but the Creator. The fear in your heart has been replaced with a lion's courage," Zion said.

"That's right. That's right." He banged a fist to his chest. "Fear don't live in my heart."

"You, all the way down," Zion said.

"A hundred feet below ground. A thousand leagues below the sea. Fear gon' grow legs and run when it see me."

"My man."

"That's right, Zee money. I am the man. I may not have a plan, but I am the man, God's biggest fan. Fearless." He gave Zion some dap, before turning the beat-up old truck off the main drag.

"You think that brotha you told me about is still working out of the Pointe?"

"Which brotha is that?" Early asked.

"The one you said has most of the dope game on lock in Dekalb County.

"Black Corleone?" Early asked.

"Yeah, that's him."

"Oh, he's still there. Old boy got the Pointe, the police, and damn near the whole county in his pocket. With power like that, ain't no need to go anywhere else."

"Good. So, when we roll up on him, I'm going to need you to grab your courage, puff out that little chest, walk up to this kingpin and, 'Pow', slap the fire out of him."

"Huh?" Early wore a deadpan look on his face.

"Don't worry, you'll be all right." Zion said. "You got the faith of a virgin Saint on communion Sunday, remember?"

"Oh, I ain't worrying. I know I'll be alright cause I ain't gon' put my hands on that man."

"But what about your faith, the mustard seed?"

"All the faith under the sun, ain't gon' make me do no fool mess like slapping Black Corleone," Early said with a serious look on his face. "Shoot, I'd be dead before I drew my arm back."

"I'm just messing' with you, Early."

"Nah, you was messin' with yourself, big homie. I'm the wrong one to put them jumper cables on. Only one that can start my engine is me, Zee." Early pulled into a parking space, put the truck in park and unlocked the door. "It's just about dark. You sure you don't wanna come back tomorrow in the daylight with the National Guard and some tanks?"

"This isn't the Pointe?" Zion said.

"It's only a ten, fifteen minute walk from here."

"Walk?"

Early hammered his shoulder against the door twice trying to open it. He looked back at Zion. "Yeah, walk. Zee, I done drove this far. I was dead serious; I am not driving this thing down in the hood. Hell, it'll attract just as much attention as Red Cherry."

Zion reached over early and barely touched the door. It opened right up.

Chapter 30

November 7, 2008
SAME DAY: **Decatur, Georgia**

Early was trying to be as inconspicuous as possible walking through the Pointe with his head down, hands in his pockets, and his red and black Miami Heat hoodie covering his badly-in-need-of-a-haircut head, while Zion carried himself with the swagger of a man that had lived in the Pointe his entire life. He greeted dope fiends, prostitutes, and even a couple lowly nickel and dime weed and crack dealers while walking to the back of the apartment complex.

"See shorty over there?" Early pointed.

"The guy sitting on the stoop?" Zion asked.

"Yeah, nah," Early shook his head. "He's a she. I mean Kill Bill is a female."

"Kill Bill?"

"Yeah," Early said. "You ain't never seen the movie?"

"I saw one and two," Zion said. "But, why would someone, especially a woman call themselves Kill Bill?"

"All I know is after the first Kill Bill movie, people that knew her started calling her that probably because her fight game is treacherous like ole girl in the movie."

"She's a martial artist?" Zion questioned.

"Zee money, she's a martial Van Gogh Picasso, and she's Corleone's number two," Early said. "Remember the two jits I pointed out that were hangin' around the entrance, the ones with the walkie talkies in they hands."

"Yeah, the two little brothers dressed like ninja DEA agents."

"They warn her of any potential danger."

"I thought you said, Corleone had the police paid off?"

"He does, but Internal Affairs, the feds, a suicidal robbing crew, anybody could present a threat to Corleone."

"If sis has a fight game like you say, why isn't she in the ring fighting professionally?"

"The fight game for women don't pay off like the dope game does. Besides, in the ring they got rules. In the streets there is only one rule, 'fight or be food'."

Zion made a beeline toward the plain-looking young lady wearing black high tech boots, a too big black Dickie button down, too big black Dickie pants and a black Atlanta Falcons hat sat on top of her head.

A kid no more than thirteen ran up to Early and Zion while they were cutting through the recently renovated rear apartment playground.

"Yo, big dog," the kid shouted as he jogged up to early and Zion.

They turned to the kid.

"Yo, I got that Bakari Osama Bin Laden dro, that'll knock you to the flo', twenty dollars a gram, how much y'all need?"

"We good, shorty," Early said.

The kid kept step with them.

"I'm sayin' though, whachu need. You name it, I got that girl, soft or hard, that boy, some ecs, you name it."

Early looked over at the kid. "I told you we good, li'l homie."

They were just about to cross the street when Early heard a bullet being chambered.

Zion turned to the kid. The kid had a gun arrowed right at Zion's chest.

"Since you done wasted my time, I'm gonna waste some blood if you two don't unass them ends."

Zion turned to the boy and locked in to the kid's eyes. "Turn around and walk to the apartment dumpster, throw the gun inside and then go home. When you get inside the apartment go to the bathroom, bathe and then go to bed. Do not leave the apartment until time for you to go to school in the morning." Zion pointed in the direction of the dumpster, "Now go!"

Without a word, the child turned, put the gun down the small of his back and started walking away.

"That's right, take you little nappy head bad behind home," Early said. "Fore I take my belt off."

While crossing the street, Zion said, "Early, please let me do the talking. No matter how bad it may seem, do not say a word. Okay?"

A moment later, the two were in earshot of Kill Bill.

"Excuse me, queen, can you get Mr. Corleone out here."

She inhaled the blunt she held between two fingers and exhaled, clouding the air in front of her with smoke and the aroma of some strong marijuana. She remained seated as she looked Zion up and down and then down and up before looking over at Early.

"Yum-Yum, who dis nigga is calling me queen?" the woman said. "You betta let that nigga know 'fore I let my hands go."

"Come on KB, chill, this my dude, Zion."

She looked at Early. "If I wasn't buzzin' I'd fist check you in the grill for allowing this fool to call me out my name. Queen." She stood up and walked up to Zion. "Nigga, do I look like a queen?"

Zion took a step forward. He was close enough to kiss the man-looking woman. "Not only do you look like a queen, sis, you are one. You are a descendant of Queen Ana de Souza Nzinga of Angola. She ruled over the Ndongo. She spent her life fighting for the rights and the freedoms of her people during the seventeenth century. Please believe Nzinga got her man most times."

"Okay." Kill Bill took a step back, and looked at Early. "If you don't get this nut job out my face."

"Pearlie Pea, I really need to see Mr. Corleone," Zion said.

"No one has called me that in twenty years," she said, a nostalgic expression branded on her face.

"Twenty-one. Henry was the last person to call you that."

She nodded. "He died when I was seven."

"Who's Henry?' Early asked.

"He was my dad," she said in a much softer tone.

"He will always be your dad, queen. He's followed your life. He was so proud when you won the school spelling Bee in the fourth grade. He cried for days when Elvin, and his two older brothers attacked you in the sixth grade."

"I was eleven."

"I know." Zion reached out and put a hand on her shoulder. "Henry worked his butt off to give you a better life than he had. This," he waved his arm in an arc, "this ain't you, queen. You know your daddy didn't want this life for you. Henry will once more be proud again when you start acting like the little girl he was raising on a day laborer's salary. He gave you a kidney so you wouldn't have to go on dialysis."

"Who are you?" she asked.

"My name is Zion."

"No, I mean who are you?"

"I'm a child of the Creator, just trying to do God's will."

Her attention turned to Early. "He's serious?"

"As a government sniper with his target in range."

"Man, look I don't know who you are, but you have to be a real somebody to know who I am." She put the blunt on the stoop next to her cell phone. "I'm gon' get you an audience with Corleone, but just remember, it's at your own risk. Corleone ain't as nice as me."

Chapter 32

November 7, 2014
SAME DAY: **Decatur, Georgia**

Zion was in deep conversation with Kill Bill when a black Hummer pulled up in front of building C.

"That's him pulling up now." She pointed.

"Thank you, Pearl," Zion said.

Early could hardly believe the exchange. Kill Bill would normally crush someone like an ant if they put their hands on any part of her body, yet Zion was calling her by her government name and had an arm around her shoulder.

A coal-skinned ox got out of the passenger seat, wearing what had to be the world's largest pair of sagging black Red Monkey jeans. A ghostly billow of smoke came out of the rear as the ox opened the rear passenger door. The chrome plated letter C shined on top of the patent leather purple shoe that touched the ground behind the Hummer's rear passenger door. The top of a suede looking purple hat appeared next. Once the Hispanic-looking driver walked around to the rear passenger door, he closed it. The three men seemed to be exact polar opposites. The driver was maybe five-four, his complexion was the color of Country Crock margarine, and he had the build of a skeleton. He wore his long black hair in a ponytail and dressed like a cowboy.

The passenger was NBA basketball player tall, pro football lineman wide, blue-black as midnight, and the sagging jeans and curtain sized red, white and blue polo he wore made him look like the world's biggest clown, while Corleone was a cross between Purple Rain-Prince and Mr. Big-Ron Isley with his tailored purple three piece suit and purple pearl handled cane. Corleone had dark beady eyes that didn't seem to go with his albino pale complexion.

Corleone and his men ignored Zion, Early, and Pearl as they took their time walking past them into the building. The Hispanic driver peeked out the building door, "Yo, Bill, give the Don fifteen minutes and send them in."

After the apartment door closed, Early looked over at Pearl. "KB, where they just come from, a wine convention?"

"Nah, why you say that?"

"Cause your boy, Corleone look like a big ass grape."

"So, she does know how to smile," Zion remarked.

"I can't help it. " She turned to Early. "You need to be on somebody's stage boy."

"So does your boy, coming out the house looking like a tired Mr. Big. His bodyguard's Mini-me and Super-size need they ass kicked."

"For what?" Zion asked.

"For letting that fool come out in public wearing Barney's Sunday suit."

"You ain't playin' with a full deck, I swear you ain't," Pearl said.

Their attention was suddenly diverted to the apartment door that was opening.

"The Don said you two can come in now," the ox said as a cloud of smoke billowed out of the apartment.

The purple double-breasted Hugo Boss suit jacket, the Hermes silk shirt and tie were replaced by a cotton, purple, Fruit of the Loom wife beater t-shirt. Corleone still had on the Hugo Boss purple suede pants though. The kingpin sat in a high back throne like chair puffing on a blunt while playing Madden on his PlayStation.

"I think I'm in love," Early said after his eyes found the three naked women that were sitting at the kitchen table cutting and bagging up white and brown powder.

Zion put a hand on the back of Early's arm before whispering, "Don't move. I got this."

Zion walked forward, leaving Early standing in the foyer ogling the three women sitting at the glass kitchen table.

"Nigga, ain't nobody said you could move," the ox growled at Zion.

"Jackson Washington," Zion said, using the name that Corleone's mother gave him, "may I have a word with you in private?"

"Playa, I know you heard me, nigga."

Zion turned toward the ox. "The word nigga is defined as one who is ignorant and or acts like an idiot." Zion smiled. "I assure you that I am neither."

"Huh?" Ox said before turning to his boss. "Who 'dis nigga think he talkin' that slick shit to?" The ox pulled a gun from his back pocket, chambered a bullet and held it sideways. The gun was pointed at Zion's head. "Let some more uppity slick shit come out your mouth, chump, see how fast I make your kid's orphans.

Zion walked toward the guns barrel. "James Baldwin once said that you can only be destroyed by believing that you are what the white world calls a nigger."

Zion wrapped his hand around the barrel as he placed it in the middle of his forehead. "Words like nigga, dog, fox, bitch, and cat have been used to address human beings, particularly black folks since they arrived on the first slave ship from the African Continent." Zion stared past the gun's barrel into the dark eyes of the man holding the gun to his head. "There have been studies done that prove that if you call a person animal names, treat them like animals for long enough they will act like the animals that they are called and they will refer to one another as the said animals. Now, look at me, Malice." Louder, Zion said, "Look at me, I said."

Ox seemed mesmerized by Zion's passion and the words that flowed from his mouth. He looked into the eyes of the man he held the gun to.

"You are looking at a man, a black man, a child of the Most High. In the beginning, the Most High did not create man in the image of a nigga. She created man in Her image. In none of God's sacred scriptures is the word nigga even used. Nigga's are man made. I am not a nigga, I am not an animal. You are not a nigga. You are not an animal. And none of us are man made. Malice Jaquavious Rogers, like me, you are a child of the Queen of existence."

Zion slowly pushed the gun away from his face. "Deep down inside, you know that my words are true. In her first trimester, Dr. Porter advised Sahara to have an abortion. He'd explained that due to her being severely anemic that it would be a fifty-fifty chance that either of you would survive."

The big man's eyes watered.

"She died so you could be here, Malice. That woman loved you more than she loved herself before you were even born. If your mother knew what type of life you would be leading, do you think she would have given her life for you to be here destroying other's lives with the poison you selling?"

"That's enough," Corleone said as he stood up from the high back chair. "I've allowed you to talk yourself into an unmarked grave." He screwed a silencer on a small gun while walking over to Early and Zion. "I don't kill kids, but I'm going to make an exception for the two of you."

"Come on, Corleone, Zion just tryin' to put you up on real game. Can't you see he more than just a kid?"

The kingpin turned to Early. "One more word and I swear 'fore God and the twelve apostles, I'm gon' unload this clip into your funny looking face."

Early put his hands up in surrender.

He turned his attention back to Zion. "Nigga, I got more money than God. In these projects, I am God." He finger-punched Zion in the chest. "You come up on my set, sounding like one of them pulpit pimps that bleed the community without giving anything back. I give the people hope and escape." He pointed to the kitchen where the girls were processing and bagging drugs. "Niggas like you don't do shit but talk about some nigga ain't nobody ever seen." The kingpin nodded. "I'm gon' give it to you though, the game y'all running is certified gangsta, pulpit pimps driving around in cars colder than mine, wearing bling more extravagant than mine and some are getting more trim than I get from way more different women. The law calls what I do illegal," he chuckled, "ain't that some hypocritical bullshit. That playground out there," he pointed to a window with burglar bars on it, "I spent twenty stacks for the renovation. I got fifty niggas in my employ, li'l niggas that would never rise above working the front counter of McDonalds. Now they earning enough cake to live like the McDonald's. But, that shit ain't good enough for you right?" He paused to look Zion up and down. "I mean you wanna help them pulpit pimps knock my hustle so them greedy mothas can milk the community for even more cake than they already eating."

The girls in the kitchen, Corleone's driver, two gun-toting young brothers that were in the back of the apartment, Early, everyone watched and listened to the kingpin as he held court.

"I agree." Zion nodded. "There are pulpit pimps all over this country and the world. Pulpit pimps have made slaves of human beings since sin was introduced. But, just as there are and have been blood-sucking vampires using the Creators words to reinterpret Her messages of love into messages of division and hate, there have been and there are more people that have fought and are fighting unconditionally for the lives and the souls of their brothers and sisters of the world. Shango, Nkondi, Horus, Imhotep, Hannibal, Moses, Yeshua, Muhammed, Buddah, Nat Turner, Martin Delaney, Marcus Garvey, Malcolm X, Martin King, Joel Naison, Louis Muhammed, George Rawlings, Hakim Fast, and I could go on for days, months, years, talking about the greatness of the Greats – Greats that everyone in this apartment has blood ties to."

Zion turned to one of the naked girls in the kitchen. "Shatonya, you of all people know about unconditional love."

Everyone but Corleone turned their attention to the beautiful twenty-one-year-old mother of four that Zion had just called out.

"Three years ago, two men followed you home from a strip club. They grabbed you and forced you..."

The young mother placed her hands over her ears and squeezed her eyes together and screamed, "No!" she ran into the bathroom and slammed the door shut.

The older woman next to her said. "There's no way you could know, unless you are," she shook her head, "no, he died before the ambulance got there."

"What are you talking about?" Corleone asked.

"The man that saved Shatonya from two rapists back when she was dancing at Magic City."

"Somebody tried to rape Shatonya?" the ox-sized man questioned.

Malice was Corleone's number three and the big man was secretly in love with Shatonya and Zion had gotten to both of them.

The albino drug kingpin didn't know how Zion had gotten so much info on his people, but he did know that the young man was using his worker's pasts to influence them. It seemed to be working, that's why he had to do what he was about to do.

"They didn't just try. They raped and beat my baby in the apartment washhouse. They would have killed her, if that homeless stranger wouldn't have came to her rescue. The man fought both rapists and somehow managed to get the knife away from one of them. When all was said and done, all three men were dead from multiple stab wounds," the woman said before going inside the bathroom to see about her daughter.

While the others were processing what had just gone on between Zion, Shatonya and her mother, Corleone had raised the silenced pistol to Zion's head.

Pow!

The sound of a muffled gunshot exploded inside the apartment.

Chapter 33

November 7, 2008
SAME DAY: **Decatur, Georgia**

"What the hell?" Corleone's driver said while pointing a tech-nine in the direction of where the gunshot was fired.

Malice stared at the life he'd just extinguished. "I couldn't let Corleone do him," he said watching his boss's blood stain the gray carpet. "I don't know who this young cat is, but I ain't never felt such a strong urge to believe in someone other than myself. And then," he made eye contact with Zion," You broke down some real shit, young buck. Put life in a whole new perspective for me." He nodded his bald head. "You right, young buck, my mother died so I could live. And now I'm disrespectin' the gift of life my moms gave me and I'm disrespecting her memory for a dollar." He shook his head. "I don't know how I'm gon' eat from this point on, but I can tell that it won't be this way." He shook his head. "I ain't 'bout that life no more, Jesús."

"Soooo, what now?" Jesús asked while pointing the semi-automatic at Malice.

"That's on you, playa," the big man said. "We can put the guns down and see what's what or we can get into some ok corral gangsta shit."

"That won't be necessary," Zion said while looking into the eyes of Jesús. "Malice is not the enemy, Jesús."

"Tell me, Zion, who is the enemy?" Jesús asked while pointing to Corleone. "The man with the hole in his chest bleeding on the carpet?"

Zion took a step toward Jesús. "No, he wasn't the enemy, but he was doing the enemy's bidding. You see, Jesús, the enemy is a mentality that upholds a system that is designed to uplift some while keeping others cultures in mental and physical bondage."

Another step.

"The enemy is the mentality that supports a system that has made a Holy day out of the mass slaughter of your Native American and Hispanic ancestors. In two weeks Jesús, family's all around this country will gather together in the name of Thanksgiving without any understanding of the inhumane horrors that this day truly commemorates."

Another step.

"The enemy is a mentality that supports a system that stole your ancestors' homeland and pushed them south, and now they have to have green cards, to come back to the land they owned, farmed and worked to make green. Nevada, Arizona, Texas, California, and I could go on. This systems constitution was drafted by thirty-seven barbarians that beat, raped, killed, and enslaved other men and women because of greed – a constitution that Americans are still governed by."

Zion took another step as he paused to let his words seep in.

"I know you were young, but you remember what happened to Marianna? José had to take her back to Belize, because every hospital your father took her to in Texas wouldn't treat her because she was an immigrant. The American doctors actually caught the little girl's Leukemia in time to save her, but too much time went by and she got sicker and by the time your dad got her to Belize, their hospitals were ill-equipped to give her the care she needed."

Jesús put a hand over his face. "We were twins. I was twelve when she..."

Zion took another step before putting his arms around Jesús and pulling him into an embrace. Although Jesús hid and buried his tears in Zion's chest, the howls of pure pain and anguish could be heard and felt by everyone in the apartment. Both men held each other tight.

"We will see to it that every single person that had a hand in Marrianna's suffering will pay if they already haven't. That's my word," Zion said as he began to cry with Jesús.

Malice began crying as he pictured his mother standing in judgment of him. Every single person he had wronged, harmed, and killed in his twenty-five years on this earth flashed before his eyes.

Everyone in the house began crying after having visions from their past – visions of past wrongs and how their wrongs affected the victims and the people close to their victims.

*****

The sound of gunshots were normal down in the Pointe, so the earlier gunfire hadn't spurred Pearl into action, but the cacophony of heart wrenching wails and sobs were abnormal and they were the reason Pearl had her ear to the dull gray steel apartment door. Finally, Malice's guttural soul stirring howls frightened her into action.

She bruised her knuckles. "Open up this damn door, now!" She banged. The only reply she received was a chorus of offbeat wailers. Not thinking, she rammed herself into the door. "Shit!" she shouted, grabbing her shoulder. She'd forgotten that the door was solid metal.

She looked down at the doorknob. She hadn't even thought to try it before now. And why should she have. It was always locked and bolted. Millions of dollars worth of drugs were processed inside this small apartment weekly. The door, the cameras, the armed men standing watch inside the apartment, and even Pearl standing watch outside were just some of the security measures that were put into place to protect Corleone's drug empire.

Pearl wrapped her hand around the knob. Surprisingly, it turned. Moments later, she was inside the apartment doubled over on her knees sobbing as people she'd victimized flashed though her mind. Everyone inside the apartment was feeling what his or her victims felt while being victimized. They felt the minutes, hours, days, months, and years of pain that their victims loved ones felt.

The pain that everyone was feeling was more excruciating than anything they had ever imagined. It was the longest sixty-six minutes of all of their lives.

Zion stood in the middle of the living room observing the nine people in the apartment as they got to their feet and regained their senses. "You have had the chance to see and experience some of what others will see and experience when they are called before the Almighty on their day of judgment. There is so much that we don't take into consideration as we go through this lived experience. Western society has brainwashed mankind into believing that we are human beings that have spiritual experiences on our days of worship; Jumah on Friday, Shabbat on Saturday, Church on Sundays. We are so much more than Western ideology suggests. Malice, Jesús, Otanya, Shatonya, Keisha, Early, Pearl, Skeet, Leon, all of mankind are Spiritual beings having a human experience and if we understand that spirit is divinely connected to every living thing and that all of mankind is responsible for the spiritual uplift of everyone else, mankind will get in line and treat others like they want to be treated."

"So, who are you really?" Pearl asked.

"I'm a child of the Creator that understands that I am because you are and you are because I am and because of who we are together is why I will lay my life on the line for the mental emancipation of everyone in this apartment just like I will do for every one in creation."

Malice frowned. "Huh?"

"Together, we are going to," he stomped his foot on the ground, "crush evil until there is not an evil strand of DNA left in creation, and that's my word," Zion said.

"I don't have no idea what you talkin' about young buck, but you got me crunk."

"Zee money, gon' bring the noise. We 'bout to send them racist crackers in power on a one way trip to the Southside of hell." Early looked at Zion, "Ain't that right, Zee money?"

"Not exactly," Zion said.

"You said we gon' destroy Evil," Early said. "I don't know of anyone more evil than white folk."

Zion put a hand on Early's shoulder. "All white people aren't evil."

"I know that, but when they go in and bomb innocents in order to rough off another country of they gold, diamonds, and oil, they call the dead victims casualties of war. So, real talk, I don't see why we just can't smoke all the white folks and call them Caucasians of war."

"Two wrongs don't make a right, Early," Shatonya's mother said.

"I know, but two Wrights did make an airplane," Early joked trying to lighten the tension in the apartment.

"Otanya is right," Zion said. "Men that do evil aren't necessarily evil. They may be brainwashed, such as Washington Jackson," he said referring to Corleone by his birth name. "Believe it or not, Washington was a man with a good heart doing bad things. Look at the playground, and he genuinely believed that he was doing more good than bad selling drugs. You have white men that truly believe that black people are lesser beings. You may think it's just skin color, but society's written and unwritten laws culminated with almost two thousand years of biblical whitewashing has caused a viral psychosis that has poisoned the minds of Eastern and Western society."

"So, you sayin' we need to be in the church or we don't need to be in the church?" Malice asked.

"No, I'm saying that we need to arm ourselves with knowledge so we can understand how to love again. You can't love God, if you don't love yourselves and you can't love yourself if you don't know who you are, and we don't know who we are because we commit acts and think thoughts that are against our very nature."

Malice crossed his arms. "Break it down so I can see what you getting at," Malice said.

"Okay." Zion nodded. "People that truly love themselves love God and would not destroy the lives of their brother and sister for a piece of paper used to exchange objects and services. The only way we can come together as a community is if we come together in truth. Truth is an unbreakable bond that ties all of creation together."

"So, after you put us up on game, we can fight the power?" Malice asked.

"Fight?" Zion said. "Malice we will be the power."

"What do we do first?" Pearl asked.

"Clean up our own house," Zion said.

Chapter 34

March 15, 2009
FOUR MONTHS LATER: **Decatur, Georgia**

"Shawty, want a thug, bottle in the club."
Snake was bouncing so hard to Li'l Wayne that he almost ran his tricked out chrome Q56 Infiniti truck into the median on I-20. While righting the vehicle, his cell phone chirped. He turned down the music and answered right as he looked at the caller ID. Damn.

"What?"

"Whachu mean, what? What kind of way is that to answer the phone, Snake?"

"Don't be callin' my phone asking me why I do any damn thing, Robyn. Now, what do you want?"

"I need twenty dollars to buy your daughter some diapers."

"I ain't got it."

"What? Negro, you movin' more bricks on the Westside than Herman Russell Construction."

"What I tell yo' dumb ass about talkin' on the phone?"

"It ain't like I said cocaine," Robyn replied. "I said bricks."

The tall lean drug dealer shook his head while looking out the window. It was still morning. There was no traffic heading to the rest stop fifty miles from the South Carolina border. If he didn't have a pass from the feds to sell dope he would've rocked Robyn and that ugly ass baby to sleep a long time ago.

"Why don't you just call the DEA and tell them what's on your mind. Stupid ass tramp," he muttered.

"So, all of a sudden after you done used me up, put a baby in me, I'm a tramp?"

"Nah, shawty, you ain't just a tramp," Snake said, "you a stupid ass tramp."

"What that make you, seven kids by five baby mommas, that yo' sorry ass don't take care of?"

"Keep poppin' off at the mouth."

"I ain't scared of you, Snake. You done beat my ass so much, I don't even care no more. All I care about is my baby that you don't do a damn thing for. At least you consistent."

"Now, what that mean?"

"It means what I said. You consistent in that you don't do nothing for none of your kids, but you ain't got no problem trickin' off thousands in strip clubs on a weekly. Calling somebody a tramp. You the tramp. Can't even buy your baby some damn diapers."

"My baby? Tramp I told yo' ass to abort the damn thing. I ain't givin' you shit."

"You gon' make me take your mother's advice and put you   on   the   state."

"What I tell you about talkin' to that trick?"

"That's yo momma."

"So? What that mean?" He paused. "Tell you what, you go on take her advice and see how fast you, the baby and my momma come up missin'. I told you when you got pregnant I didn't want no more damn kids. You knew what it was when I was tappin' that. You saw I wasn't doin' a damn thing for them other crumb snatchers I got, but yo' dumb ass still had that ugly ass little girl." He pressed the button on his earpiece, ending the call before Robyn could respond. He pulled off the highway into the rest area. He was so tired of his babies' mommas sweating him for paper. If it wasn't for his DEA contacts having connects with Child and Family Services, he'd be paying out the ying yang for kids he never wanted in the first place. When he was first approached by the DEA twenty years ago, his first thought was to murder the Uncle Tom sellout agents and have his father get him out of the country. But, the more he thought about that idea, the more he knew he would be miserable living in some rain forest in Venezuela or Columbia with his father's Medellín Cartel friends.

*****

Sandford "Snake" Carro was a modern day Nino Brown and the Westside of Atlanta had been the Black Cubans New Jack City for coming up on twenty years. Twenty years ago, in 1989, Carro's father Emilio Carro was the target of two separate investigations, one by the DEA and one by the FBI. Although the two agencies were supposed to work hand in hand they rarely did and when they tripped over each other's investigations sometimes informants were killed and millions of dollars in man-hours were lost.

The FBI was more concerned about the elder Carro's cartel ties, while the DEA concentrated their efforts on Emilio's Florida and Georgia drug operations. The DEA had several opportunities to cripple Emilio's two hundred million dollar enterprise, but they were forced to stand down by bureaucrats in Washington. As a result of FBI interference, a secret DEA task force was put together to get the FBI off of their case against the Carro family.

On March 19, 1989, DEA informant Derrick Wright was given false information and doctored tapes that looked as if Tyler Strong, one of twenty-one-year-old Sandford Carros dealers was feeding the DEA information. The DEA knew that they had just signed some innocent kid's death certificate but that was a small price to pay to get Emilio Carro's son on a murder rap. The younger Carro never suspected Wright.

Twenty-four hours didn't go by after Wright had introduced the evidence to Carro. Sandford Carro somehow got Tyler Strong to the North Georgia Mountains near Gatlinburg, Tennessee. The two men were about a half-mile into the woods when Carro stabbed one of his most trusted soldiers in the neck. Before Strong fell to the ground, a team of DEA agents had the twenty-one- year-old killer surrounded.

In exchange for Carro's freedom, he not only agreed to become a confidential informant, but he also agreed to kill his own father. After he shot his father in the back of the head, his mother was never the same. It was almost like she knew that her only son had had something to do with her husband's sudden and violent demise.

Over twenty years, Sandford "Snake" Carro had provided his handler at the DEA with valuable information that led to over a billion dollars in confiscated money, drugs, and assets from the hundreds, maybe thousand of arrests made as a result of the information that Snake had provided. In exchange for Snake's invaluable cooperation, he was allowed to purchase cocaine that had been confiscated by the DEA for thirty cents on the dollar when available and, of course he was allowed to continue his drug operations on the Southwest side of Atlanta. In the past, his arrangement with the DEA had been gravy, but times were changing and a war seemed inevitable, a war that he knew would produce only one winner and it wasn't going to be Corleone or Snake.

Snake was a lot of things, but a fool was one thing he wasn't. He'd followed Black Corleone's rise in Decatur and Lithonia. TI had even had a number one hit entitled "Black Corleone and Dom Perignon," that he'd dedicated to the kingpin. Snake had been on top twice as long as Corleone and he'd given the DEA enough info to put Corleone under the penitentiary for several life sentences, but ten years in the game at kingpin status and Corleone had never done any real time. That could only mean one or two things. The Feds had either turned him, or they were putting the wheels in motion for a war between the two most powerful kingpins in the city. A war made the most sense, because Snake knew all too well that a kingpin's reign was only for so long. Every so often the feds would set the stage for war between two hood bosses, sort of like they did between Biggie and Tupac. The government would amass hundreds of millions as a result of drug, money, property seizures and media publicity and propaganda.

New prisons would be built for the hundreds, possibly thousands that would serve time as a result of the war. While the smoke cleared from a drug war, the feds would just sit back and watch as the trickle down effect occurred. Friends would tell on friends, family, and loved ones, to prevent from serving long sentences.

Fortunately for the DEA, back in 1986, Reagan made it so two people could accuse a third party of dealing drugs without any physical evidence and this was enough to obtain a conviction that called for the defendant to serve a minimum of ten years federal time.

Snake had definitely done his share over the years by giving up info on his competitors and people he just didn't like. At least half of the hundreds of people he helped get off the streets were guilty, the other half were people that Snake just didn't like. The DEA owed him and he was coming to collect, that's why he had arranged this meeting with his handler.

Mason Terrell was in his mid forties and had been with the DEA for almost twenty years. He was a proud man that had come from a long line of men that had fought in every war since the Spanish-American War of 1898. He stood up. "Sandford." The two men shook before Snake took a seat on the picnic bench across the table from Terrell.

"This weather is crazy. It was seventy-five degrees two days ago, and now it's barely above freezing," Sandford said as he zipped up his leather coat before crossing his arms.

"Since you realize how cold it is, tell me what was so urgent that we had to meet today, of all days."

"I wanna know what's going on in Decatur and Lithonia?"

"I don't understand the question." Agent Terrell wore a befuddled look on his face.

"So, we gon' play that game?

"What game is that, Mr. Carro?"

Snake pulled out a blunt and tapped the head on the gray-blue wooden picnic table. Snake focused on the weed filled cigar in his hand. "The game where I tell you what I know and you nod and take notes."

"Uh, yes, that's the way this works. I don't answer to you, you answer to me. You inform, I listen, take notes, and process information."

Snake took out a lighter and lit the blunt.

While Snake was inhaling, Agent Terrell knocked the blunt from his mouth before leaning forward. "Look, I don't like you, Carro. I would like nothing better than to wake up and find that you have suffered some horrific violent death. I deal with you because it's my job. But, you will not disrespect me by smoking drugs in my presence." Terrell rose from the table.

Snake didn't move. "Terrell, how you gon' turn your nose up at me? I'm what I am because of Tom's like you. White man tell you to watch the niggas, let them make X amount of scratch and when they hit that X number, you swoop in and arrest them, take they shit unless they agree to turn more niggas in." He reached down to pick up the blunt that was in the damp grass. "Difference between you and me is what I do to niggas is a survival tactic, but you," Snake shook his head in disgust, "You takin' nigga's lives for a government paycheck."

Agent Terrell looked at his watch. "You have exactly sixty seconds to tell me why you asked for this meeting."

"All right, since ain't no Coke in Decatur and Lithonia, I wanna make sure I ain't steppin' on no toes by moving in on that territory."

"I'm not the one you should be having this conversation with."

"So, you saying, you don't have a problem with me taking over the Dec and Lithonia?"

"I don't, but I'm sure Mr. Washington will."

"Corleone ain't been seen in months." Snake looked up at the agent.

A questioning look shrouded the graying middle-aged DEA agent's face.

"You really didn't know?" Snake said.

Agent Terrell sat back down before he asked, "Who's runnin' Pleasant Pointe, Bosa Nova, and the Fairington apartments in Lithonia?"

"No one. I just told you that ain't no hard dope from Candler to Sigman Road."

"That's impossible," the agent said. "What else have you heard?"

Snake shook his head. "That's all I got, but once I get down inside Iraq, I'll let you in on what I learn."

If the feds didn't know about the young cat that done used the God game to clean up the hood, than I damn sure ain't gon' put 'em up on game. They'd find out soon enough when they find the kids body.

Snake was so excited he was almost skipping back to his ride. He was about to double, maybe even triple his weekly take.

We'll see how strong the hood faith is when I unload a fresh clip into they savior's ass.

Chapter 35

March 17, 2009
TWO DAYS LATER: **Langley, Virginia**

The Chairman of the Federal Reserve, the Director of Central Intelligence and the Chief of the National Security Agency were on a video conference call together.

"Why are we just finding out about the kid?" Chairman Greenspan asked. "Dammit, we been looking for this kid for seven years and he pops up in some God forsaken project apartment community in Dekalb County, Georgia. We have technology that allows us to intercept a kilogram of cocaine from a thousand miles in outer space, yet it's taken seven years to find an orphaned black kid."

Chief Lesure spoke up, "The bad news is that Zion is now a person of interest as far as the Department of Justice is concerned and we have very little sway with the DEA."

Chairman Greenspan intervened, "That just means that we have to send someone in to infiltrate the young man's circle. In the meantime, we put surveillance on the DEA agents that will soon have XR13's kid under their surveillance."

"That's it? That's all?" The CIA director spoke for the first time. "What are we trying to establish from keeping the boy under surveillance?"

"A pattern," the chairman said. "By watching his movements and his actions, we can better understand how best to destroy him."

"Seems like a lot of trouble just to kill a kid," the NSA chief said.

"From what I gathered from DEA agent Mason Terrell, his C.I. Sandford Carro will most likely do our job for us one way or the other," the CIA director said.

"How is that?" the NSA chief asked.

The chairman chimed in. "If Sandford Carro puts the boy down, our job is done and if Zion puts him down, we have the kid on murder among other charges that we will fabricate."

Chapter 36

March 21, 2009
FOUR DAYS LATER: **Decatur, Georgia**

Back in December, Zion and the Counsel of Clerics decided that it was best to move Miracle somewhere, where she would receive twenty-four hour care. Zion and Early were spending too much time away from the safehouse in Covington. They knew that Miracle needed better care. Surprisingly, Miracle's muscles had not atrophied in the eighteen months she'd been catatonic. As a matter of fact, she somehow looked more fit now than she did eighteen months ago.

Four months ago, on a cool late December night, Miracle was driven three hours away to Spartanburg, South Carolina where the late Dr. Boyce's sister resided. Orthine Evans was a retired midwife that knew more about the Creator than most theologians.

Zion instantly bonded with Momma Orthine as everyone referred to her. She's the one that told Zion that he needed to live among the wolves if he wanted to save the sheep. And since that conversation back in December, Zion had lived in Iraq (as most referred to the Pointe). Momma Orthine was the only one outside of the Clerics and Early who truly knew and believed in who Zion was. Zion often found solace in communicating with Momma Orthine, since he could no longer reach Miracle.

It was late night early morning, the first official day of Spring when Zion's eyes began to flutter. The second hand on the grandfather clock in his mind stopped moving. Soon he was drifting from the conscious world into the subconscious realm of reality. He floated through the nothingness of time and space searching for a way into Miracle's subconscious as he'd done every night to no avail since they'd moved her to Momma Orthine's in Spartanburg. And as always when he failed to enter Miracle's subconscious, Momma Orthine's hand beckoned him to come into her subconscious realm, which he often did.

The leaves swirled as they rose up from the wind that had stirred as Zion landed in front of the house next to a large sycamore tree. The first thing he heard were birds humming and chirping, the Stevie Wonder classic, *"A ribbon in the Sky"*. He looked up to where the melodic chirping was coming from. Canaries. Strange but beautiful yellow and amber fruit. That's what the five singing canaries looked like up in the tree above. A huge black O was mounted on the outside gray stone chimney wall. It obviously stood for Orthine. The address read 1444 N. Peacock road. And sure enough, there was a family of five colorful peacocks walking down the road in front of the house. The sun was going down when Zion walked through the door.

The yellow sundress, the five gold bangle arm bracelets on each arm and the simple gold chain with the peacock emblem around her neck made her look like royalty. Momma Orthine was a large woman, not unhealthy large, larger than life large. Her personality and wisdom made her a giant among men. Her smile always seemed to brighten everything around her, even the sun.

"What's wrong, sun?" she asked while sitting at the dining room table shucking corn into a large yellow bowl.

"I'm worried about Miracle. What if she doesn't come back?"

"What makes you think she ever left?"

"You care for her every day. She's a shell of the person she was."

Yellow kernels fell into the large plastic bowl. "Isn't the human body a shell for the mind and the spirit?"

"Yes." He nodded. "I guess so."

"Haven't you communicated with her since she's been like this?"

"Yes." He nodded again.

"Did she seem to be getting better or worse the last time you were able to commune with her?"

He thought back. The chocolate streets, the clothing stores and boutiques, that persistent Asian lady. "Better, I guess."

"So then, what are you worried about?"

"I was told that I needed her love in order to save mankind."

"Do you honestly believe that mankind deserves saving?"

"I do."

"So you believe in man?"

"No, I believe in the goodness of God that dwells in man."

"That applies to woman, I take it?" she asked without looking up from the bowl.

"Yes, of course."

"So, if you truly believed in the goodness of God that is inside Miracle than you wouldn't be worried."

"Last time I saw her she said that we couldn't," He dropped his head, "I mean that she could never love again."

"Boy, how are you going to save mankind if you can't even save one person from themselves?"

"I don't know." He shook his head. "Truly, I don't."

She put the cornhusk on the table, and wiped her hands on the red dishtowel before getting up and walking over to where Zion was seated. She put a hand on his shoulder. "I need you to think, sun. Use the gifts that the Creator has given you."

"I am thinking," he said.

"Obviously not hard enough. Now, what are the three L's that make up God Consciousness?"

"Love, light, and life."

"So, was that the God in Miracle speaking when she denounced love or was that her lower human self speaking?"

Zion bounced out of his seat and hugged her. "Momma Orthine, you are the bomb dot com."

"I am, aren't I?"

"And so humble," he said, his voice laced with sarcasm. He pulled back from their embrace. "So, how do I? I mean what do I do to reach her?"

She crossed her arms and shook her head. "Boy, do you want me to save mankind for you, too."

"Would you mind?"

"Yes, I mind. And no I will not save the world. Not sure if the world deserves saving."

"Okay, then how do I reach Miracle?"

"Quit trying to reach her. Let her come to you. Have faith in the God that is in her. There is only one thing that can bring her back to your world."

Chapter 37

March 24, 2009
THREE DAYS LATER: **Decatur, Georgia**

It wasn't noon yet and the sun was already beaming. The temperature reading on Pearl's watch read 72 degrees. It was the second week of the apartment wide flea market and bake sale. Last weekend, the weather was in the mid fifties and the days were overcast, but the turn out was way better than expected largely in part due to the influence of the Reverend Dr. Lomax and Reverend Daniel Kelly at First Afrikan. Dr. Lomax had prompted several local churches to bring busloads of parishioners to the Flea market. Most came because of all the talk about this seventeen-year-old young man that had inspired so much change in the Pointe and around hoods all over Dekalb County. The biggest hit of the first week was Ms. Jenkins's five-dollar soul food plates. Last week, the resident vendors trickled in and did well, but the one's who were there from Friday to Sunday sold out of everything. So, today tables and booths were set up in the grassy field to the right at the top of the apartments.

This was the first Friday of Spring and it couldn't have been more perfect. The sun was shining, and the soap opera house wives and the mini van driving soccer moms were beginning to trickle into the Pointe's huge open-air flea market and food court. There were at least a hundred vendors setting up the tents that Corleone's drug money had paid for back in January.

"Uhm, Uhm, Uhm?" Ms. Jenkins closed her eyes. "Girl, you done put your foot in them greens."

"Ahhh, come on, Ms. Jenkins," Pearl blushed, "They ain't all that."

"Chile, I'm tellin' you, these greens are the truth Ruth. I can't believe this the first time you cooked Collards."

Dora Mae Jenkins had been selling five-dollar dinners on Fridays and Saturdays in the Pointe for over twenty years. Almost everyone in and around the Pointe had enjoyed one of Ms. Jenkins five-dollar plates at one time or the other. Business hadn't been so well as of late because Zion and Malice had led the charge in cleaning up the Pointe and other surrounding drug infested apartments. Ironically, the dealers had been her best customers.

"What I can't believe is how folks are helpin' each other. It's like one big ole family. If God almighty called me home right now, I'd go smiling. Eighty-two years, chile. That's how long I been on this earth. I done seen a pregnant woman swingin' from a tree. Baby cut right out of her. Blood and guts everywhere. Law didn't do a dang thing. Klan even bragged about cuttin' the half breed baby out of the girl."

"That is so messed up," Pearl said as she set the stainless steel, rectangular food warmers on top of the fold-up tables.

"Four hundred years, black women been fighting tooth and nail to earn respect for all women and they done been forced to clean the toilets of their rapist while never knowing when they was going to be attacked again. These women didn't poison the white man, they didn't stick a knife in his neck, you know what they did, Pearl?"

"No ma'am." Pearl shook her head.

"They survived by coming back and enduring. Why? Because they had a family to raise. Why, because they had hopes and dreams that their daughters and sons would have more opportunities, a better life than they did."

"Ain't no way, I could allow anyone to violate me," Pearl said.

"Allow?" Ms. Jenkins looked at the short haired young lady like she didn't know what she was talking about. "Chile please, you either gave in to the slavemasters desires and if you resisted you would likely find yourself dangling from the end of a rope, and even then there was a good chance that white men would still take you after you was gone from this world."

"That's exactly what they would've had to do."

"If all women thought the way you do, than none of us would be here to see this day. What's happening here makes all the hell I done seen and lived worth it." The old woman waved an arm around the open field near the apartment's entrance. "I have never seen so many black folk working together voluntarily."

"That's because they making money," Pearl said.

"That may be true now, but a week ago when we had the first apartment garage sale and cookout, no one knew how successful this would be," Ms. Jenkins said.

Pearl looked up toward the entrance. Somebody was blasting NWA's old school classic *"Gangsta Gangsta."*

"Baby," Ms. Jenkins shook her head in disappointment, "now why would a young black man sing about killing other young black men?"

"I don't know," Pearl said, a little embarrassed. "It's just a song I guess."

"But baby, these is words. Words are more dangerous than any bullet or bomb." Ms. Jenkins said. "And baby, if they only knew how a black woman was treated during slavery, reconstruction, and Jim Crow, ain't no way they'd call us animals in their music. Heck ain't no way they'd refer to themselves as animals."

"Yes ma'am," Pearl replied while pulling out her cell phone.

"So much self hate. That boy done worked a miracle around here, but he gone have hell changin' the way these young folk think, and even more hell changing the way these church folk think."

"Excuse me, Ms. Jenkins I have to make a call," Pearl said while dialing Malice's number.

"Yo," Malice answered.

"Mal, Snake is headed your way. He's rolling three cars deep."

"Don't sound like he's coming to partake in the festivities," Mal said.

"Nah, it don't. Gimme a minute, I'll be down there."

"I'm good. I can handle Snake," he said before disconnecting the call.

Malice, Early, and three others were standing in front of the playground as Snake and his boys drove down the hill to the back of the apartments.

"Big Mal. What it do, cuz?" Snake greeted Mal as the Snoop Dogg look alike got out of the burnt orange '71 Charger.

"It do what I make it do," Malice said with his arms crossed.

"That's real talk, cuz," Snake said as he tried to give Malice some dap.

Instead of shaking Snake's hand, Malice opened his jacket just enough for Snake and the others to see Pete and Repeat, the names he called his two glock .40 caliber handguns.

"I know this ain't no social call, riding three cars ten men deep, so what's the business, Snake?"

"I'm here to discuss some personal business with Corleone."

"Good luck finding him," Malice said. "He disappeared months ago."

"Really now?" Snake said. "So, I guess you the new HNIC, Big Mal."

Snake's men were now behind or at Snakes side.

"You of all people know that time is money, so just state your business and move on," Malice said while stepping forward."

"As a show of thanks for all the money been coming my way cause of the sudden short supply of dope in the Pointe and around Dekalb County," Snake reached inside his multi colored Pele' Pele' leather jacket pocket.

Click-click. Like magic, five guns materialized. Malice had Pete and Repeat pointed cowboy style at Snake, while Malice's other three boys had a gun pointed in the same direction. Unfortunately, Snakes entourage of thugs had three times as many guns pointed at Malice and his army of three.

Snake slowly pulled a stuffed white bank envelope out of his inside pocket. "I come in peace, big dog." He pitched the envelope toward Malice.

The envelope dropped to the concrete near Malice's feet.

"Ain't nothin' but three stacks, but I wanted to show my new partner some good faith love."

Malice signaled for his guys to stand down. As they put their guns away, so did Snake's folks.

"I don't need any more partners," Malice said.

"Oh, but you do. I'm gon' start you off with, hmm, " he smoothed his goatee out with his fingers while he contemplated, "twenty-five kilos of the finest Peruvian flake straight from the mountains of Peru."

"These apartments are drug free and soon the whole County is gon' be."

Snake laughed before pointing to Malice. "That was a good one, and you said that shit with a straight face like, like you really meant that bullshit."

Malice and his guys just stood there waiting for Snake to finish.

"Okay now for real, it's Friday, I gotta get back to my side of town so I can check on my slaves. Now this is –"

"Snake, I need you to listen to me very closely because I'm going to say this only once." Malice stepped forward. "Ain't nobody movin' no dope in the Pointe, not as long as I'm breathing."

"You can huff and puff, big dog, but I'm the big bad wolf around here and everywhere, so if you have a death wish, you got the right one..."

Malice drew down on Snake before anyone could react. He had Pete and Repeat pointed in Snake's direction. "Kick rocks, Snake."

"Ain't yo' momma ever told you not to pull a gun if you ain't gon' use it?" Snake said.

"Oh, I'm gon' use it. Just not now."

"You got three men, five guns, I got ten guys with two guns each. No, I'm wrong. Pork Chop and Moo-Moo- have three so that's twenty two guns, well over a hundred bullets, sounds like you a little short handed, big dog."

"Sandford Carro!" Zion shouted while taking long strides across the playground.

Snake and his boys turned to the kid wearing a black Polo pull over, Levis and some Black Tims.

"Who 'dis nigga?" Snake asked.

"I don't see any niggas out here Sandford, all I see is men," Zion said.

"Ohhh, you must be the Black Jesus the hood screaming about," Snake replied.

Zion picked up the envelope full of cash. "Because you have been so generous in donating to the community, I'm going to ask Mal to allow you and your men to leave in peace instead of in pieces." Zion turned to his friend. "Malice, I'm asking you to allow these men to leave unharmed."

"What?" Snake shouted.

"Before you command your folks to draw down you might wanna look up at the second floor patios around you," Zion said.

Snake and his men looked up and around and saw a small armory of rifles pointed in their direction.

"Now, I saved your life once," Zion said. "Change your ways fast, Sandford, or you will suffer in death far more than you have made others suffer in life. Now kick rocks before we take those pretty cars and sell them out of our flea market this weekend."

Snake nodded. "This ain't over Big Mal, and you, Zion, I'm gon' see you real soon and we gon' see how bad you are without all this."

"I promise you, Sandford," Zion patted his chest, "you don't want one second of this."

"Yeah, whatever," Snake said as he turned and commanded his boys to do the same.

For the rest of the day, Snake was on one. Later that day, he pistol-whipped a crackhead half to death for looking him in the eye. He shot a pit bull for barking and he promised to kill any of his men that came up even a dollar short when they brought him his money.

"I swear on everything I love, that nigga, Zion is mine. Don't no one, and I mean don't no one handle me like that. If anyone kills him before I do, I'm going to kill them and their families for taking the pleasure from me," Snake said over and over to anyone in listening range.

It was a full moon, and Snake was mentally exhausted from thinking of different ways to kill Zion when his phone rang. He smiled upon seeing the caller ID. Just what he needed.

"Babydoll, what's the business?"

"Your baby is the business. Before you take your money and give it to some ho' in the club, I need you to bring me a little something so I can get Tiara some diapers."

"Damn, girl you just asked me for diapers a couple weeks ago."

"Uhh, yeah, she pisses and doo-doo's all day. She's a baby, Snake. Are you really that stupid?"

He closed his eyes and balled up his fists and took a few deep breaths.

"Hello. Hello. Snake, you there?"

He didn't trust himself to speak so he pressed End before pulling into the liquor store parking lot. A few minutes later, he came out with a pint of Grand Marnier and a Viagra pill he bought from Lee Wong, the liquor store owner's son.

"This was the last time, I mean the last damn time that wide mouth bitch was gon' call me stupid," he said to himself before washing the Viagra down with a swig of Cognac and Coke.

Twenty minutes later, he'd dusted off the pint of Grand Marnier, popped another Viagra and smoked a blunt before getting out of his truck. Robyn's apartment was a three-minute walk from the parking lot.

Snake's anger rose with each step he took.

"First that punk-ass-black-Jesus-wanna-be played me and then this tramp gon' call me stupid. Niggas just don't know. I ain't nothin' ta play with. I'll burn a bitch at the stake for lookin' at me sideways," he said as he half stumbled to his last baby momma's door."

Chapter 38

March 24, 2009
SAME DAY: **Atlanta, Georgia**

"Robyn!" Snake shouted while banging his fist on the door.

"Go home, Snake."

"Open up girl, I wanna see my child." He kicked the door.

Robyn's neighbor opened up his door. "Hey man, you may wanna come back another time. The lady upstairs is quick to call the law."

Snake put his foot in the older man's door, pulled out his gun, chambered a bullet and slammed it in the man's mouth. "I'm quick on the trigger. Now what?" Snake spat.

Robyn unlocked and opened the door.

The old man's chin and t-shirt were wet with blood; his eyes wide with fear. The gun lodged in his mouth prevented him from speaking.

Robyn grabbed Snake's arm. "Don't Snake. Please."

Snake's gun arm relaxed as he pulled the gun out of the man's mouth. "If five-oh, shows up I'll be back. And when I come, I'm not leaving anyone or anything breathing inside that apartment, understand?"

The man nodded with tears in his eyes.

"Go on and close the door, old man. You lucky this time," Snake said before turning to Robyn.

"Come on," she said, walking into her small low-income apartment.

"Where's the baby?" he asked, looking around the goodwill furnished apartment.

"My mother came and got her for the weekend."

"Good." He smiled before grabbing his crotch and licking his weed-stained lips.

"No, Snake, this ain't that type of party?"

He pulled his shirt over his head. "This is the type of party I say it is, tramp." He lunged forward, grabbing her arm.

"No, Snake, please." She made a feeble attempt to free her five foot four hundred twenty-pound body from Snakes clutches. "I ain't right down there."

"Tramp, don't try to play me," he said before backhanding her.

With a hand to her stinging face, she said, "I'm not. I swear. I had an abortion on Monday, I can show you my paperwork from the clinic."

He shook her by the arm. "You ain't nothing but a ho'. I can't believe I put a baby in your nasty snatch." He pushed her as he released the death grip on her arm. She lost her balance and fell to the gray linoleum floor.

She looked up at him. Pure hatred in her eyes. "If I'm a ho, you made me who I am."

"What," he said taking a step in her direction.

She scurried back against the living room wall. "You won't give me a dime to help with Tiara, I ain't got no job and even if I had one, I wouldn't be able to afford daycare and food. So yeah, I have to trick to buy your baby some damn Pampers."

Lightning fast, Snake bent down and slapped Robyn. "Tramp, don't blame me. I ain't forced you to turn the first trick."

This time she saw it coming so she balled herself into a fetal position, just like Mason had taught her to do.

"Ahhhh!" she gritted her teeth as her arm absorbed the pain of Snake's fist.

"I'm tired of you blaming me for that baby. I told you to abort the little monster." He kicked her in the stomach.

Robyn threw up her dinner.

"So, your ho' ass had an abortion Monday, but you wouldn't have one for me. You thought I was gon' be your meal ticket for the next eighteen years, huh?" He kicked her again, this time in the back of the head. "Who's stupid now, huh?" he shouted.

The pain was so intense. Every nerve ending hurt, she didn't know how much more she could take before passing out. She used her last bit of energy to pray. "No more, please God, please God, help me."

Snake picked up a metal folding chair, closed it and held it above his head. "God?" he said. "Tramp, I'm the only god that can help you. Pray to me."

She shook her head no.

"Okay then, ask God to stop me from breaking your back with this chair."

She put a hand in the air. "No, God please, save me."

Snake tried to bring the chair forward, but couldn't.

He turned just in time to see the muscles in Zion's arms contract as the young man snatched the chair from Snakes grasp.

Living in a world where the one who hesitated often ended up in a body bag, a single thought didn't enter Snake's conscious before he had his nine out and pointing straight at Zion. "What the? How'd you get in here?"

"Does that really matter?"

"Nah, but filling you full of holes does... Shit." Snake shouted before dropping the gun and grabbing his scorched and bubbling hand.

Smoke rose from the scorched area of the floor that the red-hot gun rested on.

Snake was writhing in agony.

Zion couldn't stand to see Snake suffer so he grabbed the badly burnt hand and closed his eyes. He was about to heal Snakes hand when Snake swung and hit Zion with his undamaged fist.

The blow to the ear caught Zion by such surprise that he lost his balance and was about to fall when he squeezed Snake's hand in hopes of keeping his feet.

"Ahhhhhhhhhhhhhhhh!" Snake screamed so hard that spittle mixed with blood flew from his mouth.

He let go of Snakes hand as he realized he'd accidentally squeezed too hard. "I am so sorry," Zion said, knowing just by looking at the mangled hand that he'd broken all twenty-seven bones in it. Tears welled up in Zion's eyes as he imagined the agony that Snake was suffering.

Zion reached out towards Snake midsection. He balled up his fist and concentrated. Zion was determined to make Snake suffer as little as possible.

Snake grabbed his chest. Where his heart was.

Zion slowly turned his fist.

"I, I can't breathe," Snake said as he fell to the ground not far from Robyn.

The tears were flowing freely from Zion's eyes as he continued turning his fist.

Snake started having convulsions, his body rose and fell like a fish out of water. And then Snakes arms dropped to his sides and his eyes closed.

"Is he. . . " Robyn crawled over to Snake's body. "I hope you rot in hell," she said before spitting in his face.

Sirens.

"I don't know who you are, but you better leave fast. Don't worry, I'll handle the cops," Robyn said.

Zion was at the back door about to leave when Robyn asked, "Why are you crying?"

Zion opened the back door before turning to Robyn. His eyes were glossy. "I just ended a human life."

"Dude, you just saved mine and your life," she said. An incredulous look shrouded her face.

He looked back at Snake's lifeless body. "I didn't save the brother's life." Zion shook his head in disgust before leaving.

"Call me, 770-912-9145," she shouted.

Chapter 39

March 28, 2009
FOUR DAYS LATER: **Duluth, Georgia**

She lifted her head from his lap, grabbed the remote off the coffee table and pressed pause so her husband wouldn't have to leave the room.

"Mason Terrell," he answered the call.

"Agent Terrell, I'm Mike Barnes from Surveillance and Communications."

"Okay."

"You are the agent handler for C.I. 41548-013," Barnes said as more of a question than a statement.

"I am."

"Can you verify your C.I.'s recruitment date?"

"April 1, 1989."

"Thank you, sir." Barnes said. "I think your C.I. has succumbed to foul play."

In an instant Agent Mason Terrell's heart dropped into his bowels. "I don't understand."

"We just got around to Friday's transcripts, from the bug you installed in the C.I.'s cell phone. I think you better come in and here the recordings yourself."

He shook his head before looking at his watch before letting the breath out that he'd been holding since the caller told him that his ticket out of the DEA and Atlanta were dead. "I'm on my way."

This was the second consecutive date night that they'd tried to watch "Love Jones," this time it was business, last week it was pure pleasure. His latest C.I. had done things to him that he had only seen on Internet porn sites.

"Lord, I know I haven't talked to you in a while, but please, I need your help. If Sandford Carro is dead than so are my chances at becoming a NSA senior analyst. That means no fifty thousand dollar bump in salary and no cushy desk job in DC. Lord, you know that there's no way the Chief will keep his promise if Carro is dead. So, please Jesus, let that boy be alive." He repeated a similar prayer during the rollercoaster ride he took to get to headquarters. "Lord, if you're punishing me for sleeping with my C.I., please don't. I'm sorry, Lord, the flesh is weak, but you know other than the girl, I have been a loyal servant to the law."

He made the forty-five minute drive in thirty, thanks to his supercharged company suburban and the blue light that came with it.

After listening to the recordings, and speaking with a contact in homicide at the Atlanta Police Department, Agent Terrell literally became sick. The bathroom was too far so he threw up in a Federal building lobby trash can. It was coming up on eleven PM. He debated whether to call Chief Lesure this late, but the man distinctly told him to call day or night if he had any pertinent news regarding Zion Jones.

Lord, you allow murderers to get away with killing children. Hell, you allow children to be killed. You kill so many good people. You allow the worst in society to live lavishly, but people like me, the one's who follow the law go to church every Sunday, tithe regularly, you crap on us. How can you profess to love your loyal servants when it's us that suffer while the criminals prosper? I'm done, God. I'm done with You, if there is even a you. All I asked was to keep one idiot alive long enough for me to… You know what, forget it.

He took out the phone the NSA Chief had sent him and dialed the number.

*****

Less than an hour after the Terrell debriefing, NSA Chief Maurice Lesure had CIA Director Bush and Federal Reserve Chairman Constance Greenspan on a secured teleconference call.

The chief had filled the others in on his earlier conversation with Agent Terrell.

"Something is missing here," Director Bush said. "Carro's screams are consistent with the time frame he burnt his hand. But what doesn't make sense is him picking up a gun hot enough to produce the severe first-degree burns, and what could have possibly crushed a human hand like that."

"Who knows," the chairman interrupted.

"Robyn Ross, I am willing to bet that she knows more than she's letting on," Director Bush said. "My father always said, that if something doesn't seem right, then it usually wasn't."

"Brad had a saying for almost any incident," the chairman said.

"How would you know, Connie, you weren't even born when my father passed."

A few seconds of silence followed before the chairman responded. "My uncle shared enough stories that I feel as if I knew the Senator." Chairman Greenspan said. "Why the accusatory tone?"

"Sorry, Mr. Chairman, it's late," Director Bush said.

"I know, this kid Zion is wrecking my nerves, too," the chairman said.

"So, after Carro made choking sounds and complained about not being able to breathe he just drops dead of a heart attack?" the general asked. "Something in the milk just don't smell right. We know where the kid is, I say we just send in a team, bag him and burn him," the NSA Chief said.

"And make him a martyr?" the chairman asked. "I don't think so."

"He's just one young black man, Mr. chairman." Chief Lesure said.

"So was Christ," Greenspan said. "Look, all we need to do is do what we've always done, use our resources to recreate Zion in the image we want the American people to believe."

"What about Terrell?" the chief asked.

"You trust him?" the chairman asked.

"The taps I've had on him the last couple of weeks haven't given me any reason not to."

"How far do you think Agent Terrell will go?" Gerald asked.

"As far as I push him," the general said. "Terrell will do almost anything for the senior analyst job I dangled in front of him."

"Good, I need him to get Robyn Ross to recant the statement she gave to APD. She needs to implicate Zion in Carro's death." the chairman said.

"You saw the pictures, Mr. Chairman, Sandford beat her within seconds of her life. Jones is her hero. And what about the M.E.'s report?" the chief asked.

"Let me deal with that," Chairman Greenspan said. "Maurice, you just make it clear to Terrell that if Robyn doesn't change her story within the next seventy-two hours, he's done in law enforcement. It shouldn't be much trouble for Terrell to convince Ms. Ross, she is one of his C.I.'s and once you let Terrell know that we know that he's having unauthorized relations with her, I think he'll be motivated even further to acquiesce."

Chapter 40

April 1, 2009
FOUR DAYS LATER: Atlanta, Georgia

"You do know that I can make sure that you are convicted of some serious drug charges?" Agent Terrell said while running his fingers through her Brazilian weave.

"Ouch! Be careful," she turned to Terrell. "I'm sore from Snake kicking me in the back of the head."

"I'm sorry about what he did to you, but you have to move past that, move past him and think about your daughter. You'd lose her and worse, you'd lose your freedom for a very long time."

"You must gon' plant drugs in my apartment," Robyn joked.

He sat up, turned, looked her in the eye and careful to enunciate every word he said, "That is exactly what I will do."

Robyn shook her head. "No, you won't."

"What makes you so sure?"

She stood up on top of the bed. She had her hands on her hips.

Forty-five-year-old Mason Terrell gawked at Robyn's perfect twenty-two-year-old bruised and battered naked body.

She pointed at his rising nature. "That's why. Your little head and your big head can't get enough of Ms. Kitty. Meow."

He pulled her down to the bed. "Woof, Woof," he barked.

Four minutes later, Terrell rolled over onto his back. He was panting and out of breath. "I'm telling you, I promise, you…. You will lose everything if… If you don't…."

"I said no. That boy saved my life, Mason. What part of hell no don't you understand? I don't care if you take my baby and lock me up for ten lifetimes. I am not going to lie on that man. If it wasn't for him, I'd probably be dead."

Agent Terrell sat back up and swung his legs over the side of the mattress. "How many times are you going to say the same thing?"

"How many times are you going to ask me to change my story?"

It would have been so much easier to have her killed like the NSA chief did to the Medical Examiner that prepared the preliminary report on Snake. But the NSA chief needed her and so did he, so instead, Agent Terrell picked up his pants, pulled out his wallet, opened it and laid fifteen bills out on the bed. All of them had Ben Franklins face on them.

Robyn's eyes doubled in size.

"This can be all yours if you…"

"Mason?" She got off the bed and pointed at the money. "You think I'm gon' sell Zion out for fifteen funky hundred dollars."

"No, I think you'll sell him out for ten thousand dollars. This is just a deposit."

Fifteen minutes later, agent Terrell had a signed statement from Robyn.

"So, when am I going to get the rest of my money?"

"I already told you that you will receive another eighty-five hundred when we have him in custody."

"I'm talking about my money for today," she said. "I need money for food and diapers."

"I just gave you fifteen hundred dollars."

"I can't spend that. That's my baby's college fund."

He pulled out his wallet and opened it. "I'm broke, Robyn."

She reached in his wallet and pulled out a Visa debit card. "I got a Paypal account."

"I can not believe that you are really going to make me pay after I just gave you fifteen hundred dollars."

"First," she held a finger in the air, "one has nothing to do with the other and second you didn't *give* me anything. You paid for me to lie on the man that saved my life less than a week ago."

While inputting the required credit card information, her cell phone rang. She didn't recognize the number, so she sent it to voicemail. She'd return the call after she got rid of Mason, who knows, it might be a new customer.

"All done." She handed him his card back. "See, that wasn't so bad now, was it?"

"Yes, it was." He sulked.

"You really gon' trip off thirty dollars, Mason? Do I need to let you borrow some of my tampons?"

If Robyn had known that the fifteen hundred dollars that Terrell gave her was supposed to be used to buy the "Singer Plus" sewing machine he had promised his wife on her birthday today then Robyn may have treated him with a little more compassion.

Terrell knew he should have been ecstatic about getting her to change her original statement but he wasn't. He could care less about making Robyn think that she was going to receive another eighty five hundred dollars. He felt bad for having to lie to his wife again and on her birthday but he felt even worse about the perjured statement he had in his pocket.

The second Terrell walked out of Robyn's apartment she pressed redial.

"Hello," a man said.

"I have a missed call from this number?"

"And you are telling me this because?"

"Don't play with me, little boy. I'm a grown ass woman," Robyn said before pressing the red button.

Her phone rang again.

She pressed the green button. "Quit calling my phone."

"Robyn, this is Zion, Zion Jones, remember me?"

"Boy, you was about to get cursed out."

"I see," Zion said before he changed gears. "But, anyway you gave me your number and I just called to see how you were doing?"

"Not too good."

"What's wrong?" Zion asked, his voice laced with concern.

"My check don't come for another couple days, my food stamp card don't renew till the fifteenth, and my baby is out of diapers and we don't have any food."

"Okay, I got you," he said.

"Huh, what do you mean, you got me?"

"Can you hold out until morning?" he asked.

"If I have no choice, I guess I'll have to," she said having no idea what he was talking about doing in the morning. As fine as he was he could get if for the free, she thought, but if he wanted to spend she wasn't going to deny him.

"I can't let you and that baby suffer until morning. If it's okay I can get by there in a few hours if you're available."

Just like the rest of them, he couldn't wait to test ride her, she thought. "I'm broke, where else am I going to be?" she said while stuffing the fifteen one hundred dollar bills into her pocket.

*****

It was a breezy but nice Thursday mid-afternoon day. Early, Zion and Malice were driving down the Covington Georgia, safehouse's long, gravel and dirt driveway when Zion gave Early's phone back.

"You do know she playin' you, right?" Early said.

"Never that," Zion said. "I'm not as green as you may think?"

Early looked over at Malice in the passenger seat. "Mal will you tell him?" Early slowly pulled up near the barn where the other cars were parked.

Malice turned his body so he could see Zion in the back seat of the Avalanche. "I can't believe I'm siding with this nut, but I think he's right, Zion. You call just to see how Shorty's doing and first thing come out of her mouth is how her and her baby hurtin' for bread. No offense bruh, but she was fishin' for a sucker and you took the bait."

"I appreciate you two looking out but trust me, I got her. It may be April first, but I'm no one's fool."

Moments later they were inside the safe house. The Reverend Dr. Lomax introduced Early and Malice to Reverend White, and the four other spiritual leaders that were part of the twelve that knew who Zion really was.

After everyone became acquainted, Zion said, "Excuse me everyone. Can I have your attention please?"

Everyone stopped their conversations and turned to Zion. "There's a lot of love in this house and it feels good." He paused to look at each and every one of the ten men in the house.

Reverend Kelly stood up. "Can I say something before we get started?"

Zion extended his arm. "Go ahead, the floor is yours."

The big man crossed his arms over his ample girth. He briefly met everyone's stare. His eyes rested on the second biggest man in the room, Malice. "I teach at Rainbow Elementary and I just wanna let you know that last week was our career week. I had an attorney, a police officer, an insurance professional, an actress, and a local hip-hop artist speak to my fourth graders. And at the end of the week as I always do, I gave my *real superheroes are everyday people speech* to the kids before asking them if they had any idea of what they wanted to be when they grew up." His pause caused the others to notice his squinting eyes. "Mind you, I have thirty-four kids," his voice cracked, "Fifteen said they wanted to be like Miracle Mal, twelve said they wanted to be like Zion and then they asked me what schools you two attended and what degree they had to earn to be like you two."

"Real talk?" Malice asked. "The kids are calling me Miracle Mal?"

"Real talk," Reverend Kelly replied. "And yes, you're their hero."

"What did you tell them?" Zion asked.

"What do you mean?" Reverend Kelly asked.

"You said they asked you what degree they had to earn to be like us."

"I told them that I – I didn't know." He uncrossed his arms and put a hand over his eyes before stuttering. "I – I just wanted to let you know how much of an inspiration you are to the kids in the community, how much, how much what you are doing means to me."

Reverend Kelly looked to be somewhere in his mid thirties. He put you in the mind of a biggie-sized young Isaac Hayes, a bald, dark tower standing flatfooted at six-four, six-five. He didn't fit the profile of an elementary school teacher and he definitely didn't seem like the type that easily shed tears, but sure enough, he was weepy eyed as he continued to speak.

"I have lived in this community all my life and I would've never imagined that a menace to society could become a savior to that same society."

The big man put the hand back over his face.

Malice walked up to the reverend and hugged the big man. Before breaking the embrace Malice whispered in his ear. "Thank you. What you said means a lot to me."

Dr. Lomax stood up. "I feel the same way as Reverend Kelly. Akin to Moses parting the Red Sea, you three parted the Green Sea. You got the community to see," Dr. Lomax pointed at his eye, "that the green in their wallets is not nearly as important as the welfare of others. Two years ago, if someone would have told me that Malice and his crew were going to stop dealing and that they were going to rid the community of illegal drugs I would've questioned their sanity. If they would've went on to tell me that the residents in Pleasant Pointe were going to unite and pool their resources and talents together to start a weekend open-air flea market, I would have been sure that they had either completely lost their minds or they were high on some psychotropic drug. And if they would have gone further by telling me that upper middle-class soccer moms would be shopping and donating goods and services to the vendors in the Pleasant Pointe Flea Market, there is a good chance that I would have picked up my phone quick, fast, and in a hurry and called them some professional help."

"And we would've had to break somebody out of some psych ward quick, fast, and in a hurry," Early said as the others laughed.

After everyone settled back down, Dr. Lomax nodded for Zion to take the floor.

"Like I said, a lot of love. That's all we have done," Zion said. "Malice, Pearl, Early, me, and the others, all we've done is show love to people that haven't had a lot of experience with unconditional love. It's like crack. Once you start showing love, you receive love and that's the greatest feeling in the world and it becomes addictive." Zion looked to his left. "Am I right Mal?"

The big man nodded before speaking, "I just wish everybody knew how right you were, little bruh."

"In time, big bruh, in time," Zion said before turning his attention and the conversation back to the forum of men in the room. "Because of the climate change in the community, the local media has been in the hood this past week asking questions, taking pictures, and getting video coverage. Soon, as in anytime now, the national media will be in the Pointe and the surrounding community and when that happens the powers that be will begin spinning tales in the media in hopes of getting the community to turn against us. They will use Malice's past. They will make all of us look like the embodiment of evil. That's why we have to stay strong. Our faith will be tested on more than one occasion. That's why I need all the spiritual leaders, beginning with this Friday at Jumah, to tell your congregations who I am. Show them what we have done. Bring man's religions together under one spiritual body of understanding. Show your congregations that although we are from different cultures we all come from the same Mother, that we are all one race.

Chapter 41

April 1, 2009
SAME DAY: **Atlanta, Georgia**

Malice was a man of action. He was never one to mince a lot of words, but he had been uncharacteristically quiet since the three had left the safehouse a couple hours ago. The three men were loading groceries into Malice's Avalanche truck when he said, "I been doing some thinking about what Reverend Kelly said about his kids, how they looked up to me and I think I need to go back to school and get my GED before I go to some college."

"Why you say that?" Early asked while climbing into the driver's seat.

"These kids are lookin' up to me and I don't even have no diploma."

"Education is all good, but everything ain't for everybody Big Mal, you doin' helluva good managing the community and you makin' a livin' while doin' it."

Zion just listened as the two men spoke.

"You right." Malice nodded. "Everything ain't for everybody, but education is. Everything I been reading lately, Akbr, Browder, Umoja, Jihad, Malcolm, all of them are and were able to drop mad knowledge on paper in a way that made a brother like me keep reading and it doesn't take a brain scientist to realize that they couldn't have understood the way they did if the acquisition of knowledge hadn't educated them. We give speeches and sermons, do a lotta lip smacking about our enemies, and that's all good but we need action after the talk, Mandela says that education is the best way to defeat your enemies. Toussaint wouldn't have been able to overthrow the Brits if he didn't have an understanding of warfare. If Black folks in America were educated about who they are and where they came from we wouldn't be repeating so many generational mistakes."

"You're all over the place, Big Mal, what are you saying?" Early asked.

"I'm saying, I have to go back to school."

"You don't have to go back to school to be educated," Early said as he pulled out of the Publix grocery store parking lot.

"I know that, but if I wanna stop the lies that the schools are teaching our kids I have to get a traditional education, while I continue with my untraditional reading."

"You think you wanna teach school?" Early asked.

"No, not really, but I have to teach li'l bruh. You heard the brother. These kids look up to me, so I have to be the man they think I am. Them looking up to me, shows me that I can reach them. And if they wanna be like me, I have to be like the me that my momma died for me to be."

"Man, that's a hundred leagues below the sea deep," Early said. "What do you think, Zee Money?"

"Nothing I can say to that. That's my big bruh laying down the Word," he said, reaching over the back seat to pat Malice on the shoulder. "Turn in there." Zion pointed to the parking area while picking up Early's phone from the middle console.

Zion dialed the number.

"Hello?" she answered on the first ring.

"Robyn, this is Zion, I'm pulling into the parking lot. I'll be up in a few if that's okay."

"Yeah, come on."

Robyn ran in into her room, stripped off her jeans, panties and wife beater tank top before sliding a pink teddy over her head. She put a finger under her arms and then stuck it to her nose. Satisfied, she did the same to her private area. "Damn," she cursed before running into the bathroom. She really wanted to take a bath, Zion was special, but with so little time she washed up in the sink.

Her phone beeped. She picked it up. The text read, *At your door.*

"Shit," she said aloud while straightening up her bathroom and spraying some bootleg Passion perfume in the air. She did her best to straighten up her bedroom in a minute's time. She walked to the door and was about to open it when she remembered to do the breath test. She lifted her hand to her mouth and nose and blew. "Shit!" she ran back to the bathroom and did a twenty-second toothpaste-finger brush before walking back to the door. She took the chain off and unlocked it while trying to remember what she had forgotten. She swung the door wide open.

"Damnnnnnnn?" Early said, dropping the plastic grocery bags, while gawking at the half naked beauty.

"Shit," she slammed the door. "You didn't tell me you were bringing others."

"I-I, I'm sorry," Zion stuttered. It was the first time he'd seen an almost naked woman in person.

"Give me a moment," she said.

"Ain't no way Black Cinderella got with somebody as ugly as Snake unless he was cakin' her," Early said before turning to Zion, "Look like she tryin' to give you some of her chocolate."

"Maybe you two should go wait in the truck. She's obviously embarrassed. I'll take the groceries and diapers in," Zion said. "Give me a few minutes to talk with her. I won't be too long."

"Handle your business, li'l bruh, we'll be out by the truck," Malice said.

"Don't become a baby daddy in there," Early said.

Malice and Zion looked at Early with contempt.

"Hey," he shot his hands in the air, "my post traumatic slave syndrome makes me say all type of dumb stuff that I don't mean."

Malice and Zion both shook their heads.

A minute later, Robyn answered the door, this time she was wearing jeans and a t-shirt. She still didn't have on a bra and with a chest like hers, she really needed to have on a bra.

"Where are your friends?" She looked up and down the hallway.

"I sent them away."

She pointed to all the grocery bags on the ground. "What's all that?"

"Food and diapers," he said picking up several bags and carrying them inside. She grabbed a few and followed him to her kitchen. After making two trips to the hallway her and Zion stood in the small kitchen.

She seductively walked up to the seventeen year old young man, and started unbuckling his belt.

He gently removed her hands. "What are you doing?"

"I am trying to pay for my groceries."

"They're already paid for." He took her hand, and led her to a metal fold-up chair pushed up against an old wooden kitchen table. He pulled out the chair, and said, "Please?" After she sat down, he pulled out another and sat down in front of her, never releasing her hand.

"Robyn, women would die to have your looks and your figure. Men would kill to have a woman with your physical beauty. Your life, your body is a priceless gift from the Creator. Robyn, you can't buy life, yet you risk yours every time you lay down with a man for a dollar."

She bounced out of her seat. "Man, I don't know what you're talking about. I ain't no ho'."

"I never said you were. And you do know what I am talking about."

"How you gon' tell me what I know?"

"Is all of that attitude and loud talk really necessary? You can really save your energy; I know you have fifteen hundred dollars in your left front jeans pocket. You told me you needed diapers, but Tiara has lived with your mother for the last six months. And if I open your refrigerator I'll find...."

"If you know all that, why did you bring all the groceries and diapers?"

"Because, I wanted to show you a man's love without you having to give anything up for it."

"Why?" She crossed her arms. "You don't know me."

"I know enough about you to know that I would die if it meant saving you."

"You sound like a real fool, Zion."

"Wrong. I sound like a man that knows the value of a woman, a black woman," he smiled. "You're my sister. I love you Robyn as if I had known you all my life. No man deserves to have you if they don't love and put your best interest ahead of theirs. From your womb comes life and life is light for the future." He stood up and reached for her hands. "You won't live to see your daughter graduate from kindergarten if you don't start respecting your body."

"How else can I make the kind of money I earn if I don't trick?"

"When you were younger, you used to dream about being a fashion designer. You use to redesign popular designers fashions on paper. Remember those days?"

She nodded her head.

"Besides you being black and absolutely beautiful, do you know the difference between you and say, Vera Wang?"

She shook her head no.

"After Wang dreamed about being a top fashion designer she took action to achieve that dream." Zion used a finger to lift Robyn's chin so she could look him in the eyes. "But, you Robyn, you just kept dreaming."

"I don't have money for no design school."

"There are other ways to get in school for people like yourself with low to no income. I'll help you. Tomorrow morning can you meet me downtown in front of the Georgia State University train station at nine?"

"That means I'll have to wake up at seven."

"I guess it does." He got up and started toward the door.

"Zion, I don't know why you feel the need to rescue me, but I wanna thank you."

"Earn that degree, queen. Be the number one fashion designer in the world, that's the thanks I want," he said before reaching the front door.

"A DEA agent gave me the fifteen hundred dollars to lie on you."

"I know," Zion said.

"I signed a statement saying that you killed Snake."

"I know."

"If you know so much, why are you doing so much for me?"

"You're my sister," Zion said. "I love you."

"What do I do now," she asked.

"Do what's right. But either way, I got you." He winked.

Chapter 42

April 12, 2009
ELEVEN DAYS LATER: Decatur, Georgia

The Pointe had received an ongoing onslaught of media publicity over the last few weeks since the three-day flea market began. There had never been a story such as the one that surrounded the Pointe. You could say the Pointe was living up to its entire name, Pleasant Pointe Apartments.

Media crews interviewed several residents and they all credited seventeen-year-old Zion Jones for ridding drugs from the community and inspiring them to work together. When asked how one teenage young man could inspire a community, they all said the same thing using different words. Zion had gotten them to understand who they were and how their recent and distant ancestors were resilient in resisting oppression so future generations wouldn't have to suffer as they had.

This was the fourth Friday of the bazaar. The flea market had grown to having an open-air food court, valet parking and a full service car wash, oil change and minor mechanical services. There was even a daily lottery set up to help struggling families in the community.

It was late afternoon, it was coming up on six-thirty and Malice and his crew were way behind. They had four cars to fully detail and there were six more that needed the basic exterior and interior clean.

So they wouldn't block off any viable parking spaces near the flea market field in the front, Malice ran his car wash and detail business at the back of the Pointe. Once the service on the vehicles were completed Malice would radio one of his security officers up front, tell them how much the client owed and then instruct them to come and take the client their vehicle.

Although Malice was the general manager of the Flea Market, he didn't mind getting his hands dirty when needed. And today, everybody seemed to want their car washed or detailed. Malice's girlfriend, Shatonya, had seven girls working for her, but that wasn't nearly enough if they wanted to get the cars done by nine when the flea market closed. Malice grabbed Early and a couple others to help.

While all of this was going on in the Pointe, twenty miles down the road at the Richard Russell Federal building an officer of the court read the indictment that just came across her desk. It had yesterday's date on it. After reading it, she left the office, rode the elevator to the first floor and stepped out of the building. She craned her neck left and right before she placed a call to a close friend of Dr. Lomax's.

"This is Akinyele speaking."

"Dr. Umoja, this is Tiffany Buttrell."

"Oh, hey Tiffany, how are you, queen?"

"Fine." She surveyed her surroundings again making sure no one was in listening range. "I…"

"You know, it's not to late to apply for grad school, what was your GPA again?"

"Doc, listen, I know you're tight with Dr. Long over at that church that Malice Rogers attends."

"You mean Dr. Lomax, at First Afrikan."

278

"Yeah, him. Let him know that a grand jury was convened yesterday. Zion Jones was indicted for first degree murder."

Chapter 43

April 12, 2009
SAME DAY: **Decatur, Georgia**

Atlanta traffic was the worst. On any given Friday, rush hour had no beginning and no end until late into the night. And between the hours of five and eight, traffic barely inched along.

In most U.S. cities traffic accidents caused most of the delayed traffic on interstates, but in Atlanta, it was nosy people trying to see why someone else was pulled over to the side of the highway. As a matter of fact, most highway accidents in Atlanta were a result of people allowing themselves to be distracted by what someone else was doing in the emergency lane.

It was the middle of another Friday Atlanta rush hour, traffic was worse than normal because of the five unmarked black cars pulled over to the emergency lane right beyond the Wesley Chapel exit on the I20 interstate. It took forty to forty five minutes to drive two miles to the next exit because nosy onlookers were trying to see what the ten armed men dressed in all black were doing huddled together in the emergency lane.

Over the last couple weeks, Mason Terrell's superiors went out of the way to kiss his behind. Terrell's arrogance had led him to believe that the newfound attention was due to the DEA not wanting him to go over to the NSA. Little did he know that his superiors didn't care one way or the other if he stayed, left, or died. The real reason he was garnering so much attention was because Connie Greenspan had called in some favors, one of those favors led to Mason Terrell heading up a DEA task force.

Terrell had to squint because of the sun's glare in his eyes as he pointed. "Right over there beyond that fence is Pleasant Pointe Apartments," Terrell said. "We go in, hit 'em fast and hard. By now," he made eye contact with all the men, "you should have the images of Malice Rogers and Zion Jones burnt into your mind. Am I correct?"

In unison the men said, "Yes sir."

"Yes sir, what?" he asked as he enjoyed his few minutes of power.

"Yes sir, you are correct, sir," the men said.

Minutes later they scaled the ten-foot wall separating the highway from the field behind the Pointe.

*****

"*Tomorrow is off and poppin', you hear me? The love of my life, my future babymomma, my wife, we gon' do the damn thang tomorrow night,*" Early said.

"Fool, you are screamin' over the music. The people that don't wanna hear your mouth are forced to," Shatonya said, while drying off a blue Honda Odyssey minivan.

"Soooo, what female are you going to dream about tonight, Yum-Yum?" Otanya asked.

"Oh…. The hate that hate produced," Early said looking at Otanya. "You and your daughter are just mad that neither of you will be enjoying an intimate evening with yours truly. You see my fine and unfair ladies; the ravenous beauty, Amber Jacoby has accepted my loquacious appropriated invitation to see Charlie Wilson at the Fox."

"Uh, li'l bruh? Malice tapped Early on the shoulder.

"Yes," Early turned. "You require my rapt attention?"

"Just a little advice, bruh."

"Not that I need it, Big Mally-Mal, seeing as I've captured the attentions of the finest woman on this side of Heaven.

"Okay, li'l bruh, I hear you, but if you want Amber to hear you, do not use the word ravenous to describe her beauty."

"What, you don't think she will understand my vocabularic insight?"

"No." Malice shook his head. "I don't think she will enjoy being referred to as being ravenous. The word means greedy."

Half the crew fell over laughing. They didn't even see the shadows coming from behind the buildings.

Malice had tears in his eyes. "And Early, please, please do not use words that you don't know."

"Why would I use vocabulary that I can't resuscitate the definition to?"

"That's what I was wondering when you just referred to your invitation as garrulous and arrogated."

"No I didn't. I said the invitation was loquacious and appropriated. And for all of your information, my future babymomma, wife, love of my life is greedy, so she is a ravenous booty, I mean beauty. And I usually don't kiss and tell but…"

"Since when don't you kiss and tell?" Shatonya asked. "Early you got more mouth than a bo hog got fat."

"You just mad cause you can't get none of my fineness." He turned his attention back to the others. "Now as I was saying before Oom Foo Foo interrupted me, Amber told me she loves to eat and she loves to cook, so that is why I used the word ravenous to describe her." He turned his attentions back to Shatonya, "I think you are mad cause my future babymomma is killing the game selling the hell out her homemade Red Velvet cake at the flea market."

"Ain't nobody jealous of nothing you think you have, boy. I feel sorry for Amber, she just don't know how ignorant you is. I bet you can't even spell loquacious or appropriated."

"Why don't you find another loquation to appropriate this conversation, like maybe in the fast lane on I20 right now." Early turned his attention back to Malice. "I ain't forgot about you either big boy. Now what was that you said I called my baby?"

"I said you referred to her as garrulous and arrogated."

"I don't even know what that means. So, I know I didn't call my future that."

"I didn't say you used those exact words." Malice put a hand on Early's shoulder. "I said you referred to her as garrulous and arrogated, these two words are synonyms for loquacious and appropriated."

"EVERYBODY FREEZE!" Agent Terrell said as he and his men had the car wash tent and everyone around it surrounded. Everybody on the ground. Face down, butt up!" Terrell shouted.

"What seems to be the problem officer?" Malice asked Agent Terrell.

The agent walked over to Malice, turned his AK around and hit the big man in the face with the guns stock. While Malice crumpled to the ground Terrell said, "You are the problem, Mr. Rogers."

"He didn't pose a threat or do anything to you, asshole. How'd you like it if someone hit you in the face with a gun?" Shatonya exploded.

"Baby, chill, I'm good," Malice said while holding a hand to his head where the gun had cut him.

Agent Terrell walked around all the bodies that were laying face down on the ground.

"Where is wonder boy?" the agent asked.

No one responded.

"Come on now, don't everyone speak at once. Now I'll ask again, Where is Zion Jones?"

No one responded.

"Okay, so that how it's going to be, huh?" Agent Terrell said before walking over to Malice and grabbing him by his shirt collar. "Get your big ass up."

As soon as Malice got to his feet, Terrell and another agent pushed the big man up against the Honda minivan.

"Assume the position fat boy," Agent Terrell said before going into his own pocket and pulling out something that he palmed so no one could see.

After Malice complied, Agent Terrell started patting him down. When he reached into Malice's front pocket he came out with the plastic baggie he'd just put in it."

"Well, what do we have here?" Agent Terrell held up a plastic sandwich bag filled with what looked to be a bunch of crack rocks in fingernail sized plastic bags.

"You have whatever you just planted on me," Malice said.

"You are foul man. You worse than the white man," Shatonya said. "I oughta'…

Another agent stuck a gun under her chin. "You oughta what?"

"Leave her alone." Malice shouted.

"Tell us where Mr. Jones is and we'll leave all of you alone," Agent Terrell said. "Anyone feel free to speak up, if not we'll have to take fat boy in and with his record, by the time he get's out you'll all be old and gray if not dead."

Agent Terrell shrugged. "Okay, suit yourself." Although he stood the closest to Malice, Agent Terrell turned to one of his agents and said, "Mirandize him, then cuff him."

Moments later, the agents were escorting Malice away while Shatonya unleashed a dictionary of curse words to describe the agents that were taking her man away through the back of the apartments.

"Shatonya, what's Ms. Erby's number?"

"I don't know and I don't care?" She shrugged. "What are we gon' do?"

"Stay here, I'll be right back." Early said before taking off. Ms. Erby only lived in the building across the street, but she lived all the way on the third floor. He ran inside the building. He took the stairs three at a time. "Ms. Erby," he called out as he knocked. "Ms. Erby."

"Keep your britches on. I'm coming," a voice called out from behind the door.

Early stood bent over as he tried to catch his breath when an athletic-looking sixty something-year-old tall black lady answered the door. "Early, what are you doing?"

"Catching my breath." He rose up. "Ms. Erby, it's an emergency, do you still have that camera I sold you a few weeks ago?"

"Of course, I still have it. Boy, with that super duper high powered lens, I can see all the way to Plum Nelly from here. And I can take pictures of Plum Nelly, too."

"Ms. Erby," Early made a beeline to her balcony, "get the camera, hurry, the DEA are taking Big Mal through the back."

*****

"Why are we stopping?" Malice asked one of the agents.

Agent Terrell walked through the knee-high grass up to the large man. He had to speak up, so Malice could hear him over the highway noise. "All you have to do is tell us where Mr. Jones is and I'll let you go right now."

Malice looked at the agent with disgust in his eyes and contempt on his face. "I wouldn't tell you the time of day if my life depended on it, so you know I ain't about to snitch on my peoples."

"You are as dumb as you look. You think Zion wouldn't tell where you were if his freedom depended on it?"

"I don't do unto others as they do unto me, so it doesn't make a difference if this Zion you speak of would give you anything on me."

"Okay." Terrell nodded. "I get it now. You're one of them."

When Malice didn't bite, Terrell continued, "Look it up on your cellphone after you tell me where Mr. Jones is if you don't believe that over 85 percent of convicted felons snitched on somebody." Terrell placed his hands behind his back as he walked around the big man. "You see, big boy, there are three types of people in prison. There are the ones that told, then there are the ones that wished they told and then there are the one's that wish they had someone to tell on."

"I'm the one that wishes you would shut the hell up and take me to jail," Malice said.

Terrell took out his keys before unlocking one of the cuffs on Malice's wrist.

"What are you doing?" Malice asked.

"Setting you free. We don't want you. We just want you to give a message to Mr. Jones.

Malice stuck out his arm. "What about the other cuff?"

"What about it?"

"Aren't you going to take it off?"

"Nah, I'm sure you'll figure something out, now go on back to your hoodlum friends."

"Nah man," Malice shook his head. "I done seen this movie before."

"What are you talking about?" Agent Terrell asked.

"Man, just take off the other handcuff," Malice said while extending his arm out.

"Go!" another agent shouted as he pointed toward the back of the apartments.

Malice looked at the agent without a drop of fear in his demeanor. "So one of you can shoot me in the back."

"I saw that movie, too," Agent Terrell said, "But this is real life. If I wanted to shoot you I would have. As a matter of fact, Tom," Agent Terrell called out to one of the agents.

"Sir, yes sir."

"Shoot Mr. Rogers if he isn't out of our site in," he looked at his watch, "twenty-nine seconds."

Malice took off running.

Agent Terrell took out his Browning .9mm, loaded a bullet in the chamber aimed it at Malice's head and fired.

Malice fell to the ground.

"Hmph, I guess he did see this movie before afterall ," Terrell said.

Chapter 44

October 9, 2009
SIX MONTHS LATER: **Fort Detrick, Maryland**

Thirty-eight-year-old Constance Greenspan was twenty-two years younger than the youngest member of the seven men that made up the seven body Trilateral Commission. There was not a door in America that one of these men could not open.

The Chairman of the Federal Reserve was also the Chairman of the Trilateral Commission and was leading the Commission members into a vacuum-sealed, tempered glass chamber.

"You can remove your oxygen masks and the white suits," Chairman Greenspan said while stripping out of his decontamination suit.

The Commission members were in a seven thousand square foot underground top-secret laboratory, two hundred feet below the nation's top military medical command installation. Although the underground installation was top secret, Fort Detrick Army base was not. Most people new of the military medical command installation from it's infamous history.

From 1943 to 1969 Ft. Detrick was the center of the American biological weapons program. The Army medical command installation is also the whipping boy for many conspiracy theorists who've claimed in books and Internet forums that the Ebola and HIV virus were developed at Ft. Detrick for some type of top-secret population control study.

The seven men in the radiation chamber room were the only civilians to know unequivocally that the theorists' philosophy was fact and not just theory. The Commission members knew this to be fact because for two generations their families had financed the population control study that had developed both viruses. The families of the Commission members wasted no time as they begun the study, December 23, 1913 the same day the Federal Reserve was created.

There was never any worry that either virus would travel from the Third World testing countries to the U.S. and infect anyone in the seven family Trilateral Commission circle because at the same time the Ft. Detrick scientists created the HIV and Ebola virus, they also created the antivirus just in case the viruses spiraled out of control, which to them neither had.

After the sensors had determined that the men weren't exposed to lethal levels of radiation the glass doors opened on the other side and the men changed back into their business attire.

Minutes later, the seven men were seated at a glass roundtable in the underground laboratory conference room.

The chairman stood up from his seat. "Gentlemen, we are on the precipice of controlling the world," he said as he held up a test tube half full of a transparent looking blue liquid. "Our forefathers impatience, abrasiveness and absolute lack of tact was the reason they were unsuccessful in their bid to flood China with drugs. In both Opium Wars between 1839 and 1860 thousandss died and the Chinese government still refused to buy British opium." He paused to let this little historical fact register in their minds.

The chairman continued, "In '49 right here in this laboratory," he tapped the glass table with his forefinger, "the beginning of the end was discovered. Heroine. Not just any form of heroine but a cheaper, more potent form of the drug was engineered right here, and our families increased their wealth ten fold in ten years after the government recruited and used other minorities to flood the American urban communities with the drug. If our forefathers would have used members of the minority class that they were targeting in the Orient than there would have never been one Opium War. The Heroine experiment proved that we could use drugs to control the actions of the poor, hence increasing our wealth.

"In the early '80's our scientists improved on our already successful drug/population control program by coming up with a more potent and cheaper form of cocaine. Crack. Crack is so great because unlike heroine it is a stimulant. It gives people energy, and combine energy with motivation to get more of the drug and our studies show that people more readily commit crimes for the drug as they would for heroine. The rise in crime since we introduced Crack in L.A. twenty-six years ago can be attributed to the billions we've made in the prison industry since then. But, as quick as we flood the street with mind controlling narcotics, leftwing and right wing politicians come up with laws and provisions that impede our progress. But with this agent," he waved the test tube around the room, "we will accomplish two things; effective population control and world domination."

Media Mogul Rupert Murdow said, "I don't see how. Like you just said, our efforts will be eventually thwarted by people and technology."

"Not if people and technology have no way of determining the contents of the drug." The chairman smiled. "The drug is only half of it. We are close to perfecting an agent that breaks down and takes on the molecular structure of its host. We mutate this agent with our drug and alcohol and when broken down all there will be is the ingredients used to make the alcohol.

Murdow interrupted, "So, you're saying that the scientists are close to creating an agent that let's say, you pour it on salt, when the salt is broken down and analyzed the only compounds that will be found are sodium and chloride?"

The chairman smiled. "That is exactly what I am saying."

"How long before this agent is ready?" Bush asked.

"Four to six years tops, that gives us enough time to play the world peace game with our new African-American president. We slowly pull the troops out of North Africa, and the Middle East, making the world believe that America is serious about world peace. In 2014, we roll out a huge billion-dollar media campaign for our drug. We recruit the five top rap and hip-hop artists, commission them to write, rap and sing about our product. We make them the face of our product." The chairman raised the test tube half full of the blue liquid high in the air, "Shorty Blue."

"Shorty Blue?" Rockefeller said, confusion blanketing his face.

"Yes, Shorty Blue. It's a great urban name don't you think?" Before anyone answered, the chairman continued. "The drug would be taken orally and within seconds of the drug entering the blood stream the user will feel twice the euphoria of a crack induced high. The user only has to use the drug once before the drug slowly begins killing off the users white blood cells."

"Sort of like the HIV virus?" Bush asked.

"Exactly like the HIV virus," the chairman said. "But the agents in this liquid takes between fifteen and twenty years to kill its host.

"We strictly market Shorty Blue to the urban community in America. Since it has no odor or taste, we just mix it with vodka, Gin, every hard liquor that African-

Americans regularly consume. We use food coloring and six ounce blue bottles. We set the market price at 4.99 and within five years we will put every alcohol manufacturer out of business."

"Besides the money we'll make from the drugs sells, and the prisons that will be built and filled as a result of the crimes that will be committed because of the drug, how will this drug enable us to implement our One World Order?" Bush asked.

"The urban world is led by American rappers and hip hop artists, the artists just don't realize it. What these artists wear, what they do, is mimicked all over the world. Look at the fashions today that make the most money. Do you know that over eighty-five percent of urban criminals between the ages of sixteen to twenty nine listen to rap music as a motivator before they commit crimes."

Murdow interrupted, "So, we start now using the media to build these already popular rappers into cult figures, so when they begin marketing Shorty Blue we just sit back and watch the urban world get hooked on our drug. Once that happens we begin to make the drug scarce causing a crime frenzy unlike the world has ever seen, and when governments are on the verge of anarchy, war and collapse we come in and force them to relinquish power."

Knock! Knock!

The men turned their attention to the door.

"Excuse me, gentlemen." The chairman rose and went to the door. He opened it about three inches.

"Sir, you have an urgent message from General Lesure."

"I'll head up top where I can get reception in a moment." He closed the door without saying thanks or good-bye.

He turned to the Commission members. "Gentleman, I have a slight emergency. Now that you are up to speed on what we're doing, this meeting is adjourned."

While taking the elevator back up top, Chairman Greenspan thought how quickly time had passed. It just seemed like yesterday when he was cast out of Heaven over three million years ago. He and the Creator could have shared power. He was the Creator's sun, Her light, before Horus, Jesus or Zion. Why wouldn't the Creator want Her sun's to share Her power? Three million years. It had taken three million years for the Creator to send Zion. Too bad, it was too late. The world had chosen him over the Mother. People wanted the medium that was exchanged for objects. Constance had told the Creator this time and again. He was much closer to his earthly brothers and sisters than the Mother was. People no longer believed in the Creator, but they believed in the dollar, and the dollar would be their end, before Zion could save them.

The chairman got off the elevator, took out his phone and placed the call.

"Do you have a location on Zion Jones?" the chairman asked.

"No, but we do know that he'll be addressing the nation at the fourteenth anniversary of the Million Man March next Saturday."

"Are you sure?"

"I'd bet my life on it," the head of the NSA said.

"You may just be doing that, General," the chairman said.

Ignoring the implied threat, the NSA chief said, "The people are beginning to believe the rumors and lies we're spreading through the media about the twelve clerics. Naison has taken the biggest hit, thus far. The Islamic ties culminated with the sexual deviant allegations are ruining him. In six months, thirty-two percent of his followers have dropped off.

The day before the march we will unseal the drug and money laundering indictments on some of the other clerics."

"Good," the chairman said. "I want Zion arrested on live TV. Do not allow him to speak. Any resource you think you may need let me know."

"If I arrest him in front of hundreds of thousands of people, don't you think there will be some resistance?"

"Of course there will be, but these people believe in some powerful ghost in the sky that will save them. With the exception of a small few, they won't be armed. Since this will be broadcast live, don't use any more violence than necessary."

The chairman was so engrossed in the conversation that he didn't pay attention to Sgt. Jill Simmons. She seemed to be in a trance as she stared at the chairman's head while he spoke on the phone.

*****

Sgt. Jill Simmons shouldn't have been on the base. Heck she shouldn't have been on her feet. Yesterday, she was bedridden in a hospice waiting for breast cancer to take her life. Everything had changed in a matter of seconds after the thirty-three year-old man walked into her room. He was the same government agent that had been commissioned to take agent XR13 and his family out. He was also the same agent that had gone AWOL from the CIA the same day he'd blown up Agent XR13's house in Indianapolis seven years ago.

Sgt. Jill Simmons walked out of the hospice at a few minutes before midnight last evening while Ronald "Agent FX02" Reagan lay dead in her hospice bed. And now after she had heard the chairman's plan, she was off to the airport. On her way, she purchased a red wig with the money she'd taken off of the dead ex-CIA agent.

If she hurried she could make the six PM flight to Atlanta. She was at the BWI airport ticket counter when she realized that she had no ID. She left and went to the airport parking lot. She searched for an older car manufactured before factory alarms were installed. She settled on a red Camaro that looked as if it had seen better days. The thirty-thee-year-old car was fast and it wouldn't attract much attention, she thought.

She was right. It didn't attract too much attention, but the attention it attracted cost her three precious days. The car broke down in the middle of Nowhere, North Carolina. It took the mechanic two days to get the alternator and thirty minutes to put it on. Lucky for her, she got to Arthur Strong's apartment right before he had to leave for his shift at the prison.

Chapter 45

October 10, 2009
A DAY LATER: **Lithonia, Georgia**

"Baby, there's enough niggas in here to make a Tarzan movie," the older man whispered to his wife.

His wife turned and whispered, "What I tell you about using that word, Cleotis?"

"I'm sorry, baby. I just ain't never seen the church so packed."

"Half the hood done come out to see that boy in the wheelchair," she said.

"You mean the one that the police shot a few months back?"

"Yep," she nodded. "Malice Rogers. They say he got a lot of money coming from the federal government."

"All the money in the world ain't gon' make that boy walk again," he whispered. "Damn, I mean darn shame. Black man get a little power and he shoots an unarmed black man in the back. I hope they deep fry his DEA black behind."

"I'm with you there, Cleotis. Boy stops selling that poison and gives his life over to God and another black man on the side of the law goes and shoots him in the back."

"Shhh, Pastor 'bout to speak."

The veins in his dark hands contracted as he gripped the edges of the blonde wood podium. His dark eyes seemed to search every single face in the standing room only church. Concern was etched all over his blue-black face.

"Power," Dr. Lomax said, before throwing a fist in the air. "Power!" he repeated much louder. And then in a much softer tone he said, "Walter Wink, a divinity scholar at Duke University wrote a series of books called the 'Power series.' He argues that Jesus talks more about power than he does about love, and if you go to the New Testament you will see that there are more words attached to power than there are words that are attached to the notion of love." The sleeves of his black robe fell back as he lifted both arms in the air. "So Jesus was dealing with power, issues and matters of power." He paused to survey the expressions on the faces he could see before continuing, "I wonder why we Christians are so hesitant to address issues of power. There are power issues that look us in the face every single day, and we remain silent yet we think and say we are following the One that says all power in Heaven and on Earth has been given unto me, go therefore." He paused to let his words set in. "He didn't say all love, all compassion, he said all power. Acts one and eight. And you will receive what?"

"Power!" the congregation said.

"When what? The Holy Spirit comes up on you. He's dealing with power. And you mean to tell me that we are following Jesus and we don't even want to raise the power question."

Reverend Kelly stood up from the front pew and said. "We scared."

"The bible says God has not given you the spirit of fear, but of what? Power, love, and a sound mind."

297

"Come on now Pastor, teach," Reverend Kelly said with his arms crossed in front of him.

"But, we are scared of what man will do if we stand up to a godless power. Twelve men of God from different religions and different cultures came together in the Spirit of love and truth and spoke truth to power six months ago and look what has happened." Dr. Lomax shook his head. "The godless power that is controlling the media and the government has created division in the church, the cathedral, the mosque, and even the synagogue. Because of the malicious and libelous rumors and claims made against Brother Naison over a third of his following has dropped off.

"The people choose to believe the media's lies and photoshopped photos when they know the heart of their pastor. The Godless powers have accused me of laundering drug money through the church. Fueling strife through lies to divide people is what the Godless power behind government has done for thousands of years. Look at all the different religions that pray to one singular God. The Godless powers are the ones that are and have always convinced our religious leaders into believing that the only way to salvation is through that perspective religious ideology. Divide," Dr. Lomax made a slicing gesture with his hand, "and conquer. It has always worked in the past. That revolutionary black man, named Jesus said, 'Any kingdom divided against itself is laid waste; and any city or house divided against itself will not stand.' Mathew 12:25."

Shatonya began rolling Malice's wheel chair toward the front of the church.

"Cut off the head and the body will fall. That is exactly what the powers that be are trying to do. They can't kill us or arrest us yet, why, because we still have too much power. Now, I need you men to be men and fight with me. Next weekend I want every black, red, brown, and white man to walk, jog, drive, fly, get on one of our buses, but by any means necessary get to D.C. If you haven't seen or heard the voice of God, you will. Minister Muhammad called and over a million Black men responded in '95, now we need at least that many men to respond to this one. And most important do not even leave your home if you are not willing to fight. D.C. is next weekends field of battle. Let's fulfill Dr. King's dream."

Dr. Lomax stepped down from the podium and stood at Malice's side. He placed a hand on the young man's shoulder. "This young man is my brother, he is my son, he is my neighbor, he is my hero. And as God is my witness," Dr. Lomax threw a fist in the air, "I will fight for my hero. How often do we get the chance to fight for a real hero?" An angry tear escaped the pastor's eye. "The Godless powers I've been speaking about did this to him. He is up here because he wants to speak to you. I give you Malice Rogers."

Everyone was on their feet. A few more angry tears escaped his eyes as he bent down and hugged Malice."

After the church had settled down Malice began, "I am truly honored. If I would have known I'd get this much love and attention I would've stopped gang bangin' and drug slangin' long ago."

Several attendees laughed.

"Between the three surgeries and the physical therapy I've had a lot of time to think and reflect over the last six months. What happened to me is a crime and an injustice, but what I have done to others in my past is no better than what was done to me. For the rest of my life I will look down at my useless legs and pray for strength. Not strength for me, but strength for the families of the brothers and sisters that I have had a hand in hurting. My name is Malice, but I have absolutely no malice in my heart for the agent that shot me. Too many brothers and sisters die everyday because of the malice and hatred they hold onto. The malice I carry is for the system that creates brothers like Agent Mason Terrell, like the me that I used to be. I can't stop, won't stop praying for all my brothers and sisters, just like I can't stop and won't stop fighting for my brothers and sisters. And I want you all to fight and pray for and with me."

"All day every day, Big Mal."

"Thanks, Early," Malice said. "News reporters all over the nation are interviewing people and they are saying that if Zion is the Second Coming, why is he in hiding? Why doesn't he just come out and perform some great miracle to prove he is who the twelve clerics say he is? Every time I heard this while laying in my hospital bed, I just wanted to scream. I mean, I just got my GED the beginning of the year and I can see the biblical miracles that the Creator is working through Zion. The drug problem in Dekalb County was at epidemic levels, like it is in all of the major metropolitan cities of this nation, but you'd be pressed to find a fingernail of crack or cocaine in Dekalb County now. Look at the Pointe. It was a lion's den and like Daniel, Zion walked in and walked out untouched, but he touched the lives of everyone in the Pointe. He resurrected love in a seemingly loveless community, and in a matter of months Zion got us to see God and he got us to see the God in each and every one of us and like the good reverend Doctor says, if we proclaim to believe than we must fight. And no disrespect to Dr. King's memory, but we are going to have to be ready to kill if necessary and take it from me, the government don't know the meaning of fighting fair and they will be ready to take Zion at the March."

Chapter 46

October 11, 2009
A DAY LATER: Arlington, Virginia

The church service was broadcast on C-Span, and the Atlanta public television channel. The original television broadcast received little attention, but within 24 hours, the sermon had been uploaded to the web and had gone viral. The service had been rebroadcasted in forty-three countries. Indonesia, Pakistan, Nigeria, and South Africa just to name a few.

Zion had spent most of his time praying and meditating at a safe house in Arlington, Virginia while the world became acquainted with him through sermons, history books, and Godless propaganda. He'd been living less than five miles from the capitol right under the government's nose for six months. Reverend Willie Williams of D.C. and Archbishop George Rawlings ushered Zion out of Georgia, the day before Malice was shot. That was the same day that the state of Georgia indicted him for murdering government informant Sandford "Snake" Carro.

Zion tried his best to live up to the Creator's expectations and he did, but he couldn't stop thinking about Miracle. In five days he would be on the world stage and he still couldn't reach the woman he'd been in love with for as long as he could remember. He understood all the myriad facets that motivated man to do good and evil, but for the life of him he couldn't understand Miracle. It had been almost a year since he last entered her subconscious.

Chapter 46

October 14, 2009
THREE DAYS LATER: **Atlanta, Georgia**

Arthur Strong had lived a double life longer than the thirty years that he'd worked in corrections. It was just him and Frumpy in the large two-bedroom apartment. Arthur had taken the stray cat in five years ago, the day after the worst day of his life. It was hard to believe that it had been five years since his life partner of twenty years had passed away. He used to consider himself fortunate that the virus hadn't taken his life, but now five years later, he wished it had been him instead of Carl.

The loneliness and the waiting for death was worse than death itself. With death, there was a sort of finality, with waiting to die there was fear. He'd told his peers on the job that he had the big C. He was afraid if they knew he was HIV positive they would think he was gay, and although he was, being gay in any branch of law enforcement was still a no-no. Yeah, there were new provisions and laws to prevent discrimination in the LBGT community, but the law didn't prevent the disdainful looks, the behind-the-back crude jokes, or the loss of respect that he was sure to suffer from his peers and the female inmates, some of which he just absolutely adored. What would they say? What would they think?

Frumpy and the job were his life. He was sixty-three, and he'd be dead before he was old enough to collect social security in a couple years, so why rock the boat now. It was already hard enough dying a slow death. There was no way he'd make it harder by coming out. He knew he was living on borrowed time because last month his T-cell count took a dramatic dive and he acquired AIDS.

After looking around the apartment for the better half of the last hour, he finally found his keys. They were right were he had put them, in his pants pocket. He looked at his watch. It read, 9:25. He was pushing it close. Pulaski was a twenty-minute drive with no traffic and it would take ten minutes to park and walk into the main building. After filling Frumpy's water bowl and petting the furry, gray feline's head he headed for the front door. When he opened it a tall, pale, middle-aged woman wearing a cheap red wig was standing in front of him.

"Can I help you?"

"You definitely can," she said as she stepped forward.

He stepped back. "What…" was all he had the chance to say?

Jill balled up a fist and turned her wrist. "I'm sorry, Mr. Strong. In a few seconds you'll be free."

Arthur Strong put a hand to his chest and collapsed onto the apartment's hardwood foyer floor.

Frumpy was licking Arthur's face when Jill dropped to the floor and Arthur's eyes popped open. Frumpy took off running. Her master's resurrection must have frightened her, because she ran right into the wall next to the kitchen door. She turned back to her master, and again she took off running through the kitchen and out of the back door flap.

Arthur Strong had just suffered a massive heart attack and now he was lifting Jill from the hardwood foyer floor. After carrying her to the bedroom, he gently placed her lifeless body on the queen-sized bed. Next, he said a silent prayer and left for work.

An hour later Arthur was alone with a patient in the prison infirmary. She had a fifty-fifty chance of surviving the night or so the doctor had said. Assata Che Santiago was due to be released in less than twenty-four hours but by the looks of her, she didn't wouldn't live another six.

She had served six years for taking a man's life that tried to take hers. And in all of those years she had never had one physical prison altercation, violent or sexual up until a couple of days ago.

On Tuesday, the day Jill was supposed to arrive in Atlanta an inmate had stabbed Assata because she refused to agree to leave the inmate her commissary and other personal items. The wound from the shank was not life threatening, but the sepsis infection from the dirty blade was. Tonight was critical to Assata's survival. The antibiotics could only do so much. It was up to her immune system to fight off the infection. There should have been a nurse or physician's assistant monitoring Assata through the night, but the prison didn't want to pay the overtime, so they assigned a corrections officer with no medical experience to sit with her. Earlier, the doctor had said that if she made it through the night then her chances for recovery would be about fifty-fifty.

Officer Strong stood over her hospital bed. Beads of sweat were forming on Assata's forehead. Her breathing was shallow. The only noise in the isolated area of the infirmary was a beeping sound that signaled that she was still drawing breath.

Strong took a hand in his and closed his eyes. In seconds, he had breached her subconscious. It took a second to readjust his eyes to the bright sunny day. He looked down. The white sand felt warm and tingly on his toes. Just up ahead, he saw Assata spike a ball over the volleyball net before an opponent hit the ball back over.

He was about to run to her, when he noticed a woman out of the corner of his eye. She was sitting in a chair under a beach umbrella reading a book while sipping some fruity looking drink. Upon further inspection he saw that it was Assata. He turned back to the volleyball game up ahead and sure enough Assata was standing at the net waiting for the opposing team to serve.

He shook his head before jogging over to the Assata that was reading a book. "Excuse me," he held out his hand before quickly turning it so that his palm was face down. "I'm Black," he said aloud.

Assata looked up at him. "Coulda fooled me, I thought you were a green goblin."

"No, I mean I am in my own skin," he said.

"Yeah, I can see that," she said.

"I'm sorry, you don't understand." He turned his hand to the side. "I'm Treble Frazier."

She shook his hand. "I'm Assata."

He looked back over to the volleyball game. "If you're Assata," he pointed to the woman that had just slammed the ball over the net, "then who is she?"

"She's me, of course." She looked at him like he'd just asked the dumbest question in the world. "Who else could she be?"

"But, there's two of you."

"No there's only one me. I just allowed the part of me that wanted to play volleyball to play while I allowed the part of me that wanted to sit down and relax with a good book to do just that."

He looked at her and then at the other her playing volleyball. "How?" he asked.

"It's my world, my reality. I can do anything that my mind can envision," she said.

"I'm sorry, I have very little experience entering others subconscious minds. As a matter of fact I have no experience, you're my first," he said.

She smiled, "Don't feel like the Lone Ranger, you're my first too, boo. No one has ever come into my world unless I created them," she said. "So you wanna tell me why you're here in my world?"

"It's a long story," he said.

She extended an arm. Another red and white lounger magically appeared, "Have a seat, all I have is time."

"No, we don't," he said before sitting down. "Before mankind, there was only the Creator and Her children. The same way you can create your own reality is the same way the Creator has created the reality that the conscious mind dwells. Before mankind existed, the conscious reality was the Creator and Her suns, and by suns I mean little pieces of Her light. The ancient African's referred to them as Orishas, which is another word for a god, with a little g. Today, Christians refer to them as angels."

"I'm familiar with Orisha's, my mother was Dominican," Assata said. "She was deep into Vodun spirituality."

"Well you know that the Creator blessed Shango with the power to control storms. He was known as the God of lightning and thunder. In most recent times, Shango was reborn as a man and became the third king in the West African Oyo Empire. He was reborn to show mankind who God was, just like Horus was reborn in Bethlehem and was renamed Yeshua or Jesus to show mankind who God was."

"And you are telling me this because?" she interrupted after taking a sip of her drink.

"I'm telling you this so you can have some understanding of what we have to do in order to help save mankind." He pulled his lounger closer. "Anyway, the Creator has sent messengers to save his children from the clutches of evil since sin was introduced in the garden. All have failed. And now, the Creator has sent the spirit of Horus, Shango and Yeshua back in a last effort to redeem mankind. All three spirits are alive in one young man, my sun, Zion Uhuru Jones."

"So he is the Messiah?"

"You've heard of him?"

"Everyone with a television has heard of the kid who's bringing the religions together," she said.

"Yes, well when Shango was reborn as a man, he allowed sin to divide him from his first wife, Oba. Oba and Shango had a pure love for each other that was so strong that it could bring down evil once and for good, but Shango listened to evil instead of the God in him and he banished Oba. Now, the Creator has brought the spirit of Oba back in your goddaughter, Miracle."

Assata leaned forward.

"She is the only one that can complete Zion. She is the key to peace."

"I don't see why the Creator just doesn't destroy evil Herself," Assata said.

"She can, but She won't because of Her promise."

"What promise?" she asked.

"She promised man free will and dominion over the Earth. And because of the love She has for man She has sent Her spirit down in the form of man to show humankind the way to salvation."

"Okay, so where do I fit in?" she asked.

"I need you to deliver a message and I need you to watch over Miracle. She is really going to need you."

"Why can't you watch over her?"

"I can and I am, but not as I am," he said.

"Huh?"

"Seven years ago, my body was burned beyond recognition in an explosion. Before my spirit transitioned I entered the body of the CIA agent that was charged with killing me. For six years I have been dead to my sun, and I must stay that way. The best way I could protect and watch over him was to sacrifice my physical life. Zion feels my spirit, but he doesn't understand why I haven't resurfaced, but in time he will see. If I hadn't died when I did I wouldn't have been able to keep tabs on our enemies without them knowing."

"You still haven't told me what we have to do."

"We need to share your physical body."

"We need to do what?"

"You have to enter Miracle's subconscious, like I did yours. She's been catatonic since she witnessed her mother's crucifixion and death."

She put a hand over her mouth. "Sunny was crucified?"

"I'm afraid so."

"When?" she asked.

"Two years ago."

"Who killed her?"

"Raynelle Tolliver."

"Where is he now?"

"In hell."

"Who killed him?"

"Zion."

"Good." She said. "Now explain to me what you need me to do."

"First, I have to tell you that your body will most likely recover in a few hours, but if you allow me to transfer my spirit into you, your body will die when my spirit leaves. The spirit can only transfer from one body to another only if that body is dying. Right now your body is dying, but in a few hours your immune system has a good chance of fighting off the deadly infection you are suffering from. So, what I am saying is you can die a physical death to help save mankind or you can probably wake up in a few hours and walk out of prison."

Chapter 47

October 15, 2009
A DAY LATER: **Arlington, Virginia**

Zion wasn't on a farm or in some rural area like he had been in back at the safehouse in Georgia. The murder indictment charging Zion with Sandford Carro's murder had been unsealed less than two hours before the Council of Clerics arranged for Pearl to drive Zion to a highway rest stop six months ago. Back then, Zion had climbed out of the rented Camry's trunk and was walking over to Reverend Dr. Williams' Deville in Highpoint, North Carolina around the same time the paramedics were rushing Malice to Dekalb Medical back in Georgia.

The popular and controversial African centered DC Pastor had left North Carolina and had driven six hours straight to the Landmark, an older renovated twelve-story apartment building a stones throw away from the capital. Reverend Williams had specifically chose this location a year before he'd brought Zion there. The Landmark had become a safehouse because of the sixty-seven omni directional cameras that were in and around the apartment building.

Six months ago, in the beginning, Zion was tempted to leave the apartment on more than one occasion. He had asked the Creator to allow him to enact his own form of vengeance on Agent Terrell and the DEA strike team that shot Malice in the back. Zion had been sick with regret for weeks. If he would have been there he could have prevented his friend from being shot, he'd thought.

Each time he had reached for the doorknob to leave the small eight hundred and forty square foot two bedroom apartment his subconscious took over, jolting him back to a time where one of his ancestors had acted out of anger as they attempted to exact revenge on their enemies. And each time, Zion had witnessed the severe price his ancestors had paid for their brash actions. To keep his mind off of Malice and the evil that was gaining strength in the conscious world, Reverend Williams had three hundred and thirty-three books on African and African-American culture delivered to the apartment. For the last six months, Zion had used these books like a time machine. Through them he traveled through space and time, just like he had been doing moments before he detected the two bundles of pure evil matter that were headed his way.

After placing Tony Browder's book, "Contributions to Nile Valley Civillizations" on the bed, he turned to the digital clock on the nightstand.

3:11 AM.

He got out of bed and stretched before closing his eyes and extending his arms. He sort of looked like a human cross as he hummed, summoning more positive energy. His eyelids fluttered as billions of invisible particles flew into his ears and through the canals to his brain. "Mother God you've allowed me to feel the presence of evil, now allow me to hear their footsteps, allow me to gauge what's in their hearts and in their minds, he prayed.

*****

Two middle-aged African-American men casually strolled into the historic Arlington Virginia apartment building. They were dressed to the nines, looking like popular southern prosperity preachers in their seven thousand dollar tailor made suits. The huge gaudy looking platinum crosses they wore around their necks was overkill they thought, but that's what the boss ordered. And as long as the CIA director's lackeys paid the two hundred thousand dollar fee, the two professionals didn't have a problem with wearing the get-up.

It was three fifteen A.M. No one was in the lobby – no one but a geriatric half asleep White security guard sitting behind the window in a small office that had an impressive high-tech wall full of video monitors and recording devices.

One of the pastors took a silencer out of his pocket and began screwing it onto his .22, while the other professional pressed PLAY on a digital recorder.

"Our savior, Zion Jones did say to kill the guard, correct?"

Another southern masculine voice came over the digital recorder, *"Not only did he say to kill the guard, but he said to kill anyone that looked suspicious. Zion will not let anyone stop him from blowing up the White House in a few hours."*

The gun made a poofing sound as it discharged. The kill was very clean, no blood anywhere but on the body. Satisfied that the offices recording devices had picked up the digital conversation, the two professionals took the elevator key card off of the guard before placing the body in a storage closet at the rear of the small office.

*****

Zion's eyes popped open after seeing everything in the minds of his fast approaching enemies. "Gerald Bush, the director of Central intelligence, so he was the master behind the puppets that were on the way up to his room," Zion said aloud. Zion was a constipated volcano of emotions as the truth was being revealed to him through the minds of the men that were now on the other side of the oak wood front door.

Rage was rising up from the bowels of his soul as he read more of the assassins' thoughts. He learned that NSA chief General Maurice Lesure was behind Malice being shot.

Zion balled and unballed his fists as reality pummeled his mind.

Smoke rose from the hardwood floor and the bluish-gray paint on the walls began to liquefy. Beads of paint slithered down the bedroom walls as Zion's whole body trembled.

Before Zion realized what he was doing, rage was ordering his footsteps. Revenge and death consumed him. He had a world of pain to release on the disguised men that came to set him up for murder.

As soon as he placed his hand on the knob he fell to his knees and was jolted back to 1831, South Hampton County, Virginia.

*****

Zion was helpless to do anything but watch as two hundred and thirty seven African-American men, women and children were being burned, beaten, feathered, tarred and hanged in front of angry mobs of jeering, and cheering white onlookers. There was nothing more horrifying than watching and listening to the gut wrenching screams of children as fire melted their faces. Black mothers clawed and scraped to get to their children as they were forced to watch White men pour burning hot black tar over their heads. The children were already dead from the hot tar when the angry white mobs of men, women, and children took turns throwing bags of chicken feathers on the dead children's scorched and tarred bodies. Sadly, two hundred of the beaten and murdered black slave and non-slaves hadn't even heard of Reverend Nat Turner before he set out to exact vengeance on White plantation slave owners.

*****

While Zion was witnessing firsthand what happened when a man of God allowed his anger to make him ignore the Creator's word, two NSA agents were entering the first floor stairwell.

"I thought the Chief said that there would be a guard monitoring the cameras?" one of the agents said as they both raced up ten flights of stairs.

"He did. The guy's probably somewhere napping, and if he isn't he should be, because he will not be able to get a security job anywhere in the country once the boss hears that we had to take the stairs because some guy wasn't at his post to let us up in the elevator."

The other agent chimed in. "I don't see what was so urgent about us going to the perp's room at three thirty in the morning, just to make sure he was still there. With a million cameras in and around the premises I'm sure the boss could've easily gotten Coleman Security to send over the day's camera feeds. It would only take seconds for the system to analyze the data to determine whether the perp had left the apartment."

"I know," the other agent agreed. "Knocking on the guys door at three-thirty in the morning just doesn't make sense."

The agents continued chatting as they walked down the tenth floor hallway past several apartment doors.

"That's our turn up ahead," one of the agents pointed to the hallway that led to room 1006. As soon as the two NSA operatives turned down the hall, the two pastors shot both agents in the middle of the forehead, killing them instantly.

After the two pastors dragged the agent's bodies in front of Zion's door, they took the stairs to the garage level.

Twenty minutes later, two Caucasian ex-KGB agents discarded their expensive suits and fake jewelry in the hundred-gallon barrel of acid that was bolted down in the back of the white van they were driving. The contract assassins were getting a big kick out of the American government paying them to disguise themselves as Black prosperity preachers.

"Foolish Americans," one of the assassins said while checking the passengers visor mirror. He wanted to make sure that there were no remnants of the brown makeup he wore earlier. "They pay us to play dress up. They want men killed we say we do for fifty-thousand American dollars but no dress up. They say no and pay us two hundred grand."

As the assassins pulled the stolen van to a stop before turning into the Reagan National Airport grounds, a Delta airport shuttle pulled up beside them on their left. The assassins didn't see the grenade roll under their vehicle before the shuttle driver sped off, running the red light.

Chapter 48

October 15, 2009
SAME DAY: **Spartanburg, South Carolina**

Under normal circumstances, Assata would have been released from prison at 6 AM but there wasn't anything normal about her miraculous overnight recovery and the massive heart attack that killed the guard that had been monitoring her progress. Finally, at 12:01 PM she walked out of the prison a free woman and drove away in the 1976 rusty red Camaro that was stolen from BWI airport at the beginning of the week.

Three hours after she got into the old Camaro, she was getting out.

So determined to get to Miracle, Assata hadn't realized how hungry she was until now. She wondered if her nose was playing tricks on her as she followed the aroma of her favorite, sweet and sour coconut salmon, a dish that she hadn't had since she was a child. It smelled just like her mother's special recipe, one that everyone thought she had taken to her grave.

A motherly looking woman wearing an amber colored gown opened the door and came out onto the porch. No need to be shy," she said. "Ain't nobody out in these woods but me,

316

you, Miracle, my birds and all this nature," she waved an arm around the colorful trees filled with singing yellow canaries and parrots and the leaf covered yard.

"I'm Momma Orthine baby, we family girl, now come on in this house, child," Momma Orthine waved, "before the food gets cold."

Despite Treble being in her mind telling her to relax, Assata's movements remained timid.

"Hi, I'm Assata Santiago," Assata said after walking up the yellow wooden porch steps.

"Child, I know who you are," Momma Orthine said with one arm crossed and one hand holding Assatas chin up. "Never seen that before," Momma Orthine said.

"Excuse me," Assata said.

She looked Assata up and down and then down and up as she circled the tall, coffee brown thirty something woman. "Two souls sharing one body."

How did you manage that Treble?

Prayer and a leap of faith.

Treble and Momma Orthine were communicating telepathically before she addressed Assata. "I was just asking Treble how both of your spirits were sharing one body. Seems like that would be real confusing."

"I'm kinda new to this, so I can't help you get no closer to solving that mystery," Assata said.

Momma Orthine smiled. "Gotta little spunk in ya huh, girl? I like you already. Come on in 'fore the food get cold, now." Momma Orthine led the way through the five room log cabin. "I made your favorite."

Assata was in Heaven. She closed her eyes and chewed slow as she relished the flavor and the texture of the salmon. The fish seemed to melt in her mouth and mesh perfectly with her taste buds. "Uhmph," she grunted. The vinegary onion and smoked turkey flavored collards sent tingly sensations up her spine and the four cheese baked macaroni with the cheese burnt just right at the top was perfect.

"Just like Pharah used to make, huh?" Momma Orthine said.

"Exactly like momma used to make," Assata said, wondering how Momma Orthine knew her mother's name. Her mother had died with her Sweet & Sour Coconut recipe twenty years ago. Although she wanted to ask Momma Orthine how she knew, she was afraid of what the answer would be so she left well enough alone and enjoyed her food.

"What's with all the bottles of honey," Assata asked while looking at the five bottles of honey in the middle of the table.

"Baby, that's natures sugar. Whenever you are in a sour mood, put a little bit if natures sweet nectar on your tongue and see what happens," she said. "I use honey in my food like black folks use hot sauce. I put a little honey in everything I cook."

Assata suddenly bounced out of her seat.

"What's wrong, Child?"

"Miracle," Assata's eyes were wide. "I completely forgot."

"I didn't," Momma Orthine said as she sat in her rocking chair reading on her kindle.

"Can you take me to her, please?"

Without looking up, Momma Orthine said, "After you finish your food."

"But the March is less than a day away."

"Uhm-hmm, I know."

"So, you just gon' sit there?" Assata asked.

"That's the plan, at least until you finish eating."

"I'm finished." Assata rose from her seat.

"No, you're not." Momma Orthine looked up. "Baby, everything happens the way it is supposed to happen. In my realm, we control time, time doesn't control us. Now, have a little faith, listen to Momma Orthine and sit down and finish your food."

Assata could hear Treble's laughter in her head.

I guess she told you.

"Shut up!" She covered her mouth while taking her seat. "I wasn't talking to you, Momma Orthine."

"I know." She pointed a finger at Assata, "Treble, don't make me jump in there on you."

After she finished her food and washed her hands, Momma Orthine led Assata to a back bedroom.

"Go on in, Baby." Momma Orthine stood back from the door so Assata could open it. "I'll be here when you come out."

Assata took a deep breath. She braced herself for what she might see. Two years in a catatonic state, no telling how emaciated Miracle was. "Okay." She opened the door and stepped into a world full of gray. The walls, the floor, everything was gray rock. She turned back to the door. It was gone. Replaced by a gray rock wall. The first thing that came to mind was the bat cave.

Assata turned and walked to the only door in the room. When she opened it she saw that it opened into an elevator. She stepped in and closed the door. There was only up and down, so she pressed the Up button. When the elevator didn't move she pressed the Down button.

When the elevator opened, Miracle turned to her godmother.

"Oh, my God," Assata put a hand over her mouth. Her eyes watered. "You are so beautiful."

Miracle smiled before running to Assata.

"I missed you so much, Auntie," Miracle said.

"You have no idea how much I missed you and.... And.... Sunny." Assata broke their embrace. "Miracle, this is very important."

The seventeen-year-old nodded.

"I need to know how you feel about Zion."

"I don't know. I mean he's kind, a little naïve." She shook her head, "Auntie he's…"

"He's what, Miracle?"

"He's the Messiah."

"And?" Assata said.

"I'm just me, Auntie."

"What does that mean?"

She shrugged. "I don't know."

Assata held Miracle by the shoulders and looked into her eyes. "Miracle, you are a queen. You and Zion ruled an empire. You went by the name of Oba and Zion went by the name Shango. You are a warrior goddess queen. You were the first and true wife of Shango but he was smitten with your sister, Oshun. When you asked her what she did that had Shango's nose so wide open, she lied and told you that years ago she had sliced off part of her ear and fed it to him."

"Why did Oshun lie and why was she messing around with her sister's husband and why didn't Oba break her foot off in Oshun's behind?"

"Oshun lied because she was jealous. You see Miracle, no matter how many wives or concubines Shango took, Oba's offspring were the airs to the throne. Oshun wanted it all. And to answer your next question, Oba didn't harm Oshun because she was her sister. She loved her, and that love overpowered every other emotion."

"Ain't that much love in the world. Blood or no blood, she would've had to get it and I would have given her all she could handle."

"That was a different society, different culture, different time." Assata said.

"Yeah, okay, so what happened to Oba?"

"She sliced off her ear and fed it to Shango."

"She did what?"

"She sliced off her ear and fed – "

"That's nasty." Miracle said, "So, you mean to tell me that I come from a chick that mutilated herself for a husband that was messing around on her with her sister? Hmph. Assata now you know that's some Jerry Springer mess."

"I'm telling you, Miracle, times were different back then. Shango also had another wife while he was married to Oba, her name was Oya. The real reason Shango was so taken with Oshun was because of her cooking. The woman could burn. Oshun turned cooking into an art form."

"Okay, I get it. The chick can cook, wow. So did Shango eat Oba's ear?"

"No." Assata shook her head. "He saw it in his food. He thought Oba was trying to poison him. He was so disappointed that he put her out of the palace; and grieving, she fell to earth. Some say her tears of grief formed the Oba river and she became known as the river Goddess while Shango became the God of storms."

"Zion is nothing like Shango," Miracle said. "He would never play me like Shango played Oba. That's why I like girls."

"Miracle, are you gay?"

"I guess so."

"You don't guess if you are straight or gay. You are either one or the other or you're bi. And just because you have a bad experience with a man or you hear of bad experiences women have had with men isn't a reason to become gay."

A dark skinned man walked out of the shadows and came to stand by Miracle's side.

"Baba. Baba Ududuwa," Assata said.

He put an arm around Miracle. "Tell them, Miracle."

"Baba has been teaching me the ways of the ancestors over the last year."

"So you knew who you were this whole time. Girl," Assata playfuly lifted her arm as if she were going to hit Miracle.

"I couldn't resist. I figured if Treble was going to hide who he was inside you than I'd mess with the both of you."

"So, you're not gay?"

"No, Auntie," telepathically she added, *And no, I'm not gay, Treble.*

"So, why haven't you come back into the conscious world?"

"Zion spent five years with Baba, but he needed at least seven years to obtain the forty years of knowledge it takes to fully understand the three hundred and sixty degree cipher of knowledge. Without a complete understanding of knowledge, we cannot defeat Evil. And in twelve hours I will have completed the sixty degrees that Zion lacks."

Chapter 49

October 16, 2009
A DAY LATER: **Washington, DC**

The Council of Clerics had sent out the call almost a year ago, the Sunday after Osama was elected. Although Malcolm X was not a part of the 1963 March on Washington, his spirit was an integral part of the 2009 March on the Capital. A quote of Malcolm's inspired the name for the March. He once said that *"We do not condemn the preachers as an individual but we condemn what they teach. We urge that the preachers teach the truth, teach our people the one important rule of conduct – unity of purpose."* Unity of Purpose was the name and the theme of the March.

At first, the Call to *Unity of Purpose* was met with mild enthusiasm. Whether the Council of Clerics wanted to believe or admit it themselves, most of the American people were skeptical when it came to believing that Zion was the Second Coming, heck in many minds, the jury was still out on if there was ever a First Coming.

Back in March, after CNN broadcasted interviews of low-income housing residents lavishing praise on the gangs and on Zion, skeptics around the nation became curious. When CNN followed up on the interviews by broadcasting live coverage of all the activity and commerce going on in the Pointe from noon on Friday to 6 PM on Sunday skeptics became wide eyed with amazement.

Experts, scholars and news pundits had no answer for the miraculous change in the mindset of the urban communities gangs and residents. It was as if ReShonda Tate had used actors to fictionalize last year's Emmy award winning documentary on Pleasant Pointe and other low-income housing communities in metro Atlanta's Dekalb County. The documentary "Iraq in America: A portrait of drugs, crime, and lawlessness inside the most affluent African-American County in the Nation" featured gangs that were labeled terrorists, crime lords, and drug kingpins. A year later many of these same gangs were now community heroes, leaders, and saviors, at least that's some of the praise that was lavished on them by the residents in the latest news stories.

For over a hundred years, black clergy, sociologists, psychologists, and Africana studies experts have been trying to develop and implement programs to stop the black-on-black violence that leads and has lead a grossly disproportionate number of black men and women to an early grave, to prison, and or to a life of poverty. One man has seemingly solved the genocide riddle over night and America wanted to know how. They wanted to see and hear the seventeen-year- old responsible for the miraculous paradigm shift. For these and other reasons, train and bus stations, airports and highways in and around DC had been jam-packed all week. Men from over a hundred different cultures and religions flooded into the capital.

The fact that it was unseasonably warm for October was a good thing for the herds of agnostic and atheist, Christian and Muslim, Jewish and Hebrew Israelite men that were forced to sleep in the same space.

324

Park services in and around the DC area had opened up the parks because hotels and motels had been sold out for almost three months. The closest place to get a room if you were coming from the South was around the Charlotte, North Carolina area and that was still a four hundred mile drive. If you were coming from the north the closest hotel with an available room was in New York City and that was a two hundred and thirty mile drive.

By four in the morning, men that weren't already sleeping on the national mall grounds were migrating to the mall. From the CNN helicopter it looked like a million ants moving in on its prey. A few hours later at day break, CNN reported that there were over a million men already at the mall and they expected at least a million more, blowing away earlier predictions of two hundred and fifty to half a million men.

Throughout the year, talk, news, and radio shows featured African-American, Hispanic, and other minority community leaders. For the most part, they all agreed that white patriarchal values were too deeply rooted in the consciousness of America for people of different cultures to come together, and even if uniting the religions were an option, minority leaders agreed that there was no way white society would accept a Black Messiah.

Two hours into the program, the twelve clerics had the audience fired up. The sun was at its peak. It's warmth kissed the millions of fists that were in the air as Nation of Islam leader the Honorable Minister Louis Muhammed exited the podium while pumping his fist in the air to the rhythm of rap group, Pulblic Enemy's 90's hit song "Fight the Power." The bass pounded from the five hundred mega speakers within a ten mile radius of the National mall.

There had never been a time in recorded history when so many popular religious leaders from different religions had come together under one accord. Despite the dramatic drop in membership that each cleric suffered there was still well over two million men standing as one listening to their messages. The sun was it it's zenith. It was two PM and there was no sign of Zion or the Reverend Dr. Willie Williams.

At five minutes after two, four hours after the march began, Malice was in his wheelchair on stage speaking.

"Before there were wars over race and class, men killed each other because others didn't worship the way they did. They killed because others used different names when referring to the Creator. Muslims have been at war with Christians and Christians have been at war with Muslims for 1,500 hundred years over whether Jesus was the biological son of God. Are you serious? I mean, what difference does it make? It wasn't important if Jesus walked with a strut or a limp, what mattered was, is that Jesus walked. He walked in the light of the Creator," Malice pointed a finger in the air, "that simple fact is what Muslims and Christians can agree on, and that's why we're here today, to unite so we can fight together. So we can fight with the purpose of," he shot a fist in the air, "freedom, justice, equality, and peace. In the words of the great George Clinton, we are all one nation under a groove."

Helicopter noise overpowered Malice's words.

"Look," the rapper Nas shouted, "while pointing to the caravan of military helicopters that were coming their way.

One of the Huey helicopters hovered over the middle of the outside mall area. "Attention people. May I please have your attention," a male voice bellowed from a loud speaker on the helicopter. "Please move aside, the man you have all been waiting for is here. Please move aside so we can land."

Applause rang out for miles.

Ten minutes later, the Huey landed and six men all dressed in blue and black suits ushered a seventh man to the stage. One of the suits grabbed hold of Malice's chair and whispered, "The Messiah wants you up here."

Messiah, dude looked more like the grim reaper with that black cloak over his body and head, Malice thought while trying to figure out who was under the cloak.

The other helicopters flew away as the seven men took their positions on the stage. The cloaked man walked over to Malice. Malice was too stunned to resist as the man grabbed the microphone from his hands. The man's touch felt like dry ice. A dark foreboding came over Malice as the man removed his cloak.

"My name is Constance Greenspan. Up until now I held the position of Chairman of the Federal Reserve Bank, and as of right now I am stepping down because," he pointed to the crowd, "because you need me more than ever before." He raised an old brown leather bound King James Bible in the air before continuing. "For many will come in my name, claiming, 'I am the Messiah,' and will deceive many. You will hear of wars and rumors of wars, but see to it that you are not alarmed. Such things must happen, but the end is still to come. Nation will rise against nation, and kingdom against kingdom. There will be famines and earthquakes in various places. All these are the beginning of birth pains. Then and only then you will be handed over to be persecuted and put to death, and you will be hated by all nations because of," he pointed a finger at himself, "me." Greenspan paused to let his words sink in while he looked out at the crowd. "At that time, many will turn away from the faith and will betray and hate each other, and many false prophets will appear and deceive many people. Because of the increase of wickedness, the love of most will grow cold, but the one who stands firm to the end will be saved. And this gospel of the kingdom will be preached in the whole world as a testimony to all nations, and then the end will come. Mathew twenty four, verses five through fourteen of God's only true Word."

Malice rolled his chair up to Greenspan. "Give me that, you nut." He reached a little too far and fell out of his wheelchair. Several men from behind the stage rushed forward until Greenspan's six armed men urged them to stay back.

"Oh, ye of little faith," Greenspan said into the microphone while reaching down for Malice's hand.

Malice refused Greenspan's help. He used his arms to pull himself to a sitting position by the overturned wheelchair.

Greenspan held a hand in the air. "This hand is the hand of God working through me. It is with the hand of God that caused the blind to see and the deaf to hear. This hand caused man to die and man to live and today, right now, this hand will cause a cripple to walk." He placed a hand on Malice's shoulder. "Stand up and walk my son."

Malice crossed his arms and refused to move.

"I see we have a non-believer." Greenspan turned to Malice. "I am the son of man come to bring light and salvation." Greenspan pointed at Malice before shouting, "I command you to walk."

Malice looked Greenspan up and down. "Nobody's is going to go for that boo game chump. You ain't Zion."

The averaged height, averaged built thirty-eight-year-old White man professing to be the Messiah knelt down and pulled Malice off the ground as if he weighed twenty-five pounds instead of two hundred and fifty pounds. Greenspan dragged Malice to the side of the stage and pitched him forward. "Walk, I said!"

Malice landed on his feet.

People moved back in a circle as Malice stood up.

Gasps and wows among other words were used to describe what over two million men were witnessing and millions more were witnessing on television sets and computers.

"Zion Jones is one of those false prophets that my father, our father spoke about in His Word. And how could you even consider believing anything other than God's Word." He held up the King James Bible. "Mr. Rogers asked what was so important about believing that Jesus is the son of God? It's truth. That's what's so important. God is truth, and to question God's Word and His wisdom is what men like Zion," Greenspan turned to where four of the clerics stood and pointed a finger at them, "and these hypocritical alleged men of God are calling into question. Who are they? Who are any of you to question the source of your existence, the source of all existence? Repent and bow to me now before," Greenspan reached both of his arms into the air and looked up into the sunny clear blue sky, "lightning and thunder explodes from the sky and God rains down hail that will turn into fire and brimstone – fire and brimstone that will destroy the naysayers and non-believers."

The sky began to darken. Lightning and thunder detonated.

Two million men did a mad scramble as the lightning and thunder continued. Moments later, the rain and hail began to fall causing even more panic. Thousands of men and boys were trampled to death. Fear had ruled the day.

Chapter 50

October 16, 2009
SAME DAY: **Washington, DC**

Miracle had just got off the plane in DC when the storm began. She couldn't believe that Zion had let the men take him just because they were pure of heart. Pure heart or not, men following a corrupt leader and a corrupt system could and would get it. Their hearts were pure so they'd reach Paradise quick fast and a hurry cause she'd sure send them to God if they tried that mess when she was around. The persons and the systems responsible for taking Zion thought they knew what a real jihad was.

They had no idea. The government and its minions had locked up the wrong Black woman's man.

IF YOU WANT TO READ WHAT HAPPENS NEXT.... MAKE YOUR VOICE KNOWN THROUGH AMAZON, FACEBOOK, TWITTER, INSTAGRAM, EVERYWHERE. TELL EVERYONE... I NEED YOUR HELP.... I CAN NOT DO IT WITHOUT THE VOICE OF THE PEOPLE... PLEASE ENCOURAGE EVERYONE TO SUPPORT THIS MOVEMENT. BECAUSE AS YOU CAN SEE, THIS IS SO MUCH MORE THAN JUST A BOOK. SO, RIDE WITH ME FAM. RIDE WITH ME TO SPRITUAL FREEDOM.

For life,

Jihad Shaheed Uhuru

MVP

By JIHAD

M VP is the story of two best friends and business partners. Jonathon Parker and Coltrane Jones have a history. The best

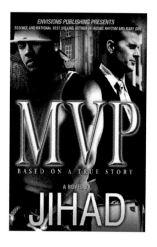

friends and business partners have been involved in everything from murder to blackmail, whatever it took to rise they did. Now they're sitting on top of the world, heading up the two most infamous strip clubs in the nation, the duo has the world at their feet. But now they both want out for different reasons. Coltrane is tired of the drug game, He's hoping to settle down with the new woman in his life. Jonathan, now a top sought after criminal attorney, is ready to get out of the game, that's because his eye is set on the Governor's Mansion. With the backing of major political players, he just might get it. There's only one catch. Jonathan has to make a major coup... bring down his best friend, the notorious MVP, Coltrane Jones. As two longtime friends go to war, parallel lives will collide, shocking family secrets will be unveiled and the game won't truly be over until one of them is dead.

ENVISIONS PUBLISHING, LLC
P.O. Box 83008, Conyers, GA 30013

MVP:Murder Vengeance Power
$12.00

Name_____

Address_____

City_____State_____Zip_____

PREACHERMAN BLUES
By JIHAD

Best friends...Mega preachers...One good....One evil....
As kids, Terrell "TJ" Money and Percival "PC" Turner had one goal

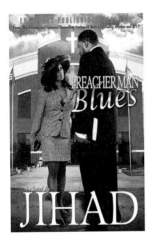

become big-time preachers. But once they accomplished that goal, heading up One World Faith; the largest church in the Southeast, the best friends disagree on just how they should be leading their flock. TJ is living up to his name and looking to capitalize on a congregation more than willing to shell out big bucks for a "man of God". Percival tries hard to walk the straight and narrow, but eventually the lure of the bling leads him astray. Can either survive? When PC tries to right his wrong ways, the battle lines will be drawn and best friends will see sides of each other they never knew existed. Soon, TJ gets down and dirty – pulling up every trick and devastating secret to keep his holy money train rolling. Will Percival learn the hard way that TJ is a sinner who doesn't want to be saved? And if he does, will it be in time enough to stop tragedy from turning his own life upside down? When the dust settles someone will definitely be singing the Preacherman Blues.

ENVISIONS PUBLISHING, LLC
P.O. Box 83008, Conyers, GA 30013

Enclosed: $___ in check or money order form as payment in full for book(s) ordered. FREE shipping and handling. Allow 7-10 days for delivery.

ISBN 978-0-9706102-2-5 Preacherman Blues $12.00

Name_____

Address_____

City_____State_____Zip_____

WILD CHERRY

By JIHAD

C herry is one bad chick. That's no surprise since she's the granddaughter of one of the most thorough hitmen in history, Daddy

Cool. An NFL Superstar and bad boy himself, Jordan Hayes is about to find that out the hard way when he decides to make Cherry a pawn in his game of lust, drugs and lies. After Jordan moves on, he forgets all about the girl he once called "Wild Cherry." But Cherry hasn't forgotten about him. In fact, he's all she can think about as she does her time in a state mental institution. You play...you pay

Jordan's twin brother Jevon has been living in his twin brother's shadow for years. When an encounter with a beautiful young lady opens the door for him to not just follow in Jordan's footsteps, but assume his whole identity, Jevon jumps at the chance. But Jevon is in for a rude awakening when he discovers the real reason his new woman is called "Wild Cherry."

ENVISIONS PUBLISHING, LLC
P.O. Box 83008, Conyers, GA 30013

Enclosed: $_____in check or money order form as payment in full for book(s) ordered. FREE shipping and handling. Allow 3-5 days for delivery.

ISBN 978-0-9706102-3-2 Wild Cherry $12.00

Name_____

Address_____

City_____State_____Zip_____

THE MESSAGE
BY J. S. FREE

T he path from boys to men is paved with obstacles...with prison rates soaring, graduation rates dropping and the streets claiming a

growing number of young black men, only the strong can survive. Now, there's help to navigate the turbulent path to manhood. It's called The MESSAGE, an easy-to-read, inspirational, page-turning book, full of true- to-life short stories that creatively attack the heart of problems that so many young men of color face growing up in today's society. Not just stocked with problems, The MESSAGE is filled with solutions. Each essay is designed to spark discussion to help young men make better decisions, motivate them to strive for more, and propel them to a lifetime of success.

ENVISIONS PUBLISHING, LLC
P.O. Box 83008, Conyers, GA 30013

Enclosed: $_____in check or money order form as payment in full for book(s) ordered. FREE shipping and handling. Allow 3-5 days for delivery.

ISBN 978-0-9706102-8-7 The Message $12.00

Name_____

Address_____

City_____State_____Zip_____

Preacherman Blues II

By JIHAD

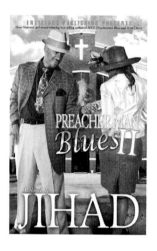

Bishop TJ Money has never made it a secret that he gets what he wants, when he wants, and by any means necessary. He has no problem robbing, stealing, and killing, to protect his holier-than-thou image. So the offer to succeed the first black US president is too tempting to resist. Who cares if the anonymous donors pushing his campaign were behind the mysterious death of the president? TJ is only focused on all the money and power the new position can bring.

But what Bishop Money and his new partners don't account for is the power of the black woman - four of them to be exact. All of whom TJ has wronged at one point or the other during his rise to mega stardom. And just as determined as Bishop TJ Money is to make his new home in the White House, these women will stop at nothing to keep that from happening.

In the riveting sequel to the best-selling Preacherman Blues, things aren't what they seem.

ENVISIONS PUBLISHING, LLC
P.O. Box 83008, Conyers, GA 30013

Enclosed: $_____in check or money order form as payment in full for book(s) ordered. FREE shipping. Allow 7-10 days for delivery.

ISBN 978-0-9706102-5-6 Preacherman Blues II $12.00
Name_____
Address_____
City_____State____Zip_____

MVP RELOADED
By Jihad

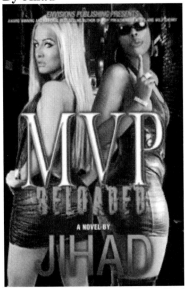

Its been five years since Karen Parker killed her father and brother. Not a day has passed that Karen hasn't regretted what she did, and now she has vowed revenge on the man who drove her to it - Coltrane Jones, the strip club mogul her district attorney brother sent to prison for life, the same man her defense attorney father helped to vindicate. For five years, Karen Parker has obsessed, plotted and planned. And now that she is in position for revenge, nothing will stop Karen from making Coltrane pay.

ENVISIONS PUBLISHING, LLC
PO Box 83008 Conyers GA 30013 (send 12.00)
ISBN 978-0-9706102-6-3 MVP RELOADED $12.00

Name_____

Address_____

City_____State_____Zip_____

WORLD WAR GANGSTER

By JIHAD

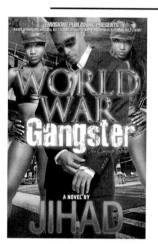

Sam Cooke said it best, "A Change is Gonna Come." But, Bo Jack Jones is tired of waiting. The world renowned Hip-Hop artist is ready to bring on the revolution himself. Tired of injustice, rampant racism and an America that is anything but "The Land of the Free," Jones enlists the help of a new group called The Truth Commission to right the wrongs of this country's past. The Revolution will not be televised The Truth Commission is working overtime to bring light, life and freedom to a New America - by any means necessary. First up, expose the real story behind two high-profile murders. Then, liberate nonviolent drug offenders who have been left to die in the penal system. The Commission was already on a mission - now with Bo Jack Jones leading the way, it's the dawn of a new day. A modern day Robin Hood, Jones is using his money, power and fame to go to war against a system that doesn't want to be changed. World War Gangster is unlike anything you've ever read. Prepare for a fast-paced, riveting ride that will blow your mind and have you rethinking everything you think you know about the country that promises liberty and justice for all!

ENVISIONS PUBLISHING, LLC

P.O. Box 83008, Conyers, GA 30013

Enclosed: $_____ in check or money order form as payment in full for book(s) ordered. FREE shipping and handling. Allow 7-10 days for delivery.

WORLD WAR GANGSTER $12.00

Name_____

Address_____

City_____ State_____ Zip_____

DARK HORSE ASSASSIN
Rise of the MESSIAH

ENVISIONS PUBLISHING, LLC
P.O. Box 83008, Conyers, GA 30013

Enclosed: $_____in check or money order form as payment in
full for book(s) ordered. FREE shipping. Allow 7-10 days for delivery.

ISBN 978-0-9706102-9-4 DARK HORSE ASSASSIN $12.00

Name_____

Address_____

City_____State_____Zip_____